Richard D. Besecker

CRESTED BUTTE
FRIENDS
OF
THE
LIBRARY

P.O. BOX 791 • CRESTED BUTTE • CO 81224

Rick Besecker was raised in the magnificent Cochetopa/La Garita Wilderness area. With life on a rustic guest ranch, one is required to contribute to the necessities for daily survival; and, at an uncommon youthful age. At five years old there was water to be hauled in galvanized buckets from the spring house, firewood to be carried from the woodshed, and kerosene lamps that needed to be filled each day. By seven, Rick was introduced to the udder end of a Jersey, and was now proficient with splitting firewood, and expected to operate a John Deere with a mower and buck rake. There was no distraction from hard work or, for that matter, hard play. Without electricity, entertainment was self-initiated and would encompass shooting prairie dogs, playing cowboys and Indians on horseback, fly fishing, hunting for Native American artifacts, and conducting Jeep tours in the back country. He shot his first deer at age 12 and his first bear at 13. And, to impress upon the man child the spiritual concept related to harvesting wild game, he was required to field dress and process the reward.

School was a 100-mile traverse each day. Although Rick was uncomfortable with the social concept of the classroom, he was ruler of the weekends and most classmates were eager to experience the "Old West" on the Quarter-Circle Circle Ranch.

Devil's Pin Cushion

By Richard D. Besecker

Devereux Publishing
159 North Road
Gunnison, CO 81230
DevereuxPublishing@gunnison.com

I wish to dedicate the inspiration for this book to Gloria, my wife of 39 years. I know what I was thinking when we got married, but I have no idea what she was thinking. I just thank God she was thinking it.

Devil's Pin Cushion

Chapter One

Everlasting Sleep

Sheila Gray studied the spender on the port side of her single engine Cessna. At an altitude of a little more than seventeen thousand feet, the lone occupant felt a safe distance from the majestic peaks and shear jagged cliffs below. At the same time, she was not so high as to miss the true depth of their magnificence in the illuminating moonlight. Great shadows cast by the fourteen thousand foot mountains gave an appearance of menacing eeriness and extended the illusion of hollow, endless depths between the uneven elevations. Still, the beautiful young pilot was content within the safety of her own ignorance.

All appeared well as every instrument gauge indicated favorable readings; a confirmation for a carefree flight. The lone occupant was home free, or so she thought. What Sheila did not know would forever change the direction of her life, if it did not cost her such. There was an undetected hairline fracture in the exhaust system. This system was designed to supply heat to the cabin of the plane. The natural vibration of the engine now spread the fracture to a significant gap. The heat diversion pipe which supplied life supporting warmth in sub-zero temperatures was now leaking deadly carbon monoxide poison into the confines of the small plane. Sheila had noted an acoustic pitch change in the engine but dismissed the sensed difference as pressure equalizing within her ears and subsequently, thought it unimportant.

As luck would have it, there would be a second stroke of peril which involved the matter of travel congestion on one of the busiest nights of the year. It was Christmas Eve, and hundreds of approaching and departing aircraft littered the controller's screens some two hundred and fifty miles away. The red, white, and blue Cessna 210 was being piloted at an elevation not registered by the flight center. Furthermore, Sheila, not wishing to bother some over worked traffic director, failed to establish radio contact. No one really knew of her existence.

As the moon slowly rose in the east, the unaware pilot was growing sleepy. Queasiness started first as a small ache, then increased in the pit of her stomach. Thinking that perhaps this would pass, she focused on the continuing journey and, with diligence, pressed on; after all, what choice did she have?

Less than thirty minutes passed when Miss Gray nodded off, causing her head to fall forward and bounce on the control yoke. With a start, the young lady raised her head and was somewhat dazed and disoriented. Not realizing that her headgear had fallen to the floor, Sheila panicked as she fought off the inevitable effects of the poisonous vapor. Frantically grasping the wing leveler, Sheila pulled hard. With her ingrained instincts guiding her response, she stabilized the level of the wing. But this did not extend to increasing, or diminishing power. By this time, Sheila knew that something was not at all right, and with vigor, the woman attempted to fight off the unavoidable sleep which was re-approaching. At this point, the fumes had increased in volume and the subsequent outcome could not be denied. The independent occupant focused the best that she could on the diodes that indicated the Cessna was on auto wing level. One last time she looked out the side window and found herself at a mystery at what was taking place. What baffled her most was the fresh realization that she was going to die and she could not muster any real concern. By her nature, she loved life and took delight in the notion of living it to its fullest. But somehow, someway, at this point she seemed not to care. Her impaired concern continued to diminish as the poison persuaded her towards predictable slumber. As she felt herself slowly drifting off, Sheila gave one last gesture to survival by simply muttering, "Oh Lord!"

*****

The large ominous figure of a man continued a rhythmic step by step up the steep slope. The snow was incredibly deep, but his snowshoes would leave only the slightest of signatures on the wind-hardened crust. After pressing more than halfway up the mountain, Jay stopped and turned. He slowly gazed at the oversized moon which began to announce its presence in the eastern sky by casting brilliance over the earth's silvery white surface. As it rose ever so slightly, the atmosphere on the horizon magnified the moon's actual appearance. The fullness of the experience was almost beyond comprehension. The unblemished snow, which rolled across the alpine mountainside, reflected the moonshine. Such illumination gave every appearance that the earth itself was like an altogether different planet.

"Come on, Wing Nut!" Jay bellowed as loudly as he could. For a moment, the large man waited, but knowing his companion would be along soon, he turned and continued the drudgery up the east face of Cochetopa Canyon towards Canyon Diablo. Soon a small, shadowy figure could be detected darting across the snow some five hundred yards away. It would only take the shepherd/chow mix a few minutes to diminish the quarter mile gap and rejoin the company of his best friend.

"They'd eat your skinny little butt in no time!" Jay once again stopped and bent down to hug his only companion. In the not-so-far distance, an eerie serenade began and then echoed throughout the canyon and seemingly, throughout the entire La Garita Wilderness. The recently planted timber wolves were breaking their silence as they began their lunar worship. Jay knew that in late January, nature influenced the starving beasts to combine their efforts in order to stalk down prey. Not wanting to pose as such, Jay slapped his partner on the backside.

"Come on girl," the bearded man ordered as he shagged the dog's head with a vigorous gesture of compassion. "We don't need complications in our simple lives right now."

As Jay increased his speed up the mountain, he glanced down at the .50 caliber Hawkins that was secured in his hands. The single shot, black powder weapon was loaded and a percussion cap was crimped in place. Feeling an increased sense of alarm, Jay understood that he and Wing Nut would not be a match for what he sensed was a large hungry pack of wild beasts. There were still a couple miles to go before he could bask in the warmth of his wilderness cabin, so the modern day mountain man began to look for the nearest source of flammable material. A stand of spruce and pine trees were several hundred yards away. Slowly scanning the terrain aft, Jay trudged toward the grove. Suddenly, a shadow appeared a half mile away and a little down the mountain. And then, another ... and another. With several years of wilderness experience, it did not take the seasoned veteran long to realize that the pack was closing in on their chosen evening meal.

Jay became even more alarmed when he realized that the cunningness of the predators had perhaps outwitted his own experience and wisdom. He could hear several of the beasts above him now and Wing Nut began to bark.

"Quiet!" the man demanded. The dog obeyed, but protested by a short whine. "We have got to keep our heads screwed on and our mouths shut; keep those silly pointed ears of yours at the ready and let me know if they are about to flank us!"

By the time the mountain man and his loyal companion reached the wooded area, thirteen shadows could be counted and each was closing in. The youngest of the approaching wolves were much more eager as they would dart toward Jay from about fifty yards away, and now, half that distance. Five older males stood, for the most part, their ground at seventy yards. Jay estimated their weight at about a hundred and fifty pounds each. The mountain man realized that the winter had been severe and these hungry canines would not be easily persuaded to detour from their natural instincts.

Jay hoped for enough time to start a fire but the aggressiveness of the pack had increased much faster than anticipated. After slowly removing his home-stitched elk skin gloves, Jay raised the fifty-caliber to his shoulder and pulled the set trigger on the replica. Now the primary trigger had become far more sensitive. So sensitive that the thought of pulling it would almost engage the mechanism. Now he would attempt to draw a bead on the closest intruder. There was a sudden eruption, a flash, and a thunderous report as the rifle responded to the master's intentions. Right away Jay would receive confirmation that his objective was successful. Through the prevailing blue smoke came a yelp from the unprepared victim. The gunman was pleased that his shot in the relative dark had found its mark. He knew however, that this was only a successful conclusion to the first battle and not a deciding factor in the war with nature!

After the smoke had finally cleared, Jay was dismayed to find that the more aggressive of the gray wolves had retreated only as far as their elders. With frantic desperation Jay searched for the powder flask in the right side pocket of his oversized coat. His hands were already hurting from the brief exposure to the freezing night air. Finally, Jay could feel the unmistaken metal container. As he attempted to reload the rifle, he glanced up to see if the dark shadows were approaching. For the moment, the aggressors were content to stand fast. They were now perfectly still as if to silently plan their next move. Their black, satanic eyes locked onto the man and his dog, steam thrusting from their mouths and nostrils; total focus, total objective seemingly theirs.

After reloading the Hawkins, the lull continued. Jay once again decided to start a fire. He felt confident that the wolves would stay away if he created a blaze. He did not relish the thought of spending the night out in the extreme sub-zero cold but at least he would not be without companionship. Unfortunately, what Jay did not know was that his main fire starting ingredient, black powder, was now gone and the gray wolves were once again feeling restless. At first, the lone man thought that the triple F powder was caked in a clump at the bottom of the metal container. Soon he would concede to his neglect and admit that he had been careless in regard to filling the flask before beginning the day-long expedition.

As if by unspoken command, the wolves were beginning to advance once again. Advancing and then retreating repeatedly, but the retreat would not be nearly as far each time. Jay wished he had brought his semi-auto Smith and Wesson handgun with multiple magazines and seemingly endless ammunition; or, even a long gun such as the Winchester model 94 30.30. It had been foolish to bring the black powder weapon but he had not planned to be out so long.

Now faith would have to carry him as he prepared himself for inevitable onslaught; a circumstance which would be the penalty of not thinking things through.

The most aggressive of the pack started to come very close and Jay placed his hand on the head of his growling ally. He instructed the faithful mutt to stay. In an abrupt instance the moment of truth was upon Jay! The wolf committed to the attack and lunged! Not wishing to chance the possibilities of an unloaded firearm, Jay gripped the weapon at the barrel with both hands and flung the rifle as though it was a club. He felt the solidness of his hit as the butt of the rifle connected with the skull of the first aggressor. Without a whimper, the carnivorous animal now laid motionless on the snow. Jay felt the pressure from a second adversary and the mountain man swung hard once again but only scored a glancing blow to the wolf's shoulder. As the wild K-9 sunk his teeth into Jay's left leg, the man could feel extreme pressure but the thick elk leather pants denied penetration. Wing Nut instinctively darted with full force at the belligerent animal and with the advantage of distraction, was able to bore her teeth into the throat of the wolf.

As if on cue, a much larger wolf was now rushing toward his prospective victim. Jay drew back a step and with a defensive stance, held the rifle correctly. As he felt the deadly jaws of the aggressor clamp with solid determination on the barrel, Jay pulled the trigger. The muffled blast whirled the blood thirsty animal twenty feet from the point of impact, and stopped the rest of the timber pack in their tracks. There was no time for the courageous human, or his dog, to celebrate. In the mere instant that it took to defeat the third wolf, the second had reversed advantage and was now at the throat of Wing Nut. With one swift movement, Jay swung his rifle in a complete circle and brought the instrument full force onto the back of the hostile beast. He could feel its back break, ultimately granting confirmation that Nut's would-be-killer was now destroyed. The wolf released its vicious hold and lay motionless.

Although he was now out of ammunition, Jay swept the muzzle of the Hawkins from side-to-side to present a deadly weapon at ever-increasing numbers of adversaries. Jay scanned the circle of wolves that now appeared to be regrouping. There were over thirty shadows that blemished the brilliant reflection of the moonlight on the silver landscape. Jay knew that neither he, nor Wing Nut, would be able to fend off another attack. The end was near.

Not wishing to concede the battle with an unconditional surrender, Jay voiced aloud a petition to a much higher authority. "Lord, you see everything. You know all that there is to know! I don't. If I have used your name in vain," Jay began his short confession, "I am truly sorry. For offending you in any way, I am sorry."

Jay stopped and peered at the enemy. They seemed to be silent as if to grant respect for one who is giving his last testimony. Or perhaps they were merely saying grace, Jay pondered. "... but I don't feel like giving up my dog to these bastards. You don't have to help us, Lord, but I would be much obliged if you at least didn't help them!"

The wolf pack began to move in an ever-restricting circle around the man and his dog. A chorus of yelps and howling echoed from the near timber and across an adjacent canyon. The younger wolves were obviously more anxious as they were again darting closer and then upon their mild retreat, they would glance at the adults as if for recognition and guidance. Jay held tightly onto the mutt of whom he passionately referred to as the Nut, a name which was acquired by the dog's unorthodox ears which constantly protruded up and outwards.

Suddenly there was an indescribable eeriness that extended beyond Jay's awareness. Jay found himself puzzled as nature's wild stalkers stopped their yelping and howling and stood motionless, as if paralyzed by an unrelated distraction. Jay mused with bewilderment at such an unexpected and unexplainable change in animal behavior. The confused man glanced down at the dog that had been licking her wounds. Now she was staring up the mountain in the same direction that the other beasts were focusing their united attention. They all were apparently alerted to the same mystery.

"What is it, girl?" Jay inquired.

Steam rolled out of her mouth as she exhaled and after a deep held breath, she once again poised herself with ears forward and taut; her eyes focused straight ahead.

Jay looked again at the dark figures a few feet away. Without warning and without any apparent explanation, the multitude of shadows split off in many directions and fled from the area. They had disappeared so suddenly, it was as though they had never existed in the first place.

Then the mountain man heard it. At first, there was a dull whisper through the trees as if the wind was announcing its arrival. But wait a minute! No, it was not the wind. It had to be something much more significant. Soon it was obvious as the whisper turned into an incredible roar and the clear sound of shattering limbs and breaking trees echoed across the mountains.

"It's an avalanche!" Jay exclaimed with a new sense of panic.

Jay smiled as he glanced up to the stars and reflected upon his short prayer to the Almighty. He had not asked for help but instead asked that the Lord not help the wolves. The Lord had apparently done just that. Jay raised his hand and gestured a thumbs up, then with a shrug shook his head. After all, he had been taught a long time ago that when you petition the Good Lord, make sure you state exactly what you need. He then braced himself, for he knew that the new challenge could also mean death. He patiently waited for whatever may be in store.

Within a few seconds, the crashing of timber was ever so close. Jay bent down and held Wing Nut tightly to his chest. Both the man and his companion looked up in time to witness the Cessna clip the last of the tree tops, glide directly overhead, and belly into the deep, hard crusted snow fifty feet away. Jay watched in complete amazement as the airplane skidded into the dense shadows of the next forest and out of sight.

Both man and beast looked at each other with a baffled expression on their faces. "Now that's something you don't see every day!" Jay understated the obvious.

Just then there was an explosion and then a second. The deep density of the black forest erupted with a brilliant double flash followed by fire. After quickly retrieving his snow shoes, Jay began to run the best that he could, down the mountainside following the approximate path of the plane.

Chapter Two

Rancid Aroma

Sheila raised her pretty head and blinked her eyes several times in an attempt to gain focus. She felt dreadfully ill and more disoriented than ever. One thing she knew for sure, was that she was on her back and she felt cold all over. Orientation would come and go as her head felt heavy. Then, with acute awareness, Sheila realized that a dog was looking at her with its face only inches from hers. It was a large, black animal with facial features not too removed from that of a wild animal.

With abrupt fashion, there was an intrusion of a second animal. A yellowish colored domestic type canine, which attacked the first. Both disappeared out of her peripheral and Sheila closed her eyes as she felt herself losing consciousness once again.

Jay reached the crash site just in time to see Wing Nut engage the young wolf pup. In the flickering firelight, he could see the two nip at each other and then tumble in the deep snow which had been breached by the yawing slide of the plane. They would surface again onto the hard crust. Jay looked around for signs of other wolves as he rushed to the aid of his pet.

Then, as sudden as the combat had begun, it ended when the two animals were thrust apart by the same will that had brought them together. For a brief moment, both stood fast, as though to stare each other down, growling and snarling. Not wishing to divert his attention, but still feeling the pressure of Jay's presence, the wolf hesitated and then chose retreat and darted from the reflective light of the now dwindling fire.   With departing determination, the wild animal disappeared into the vastness of forest shadows.

The Nut turned and wagged her tail as she sounded a victorious celebration by barking. She was proud of herself and with good reason. She had taken on the wild and now she could strut victoriously.

"And what might we have here?" Jay was still trying to grasp what all was taking place. He bent down beside the unconscious female and as he checked her pulse, he could see that she was breathing as vapor rose from her mouth. With immediate reaction, Wing Nut took to doing her own medical application by applying a warm, but wet tongue to the unresponsive face of the pretty young lady.   Jay knew he was not at all prepared for this type of an emergency, and if he was to find other victims who were still living, that would further complicate matters all the more. He took off his heavy leather coat and draped the hair clad garment over the victim. Quickly surveying the area for others that might be suffering, he found himself somewhat disturbed at failing to find the expected male associate to this young lady. After all, who was flying the plane?

The mountain man was drawn to the burning remains of the aircraft. Upon close inspection, only one wing was on fire and it had detached itself from the fuselage.   The cabin was upright and appeared virtually undamaged in the ever dwindling glimmer of the now dying flames. Upon approaching the other side of the wreckage, Jay could see that the port-side wing was practically detached as well, but again the cabin was in good repair with only the door missing. Fully expecting to find someone, Jay cautiously peered inside and called out.   No one responded.   Debris was piled in disarray throughout the passenger compartment, so it was hard to identify any particular thing. Jay climbed aboard and started to sift through the disarray of belongings. Still no one else was present. Suddenly it occurred to the one man rescue team that all the seatbelts were fastened and drawn firm to the seats with the exception of the main side pilot's position. It was unbuckled and loose. This would reveal two significant facts. First, there was only one occupant, and second, the occupant had staggered from the wreckage to where she was currently lying. Such a conclusion brought Jay to the point that time was of the essence and should no longer be wasted. Jay immediately located a lady's full length coat inside the fuselage and returned to where Wing Nut stood guard over the damsel who was still unconscious. He quickly exchanged her wrap for his own handmade cover. Ingenuity became the evening's priority and Jay did not know what ailed the woman or why her airplane had fallen out of a perfectly good sky. He was well aware though, that he would have to carry her to his cabin and this was an unforgiving two mile journey up a canyon wall of Diablo and over to Machin Lake.

It was not all that long before the unaware Miss Gray was carefully strapped to a makeshift sled that was constructed from a seven foot section of one of the Cessna wing tips. Seatbelts were used to tie the fragile cargo in place and a nylon rope found within the aircraft would serve as a pull strap. Jay estimated the combined weight as close to 180 pounds but he did not dwell on it. He understood the task at hand and absorbed himself in focusing on the finish line; the cabin beside Machin Lake which was situated near the summit of the Continental Divide.

Up the mountain the man and his burden slowly trudged. Even with the added weight, the firm snow crust showed no sign of giving under the sure footed snowshoes. All was not well, though. The slippery characteristics of the aircraft wing which made it appealing as a sled also provided equally troublesome challenges on its top side. Even with the seatbelts secured as tightly as possible, the human load naturally shifted and slipped off. After several attempts to modify the conveyance had failed, Jay conceded that the ingenious contraption simply did not work. It was not hard to measure the distance gained for there was virtually none!

Jay unstrapped the seatbelts and let out a monstrous sigh. "When you can't get out of it; then get into it!" He voiced his conclusion in the direction of the interested, but ignorant dog. "You're no help at all." With a giant heave, the dead weight of the unresponsive female was hoisted over Jay's shoulder, and he once again started the seemingly endless journey up the mountain.

Leaving the Hawkins at the crash site made Jay uneasy. He knew that it served no real purpose but still it lent its owner a false psychological advantage. At this point, he would embrace any advantage, pretend or otherwise. As the determined man lifted one tired leg at a time, he kept a sharp eye out for what he expected to be the return of the relentless wolves. He could feel their presence but as yet they dared not show themselves. The uncommon aroma of perfume reached Jay's sensitive nostrils and he did not know whether he could appreciate its apparent expense, or not. After all, he was used to the smells and odors of just he and his faithful pooch.

*****

The splendor of the moon was not only a much needed torch throughout the night but served as a "time dial" as well. It was beginning to sink behind San Luis Peak and Jay knew that this would not be good. If the predators that remained non-aggressive throughout the trip still had a mind to attack, this would be the time. Jay stopped for a few moments and set his load softly on the front portion of the snowshoes. It was with vigor that he massaged his aching thigh and calf muscles. As he did so, he could feel sheets of sweat cascading down his back and then trickle down his pant leg. This too, was not good and Jay understood it well. He recognized that if he rested too long, the sweat would turn to ice and his gallant effort to save the maiden would place them both in unforgiving peril.

As the last ray of moonlight began to diminish behind the majestic peak, the courageous man was amused if not hopeful by the lacking presence of the wolves. Periodically, he scanned the landscape but now the moon was no longer a guiding light. At this point, he narrowed his focus on one agonizing step at a time.

With stars and instinct as his guide, the self-declared mountain man proceeded in the direction which he trusted that his home would be. It was primitive by design and its distance from civilization was by choice. His preference was solitude and as rugged and unforgiving as the wilderness may be, at least he could depend on it without the human element creating an unnecessary turbulence.

With a prideful approach to the impossible, eventually the virtual unplanned mission would be accomplished. There would be no ticker-tape parade or great speeches, or even a presentation of a certificate of accomplishment; only the frosted atmosphere of the small cabin where Jay presided as king of such domain. In complete darkness, the exhausted man and his sidekick, Wing Nut, delivered the stranger to the front door of the modest residence. Jay was not certain of the time but he knew it was early morning and without realizing the true magnitude of the moment, entered the rustic seclusion of his province. It indeed was sub-zero as the coals which were glowing a few hours earlier were now black with gray powder coating and produced heat no more; only the found memory of such.

While Jay began preparations for starting a new fire, he could hear the young women turn over on the large bed on which he had placed her. Within moments, the transparent door glass of the stove allowed the reflective firelight to shine through. It was a most welcome sight, for Jay was impressed with the sudden feeling of extreme cold that came with laying down his burden. Although the temperature of the cabin was still well below zero, the man began to peel off his sweat-soaked clothing. As he did so, the most welcome warmth of the wood burner slowly but surely reacquainted itself to the familiar surroundings. As Jay dried off, he could now relinquish his sense of preoccupation with duty and realize the true depth of his fatigue. Although shivering, Jay chose to wear only a dry pair of pants as he pulled a small stump that doubled as a stool next to the cast iron stove so as to absorb every ounce of heat. He, the Nut, and their unscheduled charge were all finally safe.

*****

Sunshine began to penetrate the southeast windows, and with it, came the undesirable comprehension that the cabin was cool again. With the combination of sleeping on the floor and the extreme physical exertion of the previous night, the large man found his extremities stiff and very sore. Jay began to stretch with slow, deliberate emphasis. Wing Nut was curled next to the man's head and had her wet nose next to his ear and her beautiful reddish-blonde hair was tickling Jay's nose.

With sudden recall, Jay sat up and looked in the direction of the mystery girl. It was with hesitation that he lifted his mass to a deliberate, if not comfortable, standing position. Jay could clearly see her face and he was taken aback by the radiant beauty which he beheld. Caught off guard by such beauty, Jay found himself just standing and staring. He felt breathless as he found himself wanting to run his fingers through the beautiful long black hair which framed her olive colored face. This woman was incredibly stunning. Jay took in a deep sigh as he realized that he had apparently rescued a goddess!

Without warning, the woman rolled onto her back and produced an unanticipated nasal sound which was not unlike that of a cat regurgitating. The revolting sound broke the trance in which Jay was immersed. While chuckling to himself, Jay turned his attentions once again to the stove.

Through the clanging of the steel poker against the iron side of the firebox, Sheila began to slowly and cautiously open her green eyes. A confused expression would take over her entire face as she scanned the ceiling. She found herself engulfed in confusion while she ran her focus along the pine beams that supported the lodge pole roof. Cobwebs were thriving, and the stench of extreme body odor invaded her keen sense of smell. Where was she, she wondered? As the crackling sounds of burning pine combined with the rhythmic popping of the expanding metal stove, Sheila cautiously peered in the direction of the noise. Her eyes fell on the oversized muscular back of the mountain man. He, whoever he might be, was placing a large piece of wood through the open door of the lone source of central heating. He was unaware that he was being watched. Finally, Jay's instincts served to alert him as he felt her eyes scanning his anatomy. Jay quickly turned to face the woman in his bed. His guest was not prepared for what she was about to see. Sheila's eyes grew wide as she was certain that she beheld the elusive, maybe even mystical, "missing link"! Standing close to six-feet, six-inches, the thirty-five year old hermit felt no need to waste time or water for something as trivial as personal hygiene. This could be no more apparent than with the filthy appearance of the rugged man's face. With over five year's growth, the disgusting unwashed and matted facial hair that Jay sported with unconcern was frightful at best. But, he had no one to impress outside of himself and his best friend, and the dog seemed to think that her master was perfect as is!

Sheila let out an unexpected blood curdling scream that would emanate from the cabin, and surely stop any creature in their tracks for half a mile radius. So offset by this unexpected response, Jay took two steps back, tripped over the Nut who let out a heartbreaking yelp, and sat squarely atop the stove which, by this time, was more than just warm. Now Jay was the one who was screaming, and swearing. This served to further intensify the already charged atmosphere! It seemed that the whole alarming process gained a life of its own as the young lady began to shriek with even greater amplification.

By now, Jay was sore on the outside, as well as the inside and could no longer tolerate such an augmented disruption to his once tranquil dwelling. In as loud a voice as he could muster, he yelled, "Shut the hell up!" By this time, Sheila became aware of an ever growing nauseating grip in her throat and with immediate response, muted herself. Tears streamed down her soft cheeks with chin quivering. The combination of the carbon monoxide poisoning, unfamiliar surroundings, as well as the putrid stench and sight of the great unwashed man were suddenly too much! The lady of unmatched beauty pulled the heavy handmade quilt from atop her, bent over the side of the lodge pole bed, and expelled the contents of her stomach onto the floor.

Jay's eyes grew big and the back of his throat began to respond to the sights and sounds before him. He turned his head and simply stated, "Impressive!" For the next few minutes, he would try hard not to think about it for within a fraction of a second, his gag reflexes could betray him and he too could become an equal participant in this most repulsive episode. All things considered, he preferred the screaming.

No longer consumed with the attractiveness of the mysterious damsel, Jay sat down beside Wing Nut and began to pet the dog until he could be assured that the "hurling" was quite finished. Finally, a soft feminine voice broke the otherwise silence. "Where are my clothes?" Sheila sternly demanded. Her discovery of being clad in only her fringy black bra and bikini briefs caused her further apprehension.

The mountain man was strict in discipline and pure of heart which was not necessarily matched by his appearance or the décor of his dwelling. Nevertheless, he took exception to the possible implication that his intentions were anything less than honorable.

"The clothes, unless you kicked them off during the night, are at the foot of the bed," Jay responded.

"Who are you?" Sheila demanded.

"The ghost of Christmas present," Jay was indignant with his response.

Sheila felt somewhat amused that the individual that bore such a disgusting appearance would have an apparent sense of humor. Nevertheless she rolled her eyes. "And does the ghost have a name?" She further attempted to gain a grasp on the mystery of who he really was.

"Jason Devereux; and what is your name?"

"My, such a sophisticated name." Sheila was examining Jay's features at this point, and did not fancy that such a sad excuse of a man would celebrate such an elaborate christening. "And…"

"Don't worry. I came by it honestly!" Jay again, took offense to the young lady's presumptuousness. "Do you carry the distinction of sophistication?" The mountain man was being brusque.

Ignoring his question, Sheila hurriedly retrieved her somewhat scattered clothing and inquired as to the man's intentions of keeping her captive. "What do you think you are going to do with me? If you think …"

Again, Jay was disturbed by the implication. "I'm not doing a damned thing with you!" He made it perfectly clear. "Don't flatter yourself!" The mountain man had a high expectation of privacy, and as time progressed, he took umbrage of it being invaded by the likes of Miss Prissy! "You're the one who did the Evel Knievel thing in my back yard!"

Clutching her clothing in her hands, Sheila began to realize that there was another dimension to her existence in this strange place, and she began to weep. Jay simultaneously became aware of the void in her memory, and suddenly felt bad as he watched her sob uncontrollably. By living in the manner in which he had become accustomed, he was used to frequent death defying acts more or less, and with the lack of anyone to impress, Jay felt little reason by dwelling on them. It was just stuff that he went through and it was no more noteworthy than any other insignificant moment during the day.

"Sorry," Jason wished to start over. "Your Cessna crashed a ways from here last night. There is no other place close by, so I brought you here."

Sheila seemed a little calmer, but was still cautious. "May I use your phone?" She asked politely.

"You could if I had one, but they haven't even invented electricity yet, let alone phones up here." Jay replied.

The nearest winter neighbor was close to thirty miles to the north, and a town of significant consequence, more than twice the distance. At learning this, the young lady with the tan skin and penetrating green eyes become subdued with sadness. She sat motionless with the large quilt tucked around her as a coat of armor against the unknown. She simply stared at the flickering fire light that was dancing through the little front window of the antique stove. For the next hour, nothing was said. Jay began to cook breakfast and finally the young lady, whose name was still a mystery to him, combed her hair with her fingers the best that she could, and then draped her legs over the side of the bed and stepped from the berth. At this point, the man handed Sheila a bucket of hot water and a rag, and simply pointed in the general direction of the mess she had accidentally made. She was quick to protest, declaring herself still ill and thus unfit for such a degrading task. Jay was just as quick to point out the "no excuse" policy of his castle and ignored further protests. Soon the mess was cleaned up and she was sitting on the vacant stump next to the iron fireplace.

Upon several attempts, Miss Gray was offered something to eat, but each time she refused. Thinking that it perhaps had to do with skepticism concerning his questionable cooking abilities, Jay encouraged the fair lady to partake, nevertheless. Still, Sheila declined.

Chapter Three

Machin Lake

For several hours, Sheila stood at the frosted window next to the door without saying a word. She just stared, the best that she could, through the dirty glass. Sometimes she studied the steep slope next to the cabin, and other times she gazed at the splendor of the nearby peaks which rose with majestic appeal so much higher than the cabin. Snow was blowing from the very tip of the most northerly peak to the next, which created a constantly moving haze. Finally, she broke the silence.

"When are you going to get me to safety?" Her tone was more demanding than a question.

Jay dipped a rag into the Mink Oil container and applied a second application to the boot he was holding; he chose not to respond.

"Well?" Sheila was insistent.

Jay paused for a moment and let out a small sneer and shook his head. Still without saying a word the man proceeded with the chore at hand.

Such silence persuaded the young lady to become impatient. "I said, when are you going to help me get home?" Sheila was now glaring at Jay and had placed both of her hands on her hips as to further accentuate her point.

"No you didn't!" The man with unrefined appearance declared. "To answer your first question, you are already safe; to answer the second, about late April, perhaps early May."

Sheila was in disbelief and quite angry by now. She quickly pointed an index finger in the general direction of Jay's face, and with a somewhat spoiled tone stated, "That's unfair! It's kidnapping and that's pretty illegal!" Sheila became increasingly irate when Jay did not even acknowledge her statement. "You cannot hold me here against my will, you stinky savage!"

Jay still would not look up.

"I'm leaving!" And with such a declaration, the flustered female thrust a fist through a sleeve of her coat and began to walk to the door. "You cannot hold onto one's person without their permission!"

"Don't let the door squeeze your cheeks on the way out," Jay suggested. "Stinky savage," Jay repeated under his breath with a chuckle. "What the hell is that supposed to mean?"

Sheila fumbled with the unfamiliar door latch and, after accidentally figuring it out, stormed out, slamming the door behind her. After a few seconds a predicted muffled cry for help was audible from outside. Jay ignored the panicked cry for help for a spell while he finished cleaning off the excess preservative from his boots. He slowly placed the boots next to the stove and cleaned his hands with the rag. The commotion from outside continued. Upon opening the door, Jay would find a much humbler human being thirty or so feet from his log domain. Totally snowbound, with only her head and shoulders visible, Sheila had stepped onto a less packed area, and had broken through the snow crust. She was, once again, not that happy and the world was going to know about it! To make things worse, the ever eager Nut, who was always more than happy to aid the snowbound, ran past Jay and upon approaching the stuck victim, began to lick the woman's face with passionate vigor.

"Quit, quit, quit it, damn it!" Sheila screamed at the top of her lungs. Wing Nut cocked her head with ears forward and looked at Jay as to inquire as to what the problem might be.

Within minutes, another rescue of the high maintenance damsel was in progress. The mountain man slowly put his snowshoes on, which further infuriated the impatient woman. Then, with leisurely deliberation, he slowly adjusted his position so that he was standing astraddle Sheila's head. Sheila reluctantly raised her arms up to the waiting hands, dirty fingernails and all. With one heave, the pretty visitor was hoisted, once again, to the surface of the snow pack. The young lady's back was towards Jay while her feet were planted firmly on the snowshoes directly in front of his. Jay placed his hands upon the girl's waist and shuffle stepped the two of them back to the cabin. The faint bouquet of her perfume once again influenced Jay's sense of smell; however, this time the fragrance seemed to be somewhat alluring. Too alluring! Many years had passed since Jay Devereux had been this close to a woman and, as attractive as the aroma was, Jay desired no more complications to his chosen tranquil way of life.

As soon as the couple approached the door, the stranger released his hands from Sheila's waist and ordered her to remove herself from atop the snowshoes. Sheila was all too ready to oblige, and after doing so, turned and protested her repulse by scowling.

"And, what the hell is your problem?" In response to Sheila's ingratitude, Jay felt a surge of anger swell in his neck once again. "Are you always so surly whenever someone else rescues your silly ass? What an attitude!"

"An attitude! An attitude?!" Sheila was incensed by the man's lack of comprehension to her peril. She was obviously trying to think of a response. Unable to find the words, the angry woman took one step back and retorted, "I will show you an attitude!" With the flurry of a woman scorned, she entered the cabin, slammed and dead bolted the only door to the place Jay once knew as home. His home!

Surprised, Jay and his mutt looked at each other. Wing Nut cocked her head to one side and alerted her ears as if to ask, "What now?"

"How the hell do I know?" Jay answered to the unspoken question and began to remove the snowshoes. "I guess this means the honeymoon is over."

Realizing she had made a mistake, Sheila slowly unlatched the rustic type deadbolt and opened the door with cautious demeanor. "I want you to take me back to the airplane."

"Sounds like a plan to me." For the lack of being appreciated, Jay was still hot under the collar. "It sure will be a lot easier dragging you down this mountain than it was lugging your attitude up the damned thing. But, I got to tell ya, it's sure going take more than a couple rolls of duct tape to piece that Cessna back together... should have it done by April, maybe May! Let's go!"

Sheila was oversensitive to the man's crudeness. "I didn't ask you to bring me here!" She lashed out as, once again, she began to feel tears welling up in her eyes.

"Sorry. May I suggest that if you had not driven your airplane with the same apparent reckless abandonment in which you fail to control your arrogance, you probably wouldn't have lawn-darted the damn thing into my mountain! I guess we both will have to live with things the way they are, not the way either one of us would prefer!" Jay finished removing the wood and leather flats from his feet, and hung the pair of snowshoes on designated nails located on the outside wall. "Look, uh, uh ... what the hell is your name anyway?"

"Sheila." The girl responded as she walked over near the stove, sat down and placed her chin in her hands with her elbows resting on her knees. "Why do you feel compelled to swear all the time?"

"Actually, you haven't heard anything, yet." Jay finally smiled as he entered the room and closed the door. "Alright! So my social skills are not what you might refer to as refined. Considering that in the past half-decade I have not seen more than a half-dozen different people, it's a wonder I can talk at all. Come to think of it, you're the first woman I've seen since I have been here, and you already want me to give up my lingual luxuries."

Not quite believing Jay's excuses, Sheila looked up with somewhat pleading eyes and again voiced her desire to return to the plane.

"That would not be wise, Miss Sheila," Informed the experienced, if not pleasant looking, Mr. Devereux. "A storm is rolling off the high peaks and will produce a fierce competition with anyone who is so lame as to wander out in it. Tomorrow morning we will go; perhaps."

This did not sit well with the pretty young lady but she began to grasp the notion that she did not necessarily carry that much pull with Mother Nature or the stranger. "And when can you get me off this mountain?" Once again, Sheila's key question was posed.

"Did you have an ELT (emergency locater transmitter) aboard the Cessna?" Unknown to Sheila, Jay had been an accomplished pilot at one time.

"No." Sheila conceded. "Dad took it out because the batteries were dead, or something."

Jay shook his head and bent down to put another piece of pine in the stove. "Then you're fu... I mean screwed, I mean, your situation is really messed up." After a short pause, a new realization made its impression, and with such, Jay extended the ultimate revelation. "I mean, *my* situation is really messed up!" He just realized that the full impact of the dilemma he had taunted towards the woman earlier was indeed coming true. "April or May," he whispered under his breath.

"You have got to be kidding!" pleaded Sheila. "I can't stay here. You don't understand! I've got Christmas dinner with my parents and gifts to deliver, and, and ..." Sheila felt panicked, "... and a life to live!"

"What do you mean Christmas presents?" Jay insisted on an answer.

"Tomorrow," Sheila stopped and looked at her watch. "I mean today is Christmas. I'm supposed to be home!"

"It's supposed to be the last part of January or maybe mid-February!" Jay exclaimed. He had lost track of time before, but never this badly. Fall had turned into winter all too soon; perhaps this was the reason for his miscalculation. With such a discovery came great concerns. What first seemed a few months of extreme discomfort and certain inconvenience now turned into a question of survival; hunger and then the real possibilities of starvation.

"With your added mouth to feed around here, we will only be able to exist till the last part of March at best," Jay was quick to point out.

"First of all, I am *not* going to be around here all that long and secondly, can't you just go and shoot something?" The lady's ignorance was too obvious.

"Don't tempt me," the mountain man thought to himself. Jay was becoming disgusted with Shcila's persistence to remain stupid. She was listening, but was not hearing. Once and for all he would have to drive the point home. As he approached the woman, uncertainty was evident in her eyes. Jay quickly reached down and, without warning, lifted her one hundred-ten pound frame off of the floor with his strong hands around her waist. She was paralyzed with fear and had no reaction other than to stiffen her body and endure the man's unknown intentions. He placed her against the dusty log interior of the cabin and looked deeply into her wide eyes, which were level with his at this point.

"Did you file a flight plan before you scurried off into these parts?" The looming figure of a man asked.

Sheila slowly nodded.

"And how well did you stick with the flight plan?"

Her chin was shaking again as she did her best to respond, "I don't know where I am."

"You're at Machin Lake, near the Devil's Pin Cushion in the La Garita Wilderness!"

"No! That can't be!" Sheila was in shock. She had flown around this area for years, first with her father, and now by herself. She knew better than to "tempt the devil" as her father often said. The wind shears and downdrafts of the Sangre De Cristo and La Garita Mountain Ranges were unforgiving. Such adverse conditions were arguably unmatched anywhere in the world. Sheila now voiced her dismay, "I am way off course."

"Obviously; and, you know why I know no one's going to find you here? Because nobody in their right mind will ever fly a small search plane over and around these peaks!" Jay slowly and gently let the frightened woman down until her feet touched the floor. Adjusting his posture to once again gain eye contact, he bent and placed both hands against the wall on either side of Sheila's shoulders. "Now hear this, and take it to heart. It looks like we are going to be roomies for the duration. You obviously don't care for the idea. We have enough food for a couple months, but the snow is getting too deep for safe travel." He now turned his eyes toward the glowing embers through the stove front and thought to himself, "I will be damned if I am going to ride out the white death for this bimbo!"

Jay knew from past experiences that you must store for the winter and then live off the land until avalanche season arrives. This year he had gauged it wrong to begin with. Winter had started in mid-October, a solid month before his anticipated prediction. Jay also thought that spring would be early and what if he was wrong about that as well? With conditions marginal at best, he would have to hunt for game that had already retreated to the low lands. The whole process was a gamble at best. He feared that the task would not only prove to be fruitless but counterproductive as well. Great energy expelled meant a greater increase in appetite, and subsequently, nourishing the hunters could counter the intent of the expedition, especially if he was unsuccessful.

Chapter Four

Devil's Dining Room

As the evening progressed, Jay's prediction of a blizzard came to pass. He and the young lady spent much of the time deep in their own separate thoughts. Night fall seemed to bring the howling wind, and the snow that was within its fury pounded the windows which gave a sensation of pelting sand. Still, there was a sense of well-being as the cabin was warm and the atmosphere within its walls, calm.

*****

At daybreak the next morning, Sheila was awakened to the aroma of pancakes and bacon. As she raised her pretty head and peered in the direction of the stove, she was thankful that finally a pleasant odor had overpowered the extreme "locker room" smell. Furthermore, she was hungry. As she rose from her borrowed bed, her eyes fell upon a scrap piece of paper which was pinned to the door with a hunting knife. It simply stated:

Ms. Sheila,
Went to the plane to recover property.
Will be back before dark.
Don't wait up.
        J.

With the realization that she was all alone came an uneasiness, and for the first time, Sheila felt value in the company of the stranger. She hurried to the door and when she opened it, she would not be prepared for the scene she beheld. The woman found herself totally taken with the winter wonderland which the overnight snow and wind had left behind. Exquisite white powder had been blown into drifts that reached halfway up the cabin walls. The windward side of the nearby trees was caked with the white stuff and gigantic drifts had completely changed the landscape into a soft rolling terrain.

After consuming a surprisingly good breakfast, Miss Gray decided that she would while-away the hours by taking on the unrelenting task of cleaning the "missing link's" cave. As the morning progressed, she was amazed to find all the household cleaners necessary inside a box which was under the bed. Sheila noted that the box had a noticeable amount of dust resting on its surface.

"At least he had intentions of being less aromatic at one time," she thought to herself. "I wonder what made him want to live this way to begin with."

Around mid-afternoon, Sheila was enthusiastic as she approached the finishing touches of the now spotless living quarters. The cabin appeared much larger after things were organized. She would pause for a brief interval and take in what was not just an acceptably clean dwelling, but in all actuality, a beautiful, rustic living quarters.

A large galvanized washing tub began to rock ever so slightly as its surface began to respond to the hot surface of the stove beneath it. Sheila had placed the first batch of soiled laundry for soaking and two more piles were on the floor waiting their turn. On the back wall were two large shelves with a great assortment of books. Some were highly intellectual, some with general titles, and then there were those just for amusement. Sheila found herself becoming increasingly impressed as she scanned the entitled authors; Robert Frost, Charles Dickens, Charles Morris, and Zane Gray; even Stephen King and many others. Some were world renowned while others unknown to her. Often Sheila wondered about the mystery that surrounded the large man who had saved her life.

Thoughts of her mother and father, as well as her two younger sisters would, from time to time, intervene and otherwise cloud the pleasant success of her present toil. She missed them so much and she knew that in the coming days they would become increasingly overwhelmed with grief through their ignorance and assumptions. She knew that it was reasonable for them to believe that she was dead and such a thought made her sad beyond comprehension.

*****

Sheila's attention was interrupted as she became aware of the distant bark of Wing Nut. It was not an alarming bark. It was more like a "Mom, we're home" type announcement. The beautiful woman rushed to the door, took a quick look around to make sure all was in order, and then turned the latch as though to greet someone other than a virtual acquaintance. Although she had been engrossed in hard work the entire day, she had been aware that for the first time in her life she had been left all alone on the mountain side. A mountain that was secluded from civilization, and she had not entirely appreciated such a hollow feeling before.

Even though Jay and his faithful mutt were within sight, it was still awhile before they were able to reach the door. Jay had once again incorporated the outer portion of what was left of the Cessna as a sleigh. He strapped all the items that the intended single trip would support. Even at a great distance, Sheila could see that Jay had secured her cross-country skis to the top of the modest heap. Somehow she took refuge in the notion that she maybe had some control of destiny by such a possession.

The Nut was first to detect that something was not quite right. As she began to enter the cabin, she halted and then slowly backed out through the doorway from whence she had come. Not picking up on the dog's apprehension, Jay lumbered in and was ultimately shocked at the appearance of his domain. Everything had been rearranged. His privacy had been invaded and his solitude tampered with! Quickly diverting his stare towards the smiling Sheila, Jay realized the sensitivity of the moment. Trying his best not to hurt feelings, Jay looked down at the floor of which the likes he had not seen in several years.

"This is incredible." Jay simply said.

"Do you really like it?" Sheila asked the inevitable question. Her excitement was most evident as she solicited for a more confirming approval.

Jay smiled as he realized the significance of her labor intensive achievement. "Hell yes! It looks fabulous; don't it Nut?" Jay lied. Although the newly organized room was uncomfortable to him, he resigned himself to at least appreciate the incredible effort.

*****

It was late evening and Jay watched the once again striking features of the beautiful creature that was his guest. He found himself amused by the recent contentment she seemed to radiate as she washed the dinner dishes. In so doing, he recognized that he too felt at peace. Without knowing it, he had a smile on his bearded face as he snuggled into the depths of an easy chair which had been retrieved from the "lost and found" by way of the cleaning expedition. It had previously served as a catch all bay for everything from dirty clothes to kindling from which to start fires. He turned up a kerosene lamp and opened a book. So quickly was he engrossed that he was unaware that the new roommate was preparing for a bath. It was not until he glanced up briefly that he would experience the second great shock of the day. Jay forced himself to look at the book again, but slowly his eyes involuntarily rose again. They were to behold the sharp silhouette of the exquisite shape of Sheila. With a thin sheet hung as a blind, the woman was standing so close as to reveal every exquisite detail of her physical charm. As Jay unintentionally watched, the unaware woman slowly bent down and drew soapy water up from the galvanized tub in which she stood. She slowly straightened her body and placed the wash rag upon her chest. As the warm water gently drifted over her supple magnificence, Jay drew a deep breath and held it. He could feel his heart pounding, and was sure that the perfectly shaped creature on the other side of the thin curtain would soon detect the same. Not wishing to have his visual intrusion discovered, Jay wiped the newly formed perspiration from his hot forehead and began to stand. The now forgotten hardbound slipped from his lap and crashed on the head of Wing Nut who was content in her ignorant slumber. With a yelp, the startled dog jumped up and scurried under the bed. Now Jay was suffering through an adrenaline surge of his own. Embarrassed by the unscheduled alarm set off by his dog, and currently feeling uncomfortably obvious, Jay followed an irresistible urge which persuaded him to rush to the door and swiftly leave the cabin without a coat or footwear. It was with immediate recognition that he became privy to the miscalculation, but with humiliation as the only guide, chose to remain outside - until spring if necessary!

Fortunately, within a couple minutes the door was opened from the inside and the towel clad steaming body of unparalleled splendor appeared.

"Your turn!" declared Sheila Gray. This would prove to be the third bombshell of the day; perhaps the greatest assault of the past five years to the unwashed presence of the mountain man.

With a reaction from embarrassment more than from thorough thought, Jay soon found himself standing in the rather restrictive boundaries of the metal tub. He had not forgotten the revealing characteristics of the curtain and found himself preoccupied, more with modesty than the focus on the purpose of the task.

"And wash that beard." The house guest was becoming more like a house pest.

"*Like the herd animals we are, we sniff warily at the strange one among us,*" Jay was eager to announce his displeasure relating to soap and water so early in the winter.

Sheila found herself impressed with the quote but was not willing to appear oblivious. "I didn't understand what that really meant when Loren Eiseley said it eighty or so years ago; don't really understand it now. Besides, it isn't as though I am sniffing-I just can't avoid the obvious."

"Touché," Jay simply replied.

Within moments, a much cleaner man emerged from the makeshift bathing room. Sheila burst out with laughter as his facial expressions were not that far removed from a freshly bathed cat. Although Jay had not been that comfortable with the process, it could not be denied that he was a good sport about the entire thing. If Jay was pressed for the truth, he would have admitted that he felt better. But he was not pressed and by such, would not concede to the possibility. After his long shaggy hair had time to dry, Sheila drew a pair of scissors and a comb from her personal belongings. Jay basked in her near presence as she proceeded to cut his long mane and trim that beard with experienced precision.

*****

As the sun cast a golden glow over the eastern ridge, the very tops of the giant pines reflected the rays as if to announce the dawning of the new day. Jay scoped the ridge, and as the sun rose he directed his focus on the valley below. There was no sign of big game in the extreme depths of the snow, nor did he anticipate any. Disappointment gripped the now clean cut man as he shook his head and bent down to unlatch the bindings on his cross-country skis. He had left the cabin at four that morning and the twelve-mile journey had left him fatigued. After clearing a place in the five-foot deep snow, Jay positioned himself on his back and looked up into the heavens. Where would he find meat this time of the year? He was, in a way, relieved that the trip had proven fruitless for the distance back may have been too great to carry the spoils of success. Nevertheless, the dilemma remained the same. He missed the yellow dog but knew that the Nut would not have made the distance. Besides, if game was spotted, she would hamper the effort by unintentionally alarming the hunted. Jay also thought often about the woman who seemed to be an instant part of his life now. Although the attraction was great, he did not desire to become involved. He could not become involved! He had lived in the big city before and experienced "success" as defined by others. He had also experienced failure and, as unpredictable as the rugged mountain life was, at least he could depend on it to be constantly hard. By no means was there ever room for complacency in the wilderness!

After a brief rest, Jay chose to head back in the direction of the cabin and not to continue the elusive pursuit to the lower valleys. There had to be something edible still left in the high elevations, otherwise the timber wolves would not still be there.

Around midday, unseasonable weather began to hamper his progress. As the temperature rose, the snow began to stick to the bottoms of the skis and with every thrust, wet snow was packing against his pant legs. Jay was also worried about the atmospheric difference in relationship to the stability of the snow. With the heavier snow now on top, and the granular stuff under, the high lands became increasingly dangerous.

It was dark before the man started up the side of Canyon Diablo and towards the top of the Continental Divide. In the great distance, he could see a lamp lit window. Somehow, by the visual confirmation of his destination, Jay felt less exhausted. By this time, it was once again cold and his skis were fast. As he slid up the frozen tundra in a serpentine progression, he thought about the pleasant warmth of the stove, the dinner that would sit in waiting, and yes, the magnificent woman who would be in his home. As best he could, he tried again not to engage in such pleasant thoughts, but his mind had been touched and his heart contaminated. The pattern of wanting to be totally alone was now severely in question.

*****

The next morning, the second expedition for the ever elusive four-legged groceries had been launched. This time Wing Nut persisted in tagging along. After all, she was merely holding up to her responsibilities as partner and chief scout. Jay was compelled to start the snowshoe run in a different direction. He decided that he would attempt to scout the south face of San Luis Peak. This was something that had never been done in the winter. Perhaps there would be game on the windward side of the fourteen thousand foot treeless mountain. With her day of rest, combined with the excitement of the current campaign, the Nut preceded Jay and was able to ingress and egress atop the frozen crust with ease. The trudging man was so engrossed with thoughts of Sheila that he failed to identify the subtle hints and warnings of nature.

As Jay reached above timberline, he stopped and looked back in the direction of his log home. Smoke lazily curled from the single stove pipe and drifted in a horizontal fashion into the blue spruce. Within the confines and safety of the building was the lady who had apparently come to terms with her isolation from the rest of the world. Jay knew that when he returned he was going to have to address issues. Jay was fearful that without a defined understanding about expectations concerning roles and relationships, things would become complicated; perhaps impossible. He was not interested in, nor would he ever dare entertain the possibilities of falling in love!

As the mountain man turned and began to ascend once again, large flocks of birds which were perched in the nearby scrub oak were spooked. With apparent brisk panic, they fluttered across the path of the hunter and his dog, chirping their disapproval of the intrusion. Jay watched and marveled as fifty or more of the fair feathered friends turned, jetted up and then back down as a constant group. Not one of the birds was lost in the shuffle, nor were there any mid-air collisions.

After hours of monotonous drudgery up the steep slope, man and beast broke the summit of San Luis Peak. The view was breathtaking in all directions with magnificent sister peaks, sheer cliffs, and endless dark canyons. Jay stood in awe for a couple minutes and then proceeded down the comparably gentle grade of the southwest face. He would have done well to more closely observe the clouds which, at a quick glance, appeared to be nestled passively into the nearby La Garita Wilderness Mountains. Instead, the saturated cumulonimbus vapor was fast approaching with an ever increasing wind. There were other subtle indications of the approaching fury. There was a vapor ring around the sun. Smoke from the cabin stove had struggled to the top of the stovepipe and then, after expelling itself from the metal cylinder dropped and hung low. There was also the covey of birds which flocked so closely together. All had been signs of impending inclement weather; all had been ignored for the thoughts of a beautiful woman.

*****

Once again, Sheila spent the whole morning rearranging and straightening the common living area of the modest cabin. While she did so, she became absorbed in thoughts surrounding the mystery man with whom she found herself living with. For the most part, she found herself comfortable with the stranger, but her curiosity about him could not be denied. Such curiosity had taken on energy of its own and Sheila found herself consumed with discovering what this stranger was all about. Why was he so strong and yet so shy? He was obviously well read, but why did he choose complete solitude over interaction with the population? As she searched around the interior of the abode for clues of his past, she was suddenly struck with the realization that no trace of a past existed. None what-so-ever! Not a picture or a letter. Not even a scrap of script inside one of the books. Who was this man who had no reflection, no history?

As Sheila sat on the stump in the middle of the humble quarters, she scanned every inch of the cabin with her deep, liquid eyes. There had to be some evidence of Jay's prior life. As her gaze passed the bookshelf, something caught her eye. Looking down at the floor, her thoughts began to race as she tried to figure out what she was looking at. There were drag marks, or perhaps roller marks, suggesting that the large bookshelf was not a permanent or stationary fixture.

"You're kidding," Sheila thought out loud as she tugged at one side of the shelf. Why hadn't she noticed it before? Slowly the shelf began to move. She quickly pushed the shelf back next to the wall from which it had come. What was she doing? She had no right to further invade Jay's privacy! Deciding that a breach of such trust was not worth the risk, she perished the thought of investigating further and engaged herself with sorting through her own belongings. Soon however, her thoughts again returned to the possibilities of the mysteries behind the bookshelf. Thinking that there was no possible harm in looking around the outside of the shelf, curiosity drew her to explore further. At the other end of the rustic furnishings were two large hinges; one half of the hinges were attached to the wall – the other half, to the shelf.

Sheila's father had once told her that the devil did not want her whole soul; he would just settle for a little toe (to begin with). Then, eventually, with methodical patience, he would work his way up to her soul. Sheila had forgotten the advice, for upon seeing the hinges, her thirst for further knowledge drew her will as iron shavings to a magnet. She quickly slipped on her expensive mink collared coat and wandered outside of the cabin. As she drew near the back of the lodge, she found herself at an unexpected impasse. She simply stood and stared. There was no back side of the cabin. Or a better description would be, the cabin had a total back side. Where she anticipated an extended room was instead the face of a solid rock cliff which the cabin seemed to purposely be attached.

With excitement mounting, the inquisitor rushed back into the warm cabin, and without hesitation, secured both hands around the free end of the heavy bookshelf. Anticipation was mounting beyond measure, and consequence was no longer an element of concern. With a great heave, Sheila pulled with all her might. The cumbersome wood shelving slightly opened with a screeching sound. Sheila resituated her feet and put so much heave into it that her feet skidded forward and she landed with a thud on her rump. As momentum was gained, so was a sense of sudden apprehension. With the shelf about three feet from the wall, she would stop her effort all together and stand back as if to consider the option to abort the impromptu mission. However, it was too late, for the "devil" had already worked his way up and past her conscience. Curiosity could no longer be denied. It was with a token gesture of caution that the beautiful woman's adventurous eyes slowly peered around the shelf and into whatever mysterious depths awaited.

Chapter Five

The Devil's Kitchen

Jay's prayers had been answered. As he descended a little over a mile down the south face of the mountain, he advanced with patient faith into the tall scrub oak. Soon he detected the distinctive odor of elk. He was on the leeward, uphill side, and the smell was strong. This meant many elk were in the small meadow on the gentle slope to the south toward Creede. The wind had blown the snow shallow and feed was plentiful. He ordered the Nut to stay, and with a forlorn expression, the yellow chow obeyed by lying down and placing her head on her paws as Jay slipped his snowshoes off. Without lifting her head from its resting place, Wing Nut's eyes followed her owner's every move.

"Stop looking abused." Jay instructed his best friend. "It's not becoming and besides I'm on to you."

The dog seemed to understand but maintained the same martyred expression.

Within moments, the hunter could see movement through the thin alpine vegetation as he advanced. He slowly and carefully cocked the hammer back on the Winchester '94 as to prevent detectible noise. With periodic intentions he would take a few steps, and then stop and listen. Patience was paramount as he peered at a nearby bull. Jay's eyes grew wide as the large bull turned toward him, and with sudden admiration, Jay marveled at the seven by seven point spread which crowned the head of the Northern Roosevelt. The elk was an undeniably gigantic beast. Jay estimated the majestic king of the forest to weigh over 900 pounds, perhaps even a thousand. But this opportunity was not the one the mountain man was looking for. He knew that the larger the animal, the more meat he would waste. If at all possible Jay would wait until a yearling calf came into view.

For the next half an hour, Jay remained motionless for the bull was content to feed at the upper mouth of the high mountain meadow. His presence blocked the entire view of the other animals but Jay was content to wait. As he did so, he became acutely aware that something was not quite right. At first he noticed that there was a brisk wind flowing through the tree tops on the adjacent mountain. As Jay cautiously studied that direction, his heart sank. Storm saturated clouds were rapidly engulfing all the surrounding peaks and mountains which indicated impending blizzard conditions; this was a certainty!

Jay Devereux's first instinct was to retreat as quickly as possible and seek shelter. He half smiled as he conceded to the fact that if he could not beat the storm, he and the Nut would likely perish. He came to terms with the possibilities and concluded that he and Wing Nut would face Mother Nature on her terms here and now, on the South Face.

"How could I have been so stupid?" Jay silently conceded to his mistake. Suddenly he would recall the warning signs he had apparently chosen to ignore for the sake of reminiscing about Sheila. It was with involuntary response to his thoughts that he shook his head. By such distraction the monstrous elk lifted his massive antlers and looked in Jay's direction. Jay held his breath. He realized that he would now have to take the shot or all options would likely be lost. He could feel the cold metal trigger on his index finger as he lifted the Winchester and prepared to squeeze off the round. He hoped that the blunt-nosed round that was traditional for deer hunting was significant enough to down such a large animal. Then there was something which caused him to pause. Although the necessity for food was great, he nevertheless had reservations about taking this animal. He was committed to a more reasonable harvest.

Suddenly the king of the forest let out a large snort and swung his head in the opposite direction. It was as though the elk's attentions were directed to an unknown second intruder. Jay cocked his head as to gain an advantage on the new development. Soon things would become abundantly clear as a young five point bull rushed through eight foot scrub brush with brisk determination and advanced toward a higher form of experience. Jay watched with delight as he was able to take in an ultimate battle for supremacy.

To gain a better advantage, Jay stood upright and in full view of the unconcerned warriors of the wilderness. He expected the senior participant of this battle to engage with full massive authority and quickly snuff out the will of the youngster. Jay was to become privy to the subtle finesse in which nature educates it's young. He found himself enchanted with the concept that this was not an ultimate battle of pride or territory. Instead, it was a demonstration of posture and respect.

With total fascination, the worthy mountain man watched as the greatest act unfolded on the most magnificent stage on earth. As the young bull lunged with excessive power and youth, the elder would merely step to the side and shield himself with his superior antlers. After three or four passes, the five point bull pawed the ground with evident frustration and then stepped head to head with the master. The two locked antlers and a struggle for advantage ensued. Upon close observation, Jay could see that only the young bull was continuously expending energy. Old school dictated that the more mature of the two would constantly stand surefooted until the adolescent either got out of control or became tired.

As the wind began to pick up, so did the fury within the young animal. In an obvious fit of rage, the youngster pulled free and quickly attempted to thrust his sharp points into the chest of his adversary. Only the reactions of the royal elk would detour the sinister intentions of the five-point male. With incredible strength and unfathomable quickness, the seven point bull positioned his head low and underneath the lean mass of the aggressor. It only took a one final thrust and the smaller of the gorgeous elk was tossed into the air and came crashing onto the frozen tundra. The victor stood over the fallen ego of the now humbled male and gave a tremendous snort as to exclaim the lesson finished. The youngster flinched, but then remained still. It was obvious that the demonstration of reverence was over.

As suddenly as the event began, it had ended. Unconcerned with Jay's presence, the large bull slowly lumbered to a new location and began to graze as though the fight had not even taken place. This would open up a view of the entire park and in so doing, reminded the hunter of his purpose. Jay immediately spotted a small calf less than one hundred yards away. He quickly raised his firearm, focused through the peep sight and squeezed the trigger.

*****

Great anticipation mounted as Sheila gazed at the steel door which was framed into the wall. She tried the metal crank style handle but the dead bolt kept the barrier secure. With instant recall, her thoughts went to a gold colored key which was perched on the overhead ledge of the entry door frame on the other side of the cabin. She had discovered it while she had been cleaning the cobwebs around the ceiling. Although she had not thought much of it at the time, she was now certain that it was the key to the mystery room and, perhaps Jay's past. With undeniable haste, she retrieved the object and without a moment's hesitation pushed it into the lock slot. It fit, but at first it would not turn. Sheila pulled the key out, exhaled a breath on its surface, polished it on the sleeve of her blouse and then swiftly reinserted the skeleton styled relic back into the receptacle with confidence. This time it responded. As the resistance began to yield, Sheila whispered to herself, "Yes!"

Leaving the key in the locking mechanism, Sheila once again grasped the latch and pulled down and back. The dry hinges protested the breech with a haunted grinding resolution, followed by a creaking sound as if to extend one last chance for blissful ignorance. Sheila's focus was past the warning and she continued to pull with determination. The heavy gauged steel door began to slowly yield to her resolve. As the lone female timidly stepped into the entrance of the unknown, she would again experience doubt but somehow the point of no return had been passed. There would be no turning back for surely, discovery was now inches away.

A rush of air seemed to be released. It was cool, but not freezing. Light struggled from the partially opened doorway and even that was greatly compromised by the shadow cast by the inquisitive female. Only vague shadows loomed in the uncertain recesses of the newly discovered cavern. There was a disturbing hollow sensation to Sheila's confidence. She responded with sudden retreat, and without hesitation approached the modest table in the center of the cabin. Frantic anticipation propelled her actions as she broke several matches in an attempt to light the kerosene lamp. After six attempts, the lamp was lit and the eager lady once again focused her attentiveness to the mission at hand. It was as though she was consumed by the mystery in the walk-in vault. As she began to step through the doorway into the great unknown, the flame within the globe flickered and went out as if an omen; a last warning. At first startled but not diverted, the determined Miss Gray lit the lamp for the second time, and for the third time, launched the impulsive expedition.

This time, Sheila held her left hand in front of the top part of the globe as to prevent the draft from snuffing out the flame. She again entered the mystery room. As she slowly placed one foot in front of the other, she became aware that there were countless drop cloths that concealed the true identity of probable furniture. She was soon impressed that there were many more shelves with thousands of books. An oversized oak showcase with ornate glass doors drew her interest. With centered anticipation, she peered through the panes and found herself amazed at the many collegian trophies and mementos safely sealed in the dust resistant display. One undeniable symbol of distinction demanded Sheila's intrigue. It was a picture of Jay next to the Heisman Trophy! The unmistakable Heisman Trophy! And beside the picture was a larger framed enlargement of the Fighting Irish in their gold and blue uniforms. Sheila's eyes immediately fell on who she knew as Jay Devereux, third row and more or less, center. Although he was not sporting a beard and obviously much younger, it could not be denied, it was Jay.

Sheila felt a great sense of excitement and anticipation as she continued to scan the contents of the oak vault, which no longer concealed the stranger's past. Signatures and personal scripts were among the many valuables, and then the faded glint of a silver badge was singled out by the intruder's sharp eye. The item of fascination was at the back of the show case, and through a distance guarded by the glass and the poor lighting, Sheila squinted to read the inscription on the unmistaken shield; "City of New York, Police, #1557."

Working past the temporary intrigue of the cabinet, Sheila now stood still and surveyed the magnificent rock wall dwelling. She became increasingly content with the little bit she thought that she now knew. After all, this magnificent mystery man had saved her life. Although she continued to be confused by his apparent depth in general, peace seemed to anchor within her mind and she was comfortable with the discovery. She now was sure that the stranger possessed no dark side; or at least that is what she eagerly led herself to believe.

With a sudden start, Sheila became aware of her own presence and found herself uncomfortable with the choice of intrusion. Urgency took hold of her confidence and persuaded her to withdraw from the secret room. As she took an intentional step towards her exodus, something solid all but tripped her. She stopped and deliberately bent down and ran her hand across the most exquisite rosewood and cedar chest that she had ever seen. With care she opened the lid and laid her eyes upon its contents. Unexpected dismay gripped her as she read the front page of the New York Times which was lying on the surface. **"Cop Breaks Over 9/11 and Goes On Shooting Spree; Seven Dead!"** Jay's photograph was featured underneath the most disturbing caption. With immeasurable concern, Sheila refocused her eyes on the caption once again and read it slowly. As the shocked young lady picked up the paper and began to unfold it, her eyes grew past the printed news and refocused on the rest of the contents in the chest. It was full of money! Not just hundreds, or thousands, but definitely, hundreds of thousands of dollars in United States currency! After dropping the paper to the floor, she slowly reached down and grabbed several bundles of fifties and hundreds with her left hand while still holding the lantern with a shaking right. An overwhelming panic was taking her over, and she now wished that she had maintained the blissful ignorance and never entered the archive chamber.

*****

The fierce wind had placed the man and his dog next to the South Face wall. The formation was sheer rock which was a great distance farther from the awaiting warmth of the cabin, but was the only hope for shelter from nature's wrath. As the savage wind tore at Jay's senses and challenged his will to continue with relentless ferocity, the man searched for a cave that would lend shelter to him and his four legged companion. He felt fortunate that he even found the sheer rock face to begin with; however, the task was far from complete. He still had to find the large hole in the wall. With the added weight of the hind quarters of the calf elk on his back, he was split in deciding on keeping the spoils of his hunt, or forfeiting the important cargo.

Wing Nut sensed the urgency of the moment and taking it upon herself to seek a calm place, rushed beyond Jay's awareness. Through the deafening pitch of the wind, Jay thought for a moment that he had heard Wing Nut bark. Jay tilted his head slightly as he held firmly to the rock wall and directed an eager ear away from the gale. Yes, it was the Nut.

Jay made his way the best that he could along the wall, daring not to release the tangible touch for fear of never locating it again. As snow pelted against the back of his neck, he located Wing Nut at the entrance of the cavern. Jay was pleased with his best friend and overjoyed at the prospects of living longer.

The large man drew a deep breath and exhaled loudly. Then, with a great heave lifted the hundred or so pounds of wild game from his shoulders and allowed the elk meat to fall into the snow at the mouth of the cave. With cautious demeanor he entered the cave and attempted to adjust his eyes to the pitch black hole. Meanwhile, Wing Nut was standing at the entrance of the natural shelter with hair standing on end and bracing for the unknown. There was an incredible stench of something overly dead combined with the unmistaken aroma of rat and bat feces. The aroma insulted the usually tolerant nostrils of the mountain man. Wing Nut began to bark an alarm, and at the same time, Jay would realize anything dead at these temperatures would not abuse the sense of smell. He dared not turn his back as he slowly began a wise retreat.

From the very bowels of the earth came a low guttural protest that vibrated the ground and sent ice cold shivers up the spine of the already cold intruders. Confirmation was made; the odorous "dead thing" was not so dead! Now, there was a sobering realization that they had awoken a sleeping giant! Jay increased the speed of his retreat. Suddenly, through the depths of darkness, a large, very large, shadowy figure emerged!

Disobeying her owner's orders, the Nut rushed past Jay and immediately engaged the monster. Jay's eyes could now see the disastrous result of Wing Nut's instinctive actions. With a crashing blow from a giant paw, the 500 pound brown bear sent the dog cartwheeling twenty feet. Without a whimper, the dog now lay motionless on the dirt floor of the giant's home.

"No!" Jay exclaimed as he removed his gloves and flung them on the ground. Quickly pulling his rifle from around his back he grabbed the lever and briskly worked the action.

"Take this, bitch!" Jay yelled at the top of his lungs as he pulled the trigger.

With an irrefutable thud, the oversized bear received the full force of the bullet in her chest. However, the projectile only served to penetrate the outer skin and further enrage the beast within. Twice more Jay would shoot, but this time holding the gun near his hip. Again the lead projectiles were denied by the armor of thick skin and deep layers of fat. As the bear continued her aggression, Jay grabbed the .30-30 by the barrel and swung as hard as he could. The weapon's wood stock crashed into the side of the broad head of the carnivore and instantly shattered. Again the bear did not veer from its foe. Impulse took over and the man lunged to the dirt floor and rolled to the side of the advancing beast. Jay was only interested at rescuing his wounded pup and wished no further quarrel with the bear. The bear, on the other hand, was not content to allow the two intruders to concede and retreat. Not without suffering the supreme penalty. With the sow's winter sleep disrupted, instincts seemed to fuel her fury and thrust her to seek the final concession ... death to all who had violated her domain! With a barbaric snarl, the relative of the grizzly instantly twisted her oversized bulk in pursuit of the would-be evasive intentions of the trespasser. Jay sprung to his feet and was immediately brought down again by a head butt which took his breath away. Half crawling, half running on his hands and knees, he attempted to flee the wrath of the insane quadruped, but the beast was so much faster.   Excruciating pain pierced through Jay's lower extremities as a giant paw connected with unequal force into Jay's right hip. The sensation of being flung the width of the grotto further disoriented the unprepared Devereux.   There was no chance for compromise, and thus no chance for survival. As Jay lay in silence on the cave floor, he resigned himself to the obvious and prayed for a quick end without further pain.

"To the victor go the spoils!" Jay whispered as he watched the wallowing predator draw near for the apparent kill. Jay lay perfectly still while the large flat forehead of the magnificent bear pushed against his side. Pressing effortlessly, the bear rolled him onto his back. Jay would not resist the inevitable. As he looked into the endless depth of a black evil stare, he would realize that he was in the devil's own kitchen.

Perhaps the bear felt that she had proven her point. Or, maybe it was the faint whimper of Wing Nut that drew her focus. In any event, the meat eating monster lost interest and slowly lumbered a few feet away. With caution Jay took in a deep breath and exhaled. His right leg was growing numb, but for the most part he felt alright. He sensed that the intolerant bear knew he was still alive.

Jay could hear Nut's panting intermittently between the bear's heavy heaves of breath. Jay slowly sat up and massaged his damaged hip and leg which was becoming increasingly stiff. As he did so, he squinted at Wing Nut and his heart sank. He watched as the dog who had been his only welcome companion for the last five years attempt to make her way to him. It was clear that her back was broken by the very first blow. She concentrated her entire strength onto her front paws and elbows and then drug her body the distance to Jay.

Without regard for the beast, Jay stood up and began to hobble over to his distressed dog. Due warning was given as the bear roared her disapproval and lunged at the weary man. Jay hammered with what was left of his rifle on the head of the charging bear. Without any signs of discomfort, the giant clasped both her forepaws around the midsection of the mountain man. While holding her victim, tilted her head and opened her gigantic jaws as if to swallow the man's head whole. Jay had dropped what was left of the gun and with frantic resolve, blindly felt for his Buck survival knife strapped to his waist. Feeling the ever increasing pressure of the bear, the mountain man gripped the metal checkered handle of the large knife and yanked it from the scabbard. There was only time enough for a single assault, and Jay thrust the deadly blade into the open mouth of the oversized adversary and pushed until he could feel his clutched fist being constricted by the giant's convulsing throat. The eight foot monster choked with a grotesque guttural sound and by reflex began to gag. The superior strength of the bear was quite evident as she raised the man off the ground with only her mouth and began to shake the man back and forth as though to rid herself of the sudden discomfort the human had brought.

Jay thought that his arm would completely dislocate from the shoulder but then the ferocious head tossing stopped. Looking deep into the creature's ebony eyes, it was as though the vicious animal actually realized its own unavoidable mortality. There was even a detectable sense of disbelief. Jay could feel the throat muscles contract harder and harder around his hand as the instinct for air grew more imperative. Suddenly, with a vicious last gesture for survival, the grand beast raked the claws of both massive paws across the back of the mountain man. Jay let out a blood curdling scream and thrust his head back in response to the intense pain. The razor sharp points of each talon had penetrated the thick elk hide coat, Levi shirt, and the skin.

The instinctive brute began to lose consciousness and collapsed, which ultimately left Jay crashing to the dirt floor with the great weight of the huge bear partially on top of him. Jay could feel several ribs on his left side yield as the oxygen was forced from his lungs and back out of his mouth. One last burst of adrenalin surged through the man's veins as he began to suffocate and panic gripped his very soul. Little by little he began to squirm free. He found that by slightly lifting the head of the bear he could take a brief breath. Breathing was painful, and his arm, which was still lodged in the giant's mouth, ached. He ached all over for that matter.

*****

Jay opened his eyes and for a moment was confused. As his consciousness became clear, he realized the sight of the cold stones and rocks that made up the walls of the now serene cave. The place was much darker now, so Jay sensed the short winter day must be coming to a close. The wind had stopped and silence now engulfed the battle field. There was no thrill of victory. No feeling of jubilation or pride, or even satisfaction. Only a great sense of death and wounds along with the experience of regret and despair. God, did Jay Devereux feel alone!

Somehow he had gotten free from the tremendous weight of his conquered adversary, but he had not remembered how. He would lie for a moment and gather his thoughts. As he did so, a familiar wet tongue found its way to Jay's cheek. With breathing shallow, Wing Nut was barely alive. Jay placed his hand on the faithful dog's head and gently stroked the soft golden fur. The Nut gave one last gasp, and with half closed eyes, passed beyond. Jay knew, but continued to rub the unresponsive head. He was man among men, climber of large mountains and slayer of great beasts, but still, just a man. By such he was not only subject to scars of battles, struggles of plagues, and physical illnesses, but the emotional strife of love and heartbreak. With an endless stream of tears, Jay gathered his yellow dog in his arms and held onto his lost companion.

Chapter Six

For a Full Count

Sheila opened the door of the Earth stove and peered in. Next to the hot coals were three potatoes wrapped in tin foil. On top of the stove was a black skillet with meat of which the origin Sheila was uncertain. As the steaks sizzled her thoughts were of the hidden room and the secrets that were concealed within. How was she to reveal her discovery to the stranger with whom she was destined to spend the next several months? She kept telling herself that she should have read the entire article, but she had gotten scared and hurried out of the room before doing so.

Her concerns would change as the night progressed. Minutes would turn into hours and still there was no sign of the mystery man and Wing Nut. She often gazed through the window, hopeful that she would see Jay trudging towards the house. And, at the same time, she dreaded the thought of him being there. And then, what if he did not come back at all?

It was about midnight when she resigned herself to the concession that he would not be coming home; at least, for whatever reason, not tonight. She stoked the stove, turned down the lamp, and draped the heavy quilt over her clothed body. She would sit down in the overstuffed lounge chair and try to sleep.

At about 4 a.m., Sheila awoke with a start without any apparent reason. With her heart racing, she was pressed by extreme anxiety. She looked at her watch and then around the room. For an instant, she thought that perhaps her restlessness was a result of a forgotten dream, but she could not recall even a subliminal glimpse of such. Sheila felt compelled to rise and walk to the door. Without reasonable explanation, she was overwhelmed with the urge to open the heavy wooden barrier; still, there was doubt and apprehension causing a sensation to refrain. Nevertheless, curiosity broke her resistance and she grabbed the latch with her right hand and held her left hand flush on the door surface as a precaution. If need be, she would be able to shove it closed in an instant. Sheila released the latch on the windowless door. With tentative resolve she gave into curiosity and slowly pulled the door open. Suddenly, she felt a force from the other side and the door pushed completely open. Jay fell onto the wood floor in front of her. Clutching the dog to his chest, Jay laid face down. Sheila let out a gasp at the shock of his entrance, and then a second when she saw the extent of the open wounds on his back. With a shaking hand next to her mouth, Miss Gray reluctantly knelt over the fallen man. The silence was broken when Jay murmured something, but she could not understand.

"What?" Sheila bent close to the mutilated human as she strained to hear.

"Clooos da rooor!" Jay instructed, but Sheila still was unable to understand.

"What?" She once again pleaded.

"Close the goddamned door!" Jay made it perfectly clear.

Quickly obeying, she slammed the door but it did not latch and swung open again. This time, she pushed the door closed with both hands as to make sure it stayed secure. With mounting concern, Miss Gray rushed back to the stricken Devereux and peered helplessly at the shredded tissues of his back. Blood had intermingled with dirt from the cave floor and the matted mess was frozen.

Within minutes, Jay was undressed and wrapped in a large towel that doubled as a makeshift loincloth. With shaking hands he held onto a large steaming mug containing his favorite drink, hot lime flavored Jell-O. As he sipped the artificial flavored liquid, his memories went back to his childhood. On cold days, particularly after sledding, or walking home from school, or sick in bed with influenza, mother Devereux had always offered the young lad his favorite drink. Without exception, the offer was always accepted with enthusiasm.

"The water is ready," Sheila interrupted Jay's thoughts. "But I will need your help in getting the tub off of the stove."

It was agonizing, but the man helped the young lady lift the tub from the stove and onto the floor. He then sat in the metal tub with his feet flat on the rough wood floor outside the basin. Before long, Jay felt the painful intrusion of the warm water on his wounds. Sheila, who found herself acting in the uncomfortable role of nurse, made every attempt to irrigate the severe lacerations with a sponge. As she did so Jay would tense and then relax each time. Sheila carefully washed away the frozen blood and dirt and when she did, the large gashes began to bleed. She drew on the courageous determination of the man to pull his shoulders back as far as he could in order to assist in closing the gashes some. Other than that, the well-meaning woman knew nothing else that could be done.

"What is wrong?" Jay felt that things were not right by Sheila's tentative hesitation.

Sheila wiped her brow with the back of her hand and let out a sigh. "I can't get the bleeding to stop. The wounds are too long and won't come together."

"Then you will have to stitch 'em up!" Jay stated the obvious.

The obvious conclusion greatly dismayed Sheila. Deep in her heart she knew that there was no other way, but was persistent in debating for one. Finally, the self-appointed medical substitute yielded to the obvious and mentally prepared herself for the unfathomable task. Still feeling that the charge was beyond her abilities, and still verbally protesting the medical procedure, she began looking for a needle and some type of thread.

Jay understood the hideous chore ahead for both him as well as the helpful Ms. Gray, but he was not in the mood to discuss it. He simply declared what was most apparent, "Stop trying to make a choice about this – there are no options, just get with the task!"

With a sewing needle and dental floss, the lovely lady began the unenviable drudge of suturing multiple lacerations. Without anesthetic, the pain would be unbearable and Sheila knew it. Understanding that there was no way around the procedure, Sheila made some apologies and prepared for the long session without further tarry.

While the suturing was attended to, the battle scarred warrior kept his mind off of the agony by telling the beautiful woman the accounts of the previous day. It was not until now that it would occur to Sheila that Wing Nut was actually dead. Although she had only known the dog briefly, feelings ran deep and tears trickled down her face as she pinched the patient's skin with the thumb and forefinger of one hand and pushed the needle through with the other.

It took better than an hour for the process to conclude. The bath water was cold by this time and Jay was shivering, even though the tub was next to the stove. Sheila poured hot water from a tea kettle into a wash basin and added cold. She then applied the proper mixture to do a final wash of the wounded area. She carefully patted dry the patient and walked him to the bed where she pulled back the covers and helped him in. As she tucked the large exhausted man into bed, he gently clasped his hand around hers and simply said, "Thanks. I know you did not want to go through that-you did great."

Jay managed a slight smile as the courageous female returned a gesture of admiration by squeezing his hand.

"You didn't want to go through it either-you had the hard part," Sheila assured the mountain man that she had a grasp of the full extent of his pain.

*****

Three days would come and go without the man so much as turning over in bed. Infection had set in and with the onset of a high fever, it appeared that he was in trouble most of the time. On the fourth day, Jay opened his eyes and stared at the cobweb free ceiling.

"My Lord," he said out loud. "She has cleaned everywhere!" With vague recollection, he recalled some parts of shooting the elk and getting caught in the blizzard. He did, however, remember with distinct clarity the traumatic ordeal with the huge bear and that his dog had been killed. Everything after that was a fog and, for the life of him, he could not figure out how he got home.

"How did you get me here?" Jay broke the silence.

Sheila smiled and leaned slightly over the bed with her hands clasped behind her back. "I had nothing to do with it. Don't you remember anything?"

"The elk? Did I make it home with the elk?"

Sheila hated to tell him, but the meat did not make it. "No," she simply replied.

If predators or scavenger birds had gotten to the elk meat then it was all over. Jay knew that the high country weather would preserve the food until April, maybe even May, but time was wasting and he knew that it would be several weeks before he would be able to hunt. By that time, the high mountain peaks would be impassible.

"I've got to go," he advised as he slowly drew back the covers. What he did not know was that he was completely nude. He let out a gasp and quickly retrieved the quilt and brought it up tight around his neck.

"What did you do with my clothes?" He insisted.

"They're at the end of the bed unless you kicked them off," Sheila smiled.

*****

Jay's condition was not good. The twice-a-day bathing ritual had countered the surface infection and the hideous claw marks were healing, but not nearly fast enough for his satisfaction. And, the issue of early spring food was still critical. Upon several occasions he had tried to remove himself from bed, but without help, he could not manage.

Finally, a week and a half had passed and Jay was beginning to celebrate measurable progress concerning recovery. With thoughts of the ultimate fight still constant in his mind, the mountain man looked toward the easy chair where Sheila seemed comfortable as she read.

"You will have to do it." He could not believe what he was saying to her.

Without removing her eyes from *Mutiny on the Bounty,* she surprisingly responded. "Yes, I know." After she finished reading a paragraph, she closed the book and laid it beside the chair. "It will be a piece of cake, you'll see."

Jay took exception to her light hearted approach. "It's not like going to the supermarket! If you don't watch your ass every step of the way, know that some predator is!" He exclaimed. "Forget it. Just forget it! I will go again when I can. Besides you would get lost!" It pushed him that he was so dependent, so helpless, and, so absolutely subordinate to the female. Hell, he couldn't even make it to the outhouse without her help. And then she would stand and wait until he was finished. He needed space, especially at a time like that. And he would be damned if he was going to go in that gallon can she had brought to him.

"I've got my own skis," she broke Jay's little pity party. "They were in the plane but they came through without damage."

"What?" Jay tried to understand what she was talking about.

"They are Fisher cross-countries and they came through the crash without a scratch. I will have to borrow your poles though." Sheila seemed to be excited about the prospects of getting out of the cabin and recovering the elk meat.

She stood over him and smiled again. It was a smile that warmed his heart and placed a twinge in the pit of his stomach. He could not deny the attraction he felt for her, nor could he understand why the Good Lord would complicate his life with her presence.

"It's not safe out there," he said and feeling uncomfortable with the long eye contact, he looked away.

*****

Jay felt there was a risk either way. If something happened to the young woman, then he would never be able to forgive himself for placing her in such danger. Furthermore, he was beginning to have feelings for her. No matter how much he tried to put her out of his mind, he wasn't successful. And if she did perish, the folks from the low lands would be certain to suspect foul play and there would be explaining to do.

However, if she was successful at completing the mission, his sense of complete dominance in highland survival would be challenged. He had chosen this geographical area, as well as this impossible way of life, for two reasons. One, he wanted to be assured he would not be bothered by anyone else. And two, he wanted most to prove to himself that he could manage life off the land without any dependency whatsoever from anyone else. However, after all was said and done, he eventually yielded to good sense and placed his unreasonable pride to rest.

For the next several hours, Jay Devereux brought out maps of the region and gave precise directions to his roommate on how to find the cave from the cabin and how best to return. Not only was Sheila well-rehearsed on the basics, but dependable land marks were established within her mind as well as the intervals in which she was to confirm her location. He impressed upon her that the least miscalculation and she would be lost forever. After he was satisfied that Sheila understood the landscape and terrain in general, he went over the functions of a handgun he wanted her to carry. Although she was well prepared on the expedition and the components involved, he doubted that the excursion could succeed. As a result, he insisted the young lady dismiss the idea and that they would think of a better plan.

His back was throbbing from sitting up during the long rehearsals, so Jay had Miss Gray help him turn over onto his tummy. Without a word he heard the adventurous lady close the door as she left the cabin. An extremely lonely feeling gripped the bedridden Jay as he heard the swish, swish of the skis grow ever fainter. It was too late. She had taken it upon herself to engage in the recovery plan. He hated himself for not paying attention to the weather signs of the prior expedition, and being as neglectful and careless as to place himself and the Nut in such danger. He might as well have had his legs cut off and … Jay's awareness began to give way to fatigue and he felt himself drift towards an experience from the distant past. With sudden clearness, a different reality was unfolding; a memory so deeply hidden, so safely tucked away, that it was supposed to never rear its ugly head again. He was soon asleep and dreaming in vivid clarity.

Frosted vapor expelled from the nostrils of the eleven players in the huddle as they waited for instructions.

"An eye for an eye!" Jay bellowed as he took the time to look each of his teammates in the eye. This was a time of crowds, bright colors, and of extreme competitiveness. Jay wanted each and every member of the defense to understand his fury in case they did not realize the gravity of the moment.

"Your captain was just carried off with a shattered leg! We knew going into this game that they had a bounty on him and now it has come to pass! What are you bastards are going to do about it?!"

With the game knotted at 28 and only 26 seconds left in the contest, The Denver Broncos had just lost their quarterback, as well as the ball through a fumble at their own 36 yard line.

"Somebody's goin' to pay!" a defensive lineman intervened.

"Somebody's goin' to pay!" someone else's voice declared.

"We need to put them down for a full count!" Middle linebacker Devereux finalized.

"Shit through a goose," was the defensive signal and the Broncos broke the huddle. Preparing himself to lead the all-out blitz, Jay observed with close attention while the Raider offense approached the line. Quickly scanning the backfield, he realized that he had called the wrong defense. Due to a quick count there was not enough time to change the defensive play with an audible; the play was already set in motion. Jay back peddled with desperate response to assist the now scant secondary defenders. At least, perhaps, he could cover the short pass. Sure enough, it came. As the running back broke forward from the motion pre-snap, he cleared the end and he was free to accelerate for ten yards after he cut up field. The pass was a little behind him so he stopped, caught the ball, and apparently feeling pressure that was not really there, did a little side step. Then he turned into the open field. By this time, Jay had established the precise angle. The collision was ferocious and the subsequent result, devastating. As his helmet connected with the man's midsection, Jay could feel the ribs collapse and maybe even the vertebra give way. Jay saw the ball come loose and the critically injured player hit the ground with an earthshaking thud. The ball bounced once, twice, and on the third bounce went high into the air and then into Jay's waiting hands. Jay began to run and as he rounded the end from which the offender had come, he was free to go the distance without interference or resistance from the Oakland team.

Jay became consumed with concern as he recalled trotting the long distance back from the end zone. Several Raider players, referees and the trainers had gathered next to the injured opponent. The man had not moved and Jay knew deep inside that he never would. With mounting irritation Jay fought his way through the exuberance of fellow teammates. It was with obvious exasperation he broke through the embracing jubilance and finally made his way to the outer circle of concerned adversaries who now surrounded their fallen teammate. As he waited, he stared up at the scoreboard. It was apparent that he most likely made the "out of reach" touchdown. What was not apparent was the all-consuming concern and depression that overwhelmed Devereux. He would have eagerly exchanged the points for his opponent's good health but he knew that the deed had been done, and there was no return ticket.

Although Jay's all white traveling uniform held distinction by contrast to the sea of black and silver around him, he was not concerned about the temperament of those that he had impacted most by his previous extreme demonstration of aggression. He could only think about the man that was being lifted onto the gurney and then into the ambulance.

After several weeks, the running back for the Raiders was eventually released from the hospital, but he would never place a cleat on the gridiron surface again. Neither would Jay. Some said that he just wanted to quit on a high note, but most speculated that he no longer had the heart for it. Those who believed in the latter were right.

*****

The morning extended into afternoon and eventually long shadows stretched from the nearby peaks as to announce early evening. Jay was becoming increasingly concerned and self-condemning. Over and over he would picture disastrous scenarios which tortured his mind and placed him in a state of self-affliction.

As shadows turned into diffused reflection, Jay was near panic. He had suddenly realized that a lamp was not lit. Without a guiding light, he felt certain that the young lady could never find her way to the cabin.

Jay's back felt on fire as he slowly slid from the bed. His feet touched the cold floor and he realized that the entire atmosphere within the cabin was cold. Slowly, he made his way to the bedpost at the foot of the bed. He grabbed the standard and stabilized himself. Great pain ran the length of his right arm and he immediately began to pivot and fall. The crippled man clasped the lodge pole bed railing and suddenly ended up pivoting the other direction and smashing his nose into the railing that was supposed to support him.

Eventually, he would succeed at mastering flame and a guiding beacon was lit. As it cast a modest light about the interior quarters of the small cabin, Jay would discover that his arm was black and blue and yellow. The episode with the bear had most definitely left its mark with complete anatomic consideration.

Chapter Seven

Moment of Truth

It was about an hour after the sun snuck behind the western mountains when Jay heard the door open and several footsteps enter. Jay was once again horizontal and on his stomach. "Who is it?" He would inquire with a stern voice.

There was a pause and then a masculine voice responded, "What the hell is it to ya', ya' lazy ass?"

Jay was puzzled. As he lifted himself up with one arm, he could vaguely make out the outline of a rather tall and slender figure. The mystery man stood between the lamp and Jay which proved to eclipse the faint luster resulting in a disadvantage to Jay. "Who is it?" Jay demanded an answer.

Without saying a word, the silhouetted figure slowly raised a large knife in his left hand and suspended it in a throwing fashion. With a sudden fluid motion, the arm thrust forward and the knife instantly soared though the air and scored a stick in the log wall a few inches from Jay's head. As Jay wrenched, he would let out a shrill cry and a grimace from the pain of his pre-existing wounds. After a moment he relaxed and opened his eyes. Looking directly up, he would see the familiar metal checkered handle of his own Buck knife.

"I can't believe you sent a woman to do a man's job!" The unknown voice would taunt. "But I will give ya' one thing. She's one hell of a looker!" By this time, the man had stepped a little to the left of the lamplight and Jay could clearly see the weathered features of Mexican Joe.

Jay understood that Joe lived several miles to the north of San Luis Peak near Table Mountain but he never cared enough to find out. Joe, in Jay's opinion, was an uncouth embellisher and the only time he was not prefabricating was when his mouth was shut or he was eating something. By experience, the former was seldom.

"Yes sir," Joe continued. "I was mind'n my own business when the strange smell came out'a the mountains. I looked up and who do I see, but Miss Sweet Pants there draggin' a slab o' meat up the god damned clearing!" He stopped for a moment to look with a lustful eye at the repulsed woman. "Thought for a while that I'd run across some bad weed and I was tripp'n. Don't spose ya'd sell the bitch?" Jay did not trust the discount neighbor any further than he could pick the derelict up and toss him; especially under his present physical condition. He looked upon the revolting scavenger as an individual who was born a hundred and fifty years too late. Maybe this idiot was Bigfoot; but no, Sasquatch would surely take exception to such a filthy existence!

"Watch your language, Joe" He advised. "And I will not be telling you twice!"

Sheila approached Jay's bedside and placed her delicate hand on his forehead. The hand felt cool and most welcome. Jay fought back the irresistible urge to grab it and never let it go, but there were more pressing issues at present.

"Damn!" exclaimed Mexican Joe. "Don't tell me she's got sophistication and culture and all that shit! There goes the neighborhood!" Joe seemed to be turned off by the possibilities. "Got anything to eat?" He began to look around in a somewhat plundering manner.

As the unwelcome pest dropped the heavy bundle of elk meat that he had been dragging, he began to search throughout the cabin for whatever may be edible (traditional or not), Jay sat up the best that he could so "Sweet Pants" could check his dressing. It was evident that he had engaged in a prior tour around the cabin as the homemade sutures had torn slightly and were beginning to seep. As Sheila carefully pulled the sheet strip away from Jay's wound, Mexican

Joe's eyes grew wide and his mouth wider, revealing an old, cold baked potato, skin and all.

"Bitch'n! You really did try to make love to that 'ol sow in the cave, didn't ya?" Chunks of food and saliva fell from Joe's repulsive mouth and into the matted beard. "Pretty smart the way ya' kilt her. Who would'a figgered."

"Where you headed, Joe?" Jay was hopeful that the foul fellow had intentions of moving on.

"What's the hurry?" Joe responded. "Where'd ya' pick up the skirt anyway?" The derelict nodded in the direction of Sheila. It was obvious that Joe had come to terms with the previously observed sophistication concerning the young lady, but there was a lot more on his mind than culture. "What ya' say ya' share the squaw?"

It was obvious that the obnoxious "Skunk Ape" was born a couple centuries too late; not that such conduct was acceptable then, but this was not Joe's domain!

Jay felt the blood rush to his head as he became enraged. "Get out!" He yelled at the top of his lungs as he pointed the way. "This is not the dark ages, you missing link!"

The dark complexion of the wiry man across the room grew more apparent as the whites of his eyes enlarged. He slowly tossed what was left of the third potato on the floor, stood straight, and set his jaw. "I saved the whore's life and ya' owe me! She owes me!"

Sheila could feel the surge of blood through her veins as her pounding heart drummed the announcement of her fear. Jay softly brushed her aside and stepped from the bed without the slightest hint of pain. Pulling his knife from the wall, he fixed his focus on the pitiful excuse of a man before him.

"It is time for you to leave," Jay stated with a stern voice.

"You can't send me out at night." Joe was surprised at the posture Jay had taken concerning the female, and with his masculinity challenged, felt compelled to refute. "Besides, a slide took out my shack so I'm fix'n to stay right here."

The veins stood out on Jay's neck as his muscles drew taut and the true awesomeness of the man's physique became most evident. "If you do not leave now, the loss of your shack will have been the highlight of your day!"

The stage had been set and the issues placed forth. Taking into consideration the animal instincts of the savage, Jay understood that his territory was at stake and that Sheila was part of the quest for the uncivilized individual before him. Jay prepared for a ferocious fight if necessary.

"From what disgusting dung pile you have crawled I know not, but your future is quite clear to me. If you don't leave now I will exterminate you with greater ease than I did with the bear!"

The moment of truth had arrived. Pointing an accusing finger at Jay, the stubborn man reiterated, "You owe me, goddamn it! And I'm gonna collect!"

Jay said nothing, but gestured with the stainless steel point of the Buck, first at the intruder, and then towards the door. Joe slowly wiped the food from his lips, gave a slight shake to his head and took a step as though to exit. Abruptly and without warning, the missing link pulled his hand from his coat. Within his clutched fingers was a revolver.

"I don't care how big your knife is. You should not have brought it to a gun fight, Devy!" Joe was grinning. "Ya' may have been able to talk that grizzly outa eat'n yo sorry ass, but I can guarantee ya'll have a tougher time swallo'n a 165 grain hollow point!"

Slow and precise, the mistake of nature raised and leveled the Colt Python. The mirror blue finish of the weapon reflected the dim lamplight as the gunman paused, evidently to taunt Jay. Suddenly, there was a flash in Jay's peripheral and a loud report. It was the unmistaken loud report of a gunshot! Jay flinched as he witnessed a massive amount of sparks flare from the pistol that was being held by Joe. But, Jay felt no pain. Furthermore, the scream that he heard was not coming from his own lips. The shrill octave that could have been mistaken as from a feminine source reverberated throughout the rustic cabin. Jay's reaction was swift and deliberate. He lunged at the villain, but he no longer had the knife for it had slipped from his weakened right hand. Old instincts surfaced as he hit the scoundrel low, driving the man back and to the floor. The two hit the floor simultaneously, and Jay rolled to his feet and stood over the now cringing coward. There was excruciating pain from stitches torn and wounds now gaping combined with alarming certainty that Sheila had to be injured. Jay kicked the unwanted intruder in the face and then leaned against the bookshelf and let out a groan.

Devereux placed his foot on the drifter's throat and squinted across the room at where Sheila was still standing.

"What the..." Jay was confused.

"Is he dead?" The woman was hesitant to ask.

Jay could then see the semiautomatic in her trembling hands. It was the nine millimeter that he had given her to take on her mission and the weapon he had forgotten she had.

As Jay's comprehension took hold, he realized that Sheila had fired the round, not Mexican Joe. The blaze and sparks from Joe's weapon was by coincidence and it would take time to piece the circumstance together.

"You saved my life!" Jay said in a little more than a whisper.

Sheila was no longer innocent or removed from the relativity of necessity and harsh realities. She was instantly nauseated by the sudden and complete recognition of what she could be capable of. She flung the firearm down on the bed as if not only to rid herself of the weapon, but of the possibilities associated with the destruction she had just imposed. She then returned her stare at the pitiful mass of repulse lying on the floor.

"Is he dead?" She repeated the question.

"No," Jay answered. "It takes a lot more than that to kill a snake. Sometimes you have to remove the reptile's head." He added more pressure to his foot, which was now on Joe's neck. Jay once again directed his observation towards the damsel, "You saved my life."

"If it hadn't been for me, your life would not have been in danger in the first place." Sheila was quick to retort.

Joe let out a groan with every exhale, but Jay did not care. Sheila sat down on the corner of the bed and placed her hands between her knees. Jay lifted his foot off the gasping man's throat and bent down to get a closer inspection of the damages. He secured the Python, but then quickly stood straight up again and slammed his foot down hard on Joe's arm. Joe let out a shriek and released a crudely made knife which he was slowly extracting from a coat pocket. Jay picked the blade up and briefly looked at it. Diverting his attentions back to the man on the floor he conveyed his discovery.

"What's this, Joe? Looks to me like a memento from a prison gift shop; what do you think?" Still holding his foot on Joe's arm, Jay brought the knife close to the intruder's face. "At least it's made in America, right?"

"What are you talking about?" Sheila asked.

"Our boy has been building a portfolio in the prison system. Probably for burglary or nickel hauls from midnight convenient stores." Jay reached down and placed his fingers through the dirty hair of Joe and gripped a hand full. "Get up! What else do you have?"

After getting Joe to his feet, Jay escorted the thug to the door of the cabin and placed the man up against it. "Spread 'em," he said, and with obvious reflective training, Jay kicked Joe's feet apart and began to frisk. Still maintaining the grip on the man's hair, Jay removed the heavy coat and then the soiled shirt. Underneath would be discovered a broad spectacle of incredible art work and various degrees of artistic ability in tattooing. The spectacular, if not vulgar, fantasy of a street scene lined with Harleys and naked women in various unflattering poses took up most of the human canvas. The already busy scene was further complicated with satanic insignias and sacrificial suggestions. Although there was evidence of significant trauma that suggested an uncomfortable history, there was no sign of current wounds. Front to back, there was not a bullet hole! Jay was puzzled. Where had the bullet gone? Satisfied that Mexican Joe no longer possessed a weapon, Jay escorted him next to the stove and secured the thug with a leather ligature.

Jay picked up the revolver that was in Joe's possession and began to laugh.

"Sweet!" Jay declared and held the gun up so that Sheila might see. There was a fresh blemish that extended down the outside of the barrel all the way to the cylinder where bullet fragments were embedded. The bullet that Sheila fired had rendered the Python useless and with subsequent result, placed Joe at an instant disadvantage.

*****

The night was long and drawn out, but went without incident as both Jay and Sheila took turns standing guard over their prisoner. With the rising of the sun, the next day would come with the unavoidable task of relocating the loathsome individual.   Still suffering the ill effects of the misunderstanding with the oversized carnivore, Jay had no choice but to embark on a rather distant journey. The purpose of the journey was to hopefully cause enough distance between Joe and them, that Joe would lose interest or option to come back. The only other choice was to shoot the bastard outright or chain him up for the rest of the winter. Declaring that the unwelcome guest was not worth the expense of a bullet and recognizing the extreme displeasure, as well as risk of caretaking the repugnant individual, Jay decided on the choice of relocation. This would be a merciful decision that Jay would regret in the not too distant future!

Chapter Eight

Last Chance

Beyond the North Face was Canyon Diablo. The actual depth of the canyon was greatly exaggerated due to the sheer characteristics of Table Mountain to the east and two enormous peaks to the south and south west; San Luis Peak at 14,014 feet and its twin, Stewart Peak at 13,917. On the southeast face of San Luis was a long canyon with signs of seasonal destruction. Avalanches were traditional and dependable as clockwork each year. Mexican Joe's previous place of humble residence used to be at the base of Stewart Peak. It was regarded as quaint at best; that is until Mother Nature cancelled the certificate of occupancy.

In the five years that Jay had embraced mountain life, he had spent all his summer days exploring and acquainting himself with God's most majestic creation; the northern most regions of the Devil's Playground. He had scaled all the peaks several times, fished the ice cold rivers and on calm winter nights, laid back and took in the most wondrous theater of all, the northern lights from 14,000 feet. Although Colorado was a great distance from Alaska, atop the highest mountains one could often take in such delights. He knew this territory intimately and had, with legitimate passion, built a respect, as well as an incalculable love of this land. He would harvest the wild game that he needed and out of respect he so claimed, knew every rock by its first name.

Although Jay was not up to the task, he persuaded Joe along at the point of a pistol. Past the snow slide area that was familiar to the captive, towards a destination not disclosed unto Mexican Joe, the two men skied.

"Where the hell ya' tak'n me, ya' son-of-a-bitch?" Joe was tired and cold and was beginning an incessant whine. Jay prompted Joe with the sharp point of a ski pole. Joe dropped the protest and skied onward. Although they had begun the drudgery several hours before, it was not long now and Jay was anxious to rid himself of the unwanted man once and hopefully, for all.

In the distance, a faint roar was detected. This indicated that they were closing in on the boxed portion of the canyon and Joe was becoming more concerned. He knew that there was no way out and he began to suspect that Jay's intentions were less than honorable. As they approached Shadow Falls, the roar was so great that one could not concentrate. The view was breathtaking, however. For several hundred feet, the plunging water could be seen as it cascaded under a transparent ice shell.

Joe's eyes wandered from the small Shadow Lagoon at the base of the falls, then slowly up the sheer rock of Table Mountain. Joe was confused; there was no earthly way that Jay could expect him to scale the cliff. Joe now studied his captor. Placing his hands outward from his sides with palms up Joe gestured as if to ask, "what now?"

Jay nodded in the direction just to the right of the falls. Joe squinted in an attempt to see through the now dusking sky.

"That is your passage way to your new world," Jay declared.

"I see nothing." Joe still thought that this was a mission ending in his demise and although hopeful that Jay was true to his word, Joe could not help but think that the moment of truth was present. For sure, one way or another, the end was near.

"Get your useless carcass over there," Jay instructed as he pointed his Glock handgun at the Mexican. "There's a mine drift that goes from here, all the way to the other side of Table. Once you get on the other side, there are abandoned buildings for your shelter."

Joe could now see the dark hollow of emptiness that was framed by old broken timbers. "It looks pretty much a passage way to nowhere - and if I refuse?"

"Then you can kiss your ass adios," Jay was matter of fact. "For then I would be forced to leave you out here without skis."

"That would be murder!" Mexican Joe protested.

"No it wouldn't. It would be suicide for the choice is still yours. You could still go through the tunnel. The way I figure it, it would be nature's way of weeding out another undesirable, if you know what I mean." Jay had not come all this way, suffering constant physical discomfort to let bygones be bygones. He knew that the first chance Joe got he would stab Jay in the back and ultimately make his way back to the beautiful Sheila.

"So you're gonna just leave me here to die rather than have integrity to do the job yourself?"

"You don't listen all that well, do you," Jay replied. "That's all right. You're an idiot and I guess that you can't help it. Now, take off your skis." While Joe tripped the bindings, Jay removed a large stake from his backpack and began to pour kerosene from a bottle onto a cloth wrapped end. As soon as the bottle was empty, he lit the rags and tossed Mexican Joe the torch. Then he threw the backpack to Joe. "There are staples enough to keep you from starving for a while; if I were you I would be conservative about catering to you appetite."

Jay then nodded towards the mine drift, "If you don't tarry, you should be through the shaft within an hour or so. The torch will last about 90 minutes. It's only about a couple or so miles to the other side."

"What if the shaft is caved in?" Joe made a valid point. "Besides, I don't like closed in spaces!"

Jay knew that he could not be concerned with such details, "Look at it this way, if you make it, then you owe me."

"How do you figure?"

"I got you over your fears."

"And if I don't make it?" Joe sneered.

"Then I guess I will owe you," Jay responded with a matter-of-fact tone.

The bad man was still having difficulties comprehending the true gravity of Jay's sincerity. It had been at least a ten mile trip to this point and darkness was closing in fast. Thoughts of overpowering the injured Jay seemed to be crowding the already narrow capacity of Joe's ability to reason. Jay picked up on the signal from the transparent individual and responded by once again pointing the Glock at Joe's head.

"Don't even give it a thought," Jay said. "Now get in the shaft and stay in the shaft!"

When Joe was out of sight, Jay approached two trees that were close together and wedged the derelict's skis and poles between them. With some effort, he was able to bend them to the point that they broke. He then took a hatchet and began to chop a hole in the ice that covered the lagoon. Within a few minutes there was a hole large enough to accommodate what was left of the sources of winter conveyance, and it was with a sense of urgency that he plunged the ski fragments through the hole and out of sight. He knew that within a couple hours the ice would be reformed and ultimately serve as a lasting barrier.

Even though Jay was convinced that a ten mile hike without skis would be a certain death march, he had no intentions of chancing the odds. He knew that he would have to create a permanent barrier between Joe and Jay's own small utopia. Although Jay could no longer see Joe or the light from the torch, he could feel that the dreadful individual was still standing close to the entrance of the mine drift.

"It is in your best interest to go on now," Jay was anxious to proceed with the final stage of his plan. "You will make out just fine when you get to the Sky City Mine. They left fuel oil and maybe some food there. Don't come back on this side of the mountain, for I will surely place you under; and it really isn't likely that anyone will miss you!"

With the final farewell advice, Jay placed the semi auto handgun back in his pocket. This would serve to peak Joe's interest. Jay was right in anticipating that Joe was still observing him from a vantage point just inside the man-made portal. The interest would soon change to unadulterated terror, however. Jay's hand would reappear from the coat pocket, but this time he was holding a full stick of dynamite! Without hesitation, Jay struck the phosphorus tip of a kitchen match on his thumbnail and placed it close to the fuse. He then looked at the shocked expression on the adversary's face. By this time, Joe had reemerged from the mine entrance and was attempting to comprehend the peril which was at hand.

Jay made his last announcement, "You best split Joseph; 'cause this portion of this mountain is coming down!"

Joe stood for a second as though to wrestle with the full gravity of the moment. Devereux shook his head with the lack of conception displayed by his rival. He then lit the fuse and gave a mighty heave with his sore arm. The stick with the sizzling tail propelled upward and onto a small ledge twenty or so feet above the entrance of the drift.

"The way I figure it, you have about thirty seconds at best." At this, Jay quickly turned and began a hasty retreat on his skis back along the same snow packed route in which they had come.

For a split moment, Joe decided to exit the damp recesses of the uncomfortable mine in an attempt to remain on the outside. Without skis, the snow instantly swallowed his body and he began to flounder in its depth. As the mad man crawled his way back to solid footing, he took one last glimpse at the fleeing enforcer and muttered under his breath, "Paybacks are gonna be a bitch, pretty boy!" He then submerged himself into the depths of the black hole, picked up the torch from the dirt floor and disappeared.

After swiftly traveling over a reasonable distance on the dual trail in the snow, Jay began to worry about the dynamite. Perhaps the explosive had not been turned properly while it had been stored and the Nitroglycerin had leaked out rendering it useless. Or maybe the fuse was faulty. In any event, the planned avalanche, which was to further insure against Joe's return, was not taking place. Jay stopped to rest. With mounting anticipation, he scanned the formable profile of Table Mountain; a mountain that would have otherwise fortified his cabin from further intrusion by the misfit. Twilight was now immersing the deep canyon in darkness and the lone mountain man could vaguely see where the mine entrance might be. He was satisfied that the vulgar man was not following him but was deeply concerned at the prospects of not knowing if he would try later if indeed the explosive did not go as planned. With such a possibility, Jay decided to return to the base of the portal and crawl up the mountain face to recover and inspect the explosive.

As he redirected his travel once again, there was a sudden brilliant flash of light followed in a split second by an unfathomable clap of thunder. It was most apparent that the explosive had ignited.

Now the only question was if it had worked as intended. Within moments, Jay would receive confirmation. First, the beautiful crystal ice globe which stood as a funnel for the water fall, collapsed. With the force of unbelievable magnitude, the great natural structure slid slowly at first, downward and then plunged into Shadow Lagoon. A large geyser shot straight up and then plummeted back into the icy water.

While Jay watched and waited, he felt it. First, just a slight tremor as the earth began to vibrate, but then it increased. He felt the pulse within his neck race and his breath became labored as he began to question the apparent modest distance he had placed between ground zero and where he was standing. Accepting the situation as it existed, Jay concluded that there was little ground to be gained by fleeing further and chose to stand and bear witness to the spectacle which he caused.

As the visual dynamics increased with the instability of the snowfield, so did the audio. The vibration underfoot grew greater by the second and Jay suddenly became aware that several secondary slides were simultaneously triggered by the blast. All around him, the combined energy of each escalated and gave the irreversible impression that he indeed initiated the device that triggered Armageddon.

He watched with interest as the main slide picked up speed and began to cover the entrance to the Sky City prospect hole. Tons of snow and debris began to hard pack and build up. The visibility of the drift no longer existed. If all else failed, at least the main objective had been accomplished.

For close to ninety seconds, the rumble would continue, but Jay could no longer see how close to danger he might be. Waves of granulated snow were constantly sifting out of the sky and engulfing Jay where he stood. He had created a blizzard of sorts and all his senses were challenged. After a while, the roar subsided and he was able to make out the dim outline of Table Mountain. Darkness of nightfall had replaced the manmade whiteout conditions, and wisely, Jay decided to bed down for the night. His body was fatigued beyond pride or desire, and the aches and pains of his wounds were once again pressing his conscious awareness.

*****

Sheila flinched with a start as she felt the small tremor from the table on which her elbows were resting. Then there were the multiple reverberations as the distant explosion echoed throughout the mountains and canyons. She was well aware of the distance that the sound had traveled and she took comfort in knowing that it was probable that things were progressing as Jay had planned. She marked and closed the book she was reading, got up and walked to the window. As she attempted to peer through the single pane, the outside darkness would only yield her reflection as if the window was a flawless mirror. For just a moment, she would look at her own beautiful features of which she had not seen for several days. With hesitation, she resigned to the notion of a lonely night and recessed to the comfort of the lazy chair. Her thoughts were of the man who stood up for her the previous night. Many times she had been fought over, argued over, and made over, but no man had ever placed his life on the line on her behalf. And what had confused her all the more was there was no apparent hidden motive or reason for such gallantry; only pure chivalry as defined by the medieval institution of knighthood. The thought of such made the young lady smile with almost a juvenile fixation.

Her thoughts also gave way to the realization that she, for all intents and purposes, had resigned herself to kill someone. Yes the man, using the term loosely, was an unwelcome intruder who was obviously embarking on an ultimate transgression of deadly intentions. But nevertheless, he was one of God's creatures. The awareness of her newly discovered abilities made her shudder, and she found herself thanking the Good Lord that the actual result was much better than the reactionary intent.

Again, Sheila found herself thinking with attraction about the self-made mountain man. He was courageous, gallant, extremely strong, good looking, and… and … and wealthy! As suddenly as she found herself smiling with favor, even more quickly she was reminded of the reason to be concerned. Drawn by the hidden passageway behind the bookshelf, the beautiful woman swiftly removed herself from the luring softness of the chair and threw herself into the uncomfortable recesses of discovery once again. This time she was on an expedition of complete discovery and would not be denied the whole truth.

With swift determination, Sheila pulled the shelf from the wall, unlocked the walk-in safe and placed her purpose past the point of no return. After carefully putting the glowing lamp on top of what was believed to be a draped table, Sheila slowly descended to her knees and rubbed her hands together. Cautiously applying both middle fingers of each hand at the corners of the lid, the self-appointed investigator lifted the cover and then just sat back on her heels for a moment and stared at the contents. If she was exposed to a killer she had a right to know. On the other hand, ignorance could indeed be bliss. Choosing the former, she reached down without further hesitation and lifted the two newspapers out of the ornate trunk. Sitting back onto an apparent sofa, she began to immerse herself in the depths of Jay's history.

NEW YORK TIMES   SEPTEMBER 12, 2001

COP GOES ON SHOOTING SPREE

At approximately 1:25 A.M. this morning, several 911 calls were received by the 5th precinct in regard to what at first appeared to be a gang related street battle in the Bronx. As police converged on the 3600 block of Jerome Avenue, they would discover what greatly resembled a war zone. One responding officer, who was a Vietnam veteran, advised the Times that the street scene compared greatly to his experiences overseas. "When we arrived, there was death everywhere," Stated Officer Costello.

After the final tally was released, seven boys ranging in age from thirteen to sixteen were pronounced dead at the scene by the coroner's office. Four others were transported to nearby hospitals where one was pronounced dead upon arrival. The condition of the three others is still unknown at this time.

Nearby residents, who wished to remain anonymous, witnessed the shooting and told reporter Clara Johnston that a police officer had engaged in an argument with several youths yesterday afternoon. The police officer, known as Devin Pierce, has a reputation of being "hardcore" in the neighborhood and is not well liked. Several eye witnesses claim to have seen the off-duty beat cop return to the area late last night in his personal car. Pierce allegedly waited until the time was right and then shot several members of the S.C.F. (Satan's Chosen Few) as they were walking across Jerome Avenue.

Police Chief McMillan confirmed that in fact, Officer Devin Pierce III, is a prime suspect in the late night shooting. He advised that the City deeply regrets the actions of Pierce. He was also quick to point out that the officer's actions were of his own volition and in no way represented the sentiment of NYPD or any of its members toward the city's citizens. When asked if he felt the slaying was somehow connected with 9/11, the Chief simply replied that there was no evidence that linked the two. The Chief refused to comment further stating that the case was still under investigation and that an undisclosed outside agency would conduct the investigation.

The Times has it on good authority that suspect Pierce is not in custody at this time as he has apparently fled the City and perhaps the state.

Sheila closely studied the photograph of the man she knew as Jay. Although she did not know the man all that well, somehow the profile just did not fit. During the short time she had spent with him, he had never once given her reason for fear or doubt.

Slowly she folded the paper back in half and placed it beside the wood cabinet. She then leafed through the next paper but was unable to locate the significance of why it was treasured. Placing the second paper on the first, she began to sift her hands through the large bundles of currency. There was even more money than she had first thought. As she struggled to locate the bottom of the box with her fingers, she would find the money took up the entire volume of the trunk. Such a realization was astounding and the discovery made her feel all the more ill at ease.

Miss Gray replaced the newspapers and gently lowered the lid back on the handcrafted chest. She sensed the air escape from the container as the lid snapped in place. She sat back on the couch and just looked around. On the walls hung many portraits that Sheila had failed to see upon her rather hurried first tour. She noted that there was a peculiar mixture of Picasso and Norman Rockwell pieces, hung side by side. As she gazed around the room of the apparently rich and famous, she was confused by what "Devin's" purpose was for all the treasures? Why would he hoard the belongings and what was his plan for her future? Was she just another prized possession that would be placed at some point within the stone archive? In any event, she had pretty much discovered what she had embarked on and now was the time to start preparing for the future and self-preservation. She realized that she was going to have to make decisions on whether or not to square up with the apparent fugitive. If she did, and things did not go well, what would she be able to do? Perhaps things would go well and he would have a reasonable explanation for murdering eight or more teenagers. Such a notion was ridiculous and Sheila quickly dismissed it.

With a thorough last study of the room, she stepped back into the cabin and closed the heavy steel door. All the while, she was secure in the thought that nothing would give away her encroachment. She realized that her first step towards self-defense was gaining control of the Glock 9 millimeter. At least she knew that if forced, she would now be able to use it.

Chapter Nine

Final Judgment

Jay pulled the thick winter glove from his right hand and gently stroked the frost from his short beard. After he placed the glove back on his hand, he emerged from the small snow cave with slow and deliberate motions. Every muscle was stiff and aching. His body not only endured the agony of battle with the angry bear but an unscheduled expedition into the wilderness with Mexican Joe.

The sun was high in the sky, and he could feel its radiant heat off the brilliant snow. He had slept much longer than he had planned, but the added time had done the contemporary mountain man a world of good. He felt marvelous as he chewed on a stiff piece of jerky. He now would be able to give a daylight evaluation of the success of the previous evening's undertaking. He was amazed at the amount of snow the dynamite had influenced. Snow and debris had clogged the free running waterfall to the point that the water was now diverted near where he estimated the mine drift to be. As a result of the unplanned diversion, the snow was now turning to solid ice which created a monstrous glacier over the quarry entrance. The consequence was far better than previously intended and the mountain man could now make his way home with secured peace of mind.

*****

The trip home went without incident and only took half the time as did the trip to the Shadow Lagoon. Along the way, Jay thought often of the elegant lady who was waiting at his humble abode. Yes, complications did exist. Even if nothing was to become of any sort of relationship, a change within him had transpired and with that change would come the realization that loneliness is everything it is cracked up to be. He no longer desired to be left alone and now that Wing Nut was gone, consideration against that lonely feeling became more important, more relevant. On the other hand, he did not relish the thought of returning to the lower lands, either.

It was late afternoon when Mr. Devereux finally reached the log structure. As he made his entrance, he rushed in through the door and jokingly announced his arrival, "Honey, I'm home." Jay was somewhat puzzled at the less than warm reception Sheila returned. Thinking that perhaps she was upset about his late return, he backed off and waited to share his experiences.

The pleasant fragrance of chunky meat and canned vegetable stew was simmering in a large kettle on the stove and Jay was past the stage of hunger. Recalling etiquette from long past, Jay first asked as not to appear to be presumptive. Upon receiving a cool nod he proceeded to help himself.

"You did really well the other night, Sheila." Jay attempted to at least soften the glacier cool atmosphere.

The young lady did not respond, but continued with her plans of sitting down in the favored overstuffed chair with intentions of reading. Jay sat quietly and made sure he did not make noises as he ate the feast. As he risked a second helping without prior notification, his conscience got the best of him and he would mask the action by asking a question. "How were things while I was out goofing around in the snow?"

"Fine," Sheila simply stated.

"This is ridiculous." Jay thought to himself. Perhaps he was right all along about the no hassles approach of living alone in the mountains and answering to no one else. He had done nothing to bring on such refrigeration and the female's indifference was extremely annoying.

The rest of the evening, the two adults immersed themselves in separate interests. Jay whittled on a cedar stump and the moody Miss Gray continued to read. By midnight, Jay had already crawled into his sleeping bag which was on the floor and without so much as a word, went sound asleep. At this point, the insecure young lady was able to place the bulk of her fears on hold, snuggle under the heavy quilt and drifted off to sleep as well.

*****

The sound of late morning silence was deafening as sleeping beauty awoke with a start and sat up in the bed. Where was Devin? She quickly looked around the room and discovered he was nowhere to be found. Still wearing the clothes of yesterday, she quickly scooted from the bed and placed her petite feet in her boots. Without tying the laces, and only having one of the boots all the way on, she hobbled across the floor and unlatched the heavy pine door. As the brass hinges creaked and the door opened, she became bewildered by the sight of the mountain man loading the makeshift sleigh with his belongings.

"What are you doing?" She asked.

He would stop for a brief moment, take a quick glance at the beautiful woman and then refocus on the tie downs, "She actually speaks," he observed with a facetious expression.

"What do you think you're doing?" She asked.

He did not answer, but continued to concentrate on the task at hand. Becoming increasingly agitated she hobbled out to where the uncooperative man was and placed her hands on her hips, "What is your problem?"

Without taking his eyes off his chore, he simply replied, "And I'm the one with the issues! My only issue is you and that will not be for long! I'm leaving."

"When will you be back?" She asked.

"When will you be gone?"

"What?" Sheila was confused. "What are you talking about?"

Jay bent down and started to fasten the ski bindings to his boots. "I'm talking about having better conversation with a tree stump. It is all too obvious to me you are not all that taken with my presence, so I'm changing my address." The large man reached down and picked up his heavy backpack. Adjusting the straps and then heaving the heavy load onto his back, he looked directly at the confused young lady.

"I will not engage in mind games, Miss Gray. If you want the straight up, you've already got it. I just expected the same courtesy." Checking his pocket for the handgun, he withdrew the weapon and handed it to her grip first. "Watch it. It's still loaded minus the round that you shot at Joe." Jay paused and then pointed at a general area on the other side of the canyon, "I will be at the old line-rider's cabin on the other side. I will be back in a day or so to collect half of the elk meat."

Sheila's mind was spinning and she could not decide what would be best. "Bull!" She finally responded as she gave into an urge and pushed the shoulder of the unprepared man. At first, Jay attempted to maintain his balance by flapping his arms like a chicken trying to gain flight. Realizing the inevitable, he finally rolled his eyes and prepared himself for a rough landing. With a noteworthy thud, Jay fell onto and through the crusted surface of the snow. Although pain was evident by the expression on the man's face, he found himself more angry than hurt.

"You give the straight up all right!" And with that, Sheila marched back into the cabin mumbling something about "keeping secrets." She slammed the door but the latch mechanism did not have time to slide in place and the door swung open again.

"Now I know what it feels like to be a helpless turtle!" Jay acknowledged as he struggled to get off his back. At least a turtle didn't have snowshoes to further complicate the already impossible inverted experience. It took several minutes for the angry man to gain vertical advantage once again. With a volley of choice swear words under his breath, he removed the backpack and released the ski bindings and stood upright. Half chuckling, half seething, the extra-large human stomped into the cabin and slammed the door as if to draw special exclamation to his entrance. Once again, it voluntarily opened on its own accord.

"Now," he said through clinched teeth. "What is with all the hostility?"

Jay's eyes took a moment to adjust to the dark room after the extreme contrast of the brilliant sunshine outside. Finally, his pupils became accustomed and when they did, he did not like what he was about to behold. The barrel of the gun that he had given Sheila seemed to be much larger than he had remembered and it was pointing directly at his head. Slowly he removed both of his gloves and tossed them on the floor near the stove.

"My question is more justified than ever; is it not?" Jay was attempting the impossible task of reading what was on the young woman's mind. "What is with the hostility? Cabin fever doesn't usually kick in until the second or third month."

"I just want to know why a somewhat polished, intelligent human being feels compelled to live like this." Sheila asked.

The mountain man removed his coat and hung it on a nail next to the door. "And you feel you have to ask that at the point of a gun?"

"You're the one that came barging in here as though you were going to make something happen!" Sheila was eager to make a point as she made a swaggered motion with her head.

"You're the one that dumped my ass off into the snow for no reason." Jay's apprehension was growing and with the anxiety was the irresistible urge to spank the spoiled brat that was resorting to violence. Confused by the whole overreaction thing, Jay removed the coat from the nail and hastily put it back on. "I guess what pushes me most is the silent treatment from last night! I told you once and I'm telling you…"

Sheila would interrupt the large man by throwing the gun near his head. "You're the one that was going to leave without letting me know!"

After catching the weapon in his left hand he walked over to the table and picked up a small piece of paper. He then approached Miss Gray and placed it in front of her face and tilted his head and gave a mocking smile.

"The next time that you point a gun at me, Miss Prim and Proper, you goddamned better well use it!" Jay explained with no uncertain terms in a whisper next to Sheila's right ear. The situation was tense to say the least, and she would flinch as he pushed the weapon's magazine release and then removed it. He worked the action in front of her face. The chambered bullet ejected and landed on the floor. Paying no attention to it, Jay tossed the weapon across the room and onto the unmade bed and then the loaded magazine as well.

Jay felt compelled to state the obvious, "I have no idea what this female moment is all about! I do know that this little *get to know each other better moment* has nothing to do with the silent treatment, or leaving and not telling, or dumping my butt in the snow bank, or even the gun in the face thing." Jay paused for a moment and shook his head, "a gun in my face!" He dwelled. "Those are just symptoms. Those are just things that enrage and incite. Look Sis, I don't even know who you are, but..."

Terror began to shadow over Sheila's face and grip her very soul as she had made the ultimate choice to interrupt the angered highlander for the second time. It was now or never.

"That's just it, *Devin*!" Sheila was compelled to take a safety step back and hold her breath. My God she had done it. With four small words she had revealed her discovery and revealed all the hidden demons! She felt instantly vulnerable and wished she had not said it! But she had and some things just can't ever be taken back!

As she looked at the gun lying on the bed, Jay instinctively looked in the direction of the book shelf. "What did you call me?" Jay's eyes narrowed, his forehead rose, and a most sobering expression was now displayed on his face. Slowly he began to walk away from the woman and then he stopped and glared at her. He then walked towards the easy chair.

"So now the cat is out of the bag," he stated the obvious. He would sit down and begin to nervously pick stuffing out of a preexisting hole in one of the chairs arms. "Well ain't you quite the little Sherlock; didn't take you all that long either!" Jay slowly ran his hand through his hair as he struggled with his own composure. "So sis, ya' got it all figured out, don't ya?"

"Why did you do it?" Sheila could feel her hands tremble and her feet grow cold.

"Cause they pissed me off!" Jay had just confirmed his action as illustrated in the New York Times. "Not that far removed from what you are doing to me right now! Pissing me off!"

Sheila was shocked at his matter of fact response and felt paralyzed with his abrupt demeanor. Hoping to gain a better advantage to the bed she slowly began to advance. "There has to be a better reason than that," she murmured.

"I can't believe you betrayed a trust, violated common courtesy... my obvious expectation of privacy!" Jay appeared stressed. "Females just can't help it can they! Why?"

"I was searching for the truth!" Sheila defended her actions.

"And now that you have found it, has it set you free?"

"No! But it's pretty well spelled out in black and white!" Sheila now had the best angle to the bed.

Jay repositioned himself to gain a better view of the Glock. "You ever see a chicken with its head twisted off?" Sheila was caught off balance by the question and withdrew her gaze from the bed. "Damned thing will run around the barnyard several minutes spraying blood all about and still living. It's the darnedest thing you'll ever see. They say it's because of the total lack of intelligence."

Sheila was further confused by the analogy and thus asked for clarity by her mere expression.

Jay went on, "As stupid as that two legged creature is, I would bet he would be smart enough to figure out that it would be in its best interest not to go for the gun."

Sheila retreated back to where the stove was and placed another log on the dying embers. The act was more an attempt to a graceful retreat, a nervous diversion than a necessary task. As she sat quietly on the stump, Jay wrestled once again with the removal of his coat while still sitting.

"Seek the truth and the truth will set you free, huh, Sheila?" Jay asked. "Ya' feel all freed up?" It was obvious that the mountain dweller's anger was not subsiding.

With another attempt to retain an explanation, the now worried female would try again, "Why did you kill those boys?"

"Does it really matter to you? I mean, I haven't even had my day in court and you have already passed judgment," Jay paused, "and you know what really chaps my butt, I never will have my day in court!"

"This is not a court of law but I will listen," the young Sheila would try to steer things in a more positive direction, but regretted the offer as she realized it sounded less than sincere, even condescending.

Her fears were valid as Jay became more upset with such prospects. "And I can see you are real impartial. Which has more strength, truth or perception?"

"Truth, without a doubt." Sheila felt confident.

"Dead wrong!" Jay insisted. "After life, there is nothing but truth. Here on earth you may see from time to time subliminal glimpses of truth, but perception, by a long shot, rules!" Jay picked the book off the floor which the young lady had been reading and aimlessly leafed through the pages. Finding nothing to catch his eye, he slammed the book closed and tossed it in the direction of the table. The book slid across the surface of the table and crashed to the floor on the other side.

Sheila said nothing as Jay got up and with a single thrust, swung the heavy bookshelf open. She stood frozen as the case reached the end of its track and stopped resulting in more than half the books tumbling in abrupt fashion onto the floor.

Trying the handle and finding it unyielding, Jay looked at the terrified woman. "The key," he ordered. "If you are going to draw a complete conclusion and judgment, you best learn how to tidy up on your investigative skills."

Within a short time the two entered the stone clad chamber, and Jay held tightly onto the kerosene lamp. With firm conviction, he placed the lamp on the drop clothed table and sat back onto the covered davenport. Jay nodded at the now reluctant female and looked in the direction of the wooden vault of secrets. "Go ahead prosecutor, present your case!"

"I don't want to do this." Sheila protested.

"What made you think that there was an option?" Jay was stern. "You compiled the evidence and filed the accusations. Hell girl, you even passed final judgment and the only reason you are searching for answers for my apparent indiscretions is because you're not prepared to be the executioner." Jay was unsympathetic and relentless in proving his point. "So, my fair guest, you open Pandora's box and present the evidence."

It was with reluctance that she opened the lid and once again viewed the front page of the Times. Sheila's apprehension showed as she paused.

"I insist that we get on with it! After all I have a right to a speedy trial, don't I?" Jay's anger would not subside as he was forced to relive the past.

Sheila finally lifted the newsprint from the once secure depths of the chest.

"Read out loud Ms. Prosecutor; I insist!" Jay ordered.

Knowing well that declining would be futile and perhaps even fatal, she forced herself to read the front page aloud and did not stop until she had completely finished. After doing so, she was more certain of his guilt than ever and subsequently puzzled as to why he was forcing her to indulge in such useless quest.

When she finished she simply stated, "No matter how many times I read it, the kids are still going to be dead!"

"What's the date?" The accused would ask.

"September 12th, 2001," Sheila answered.

"And what is the date of the next paper?" Jay would initiate a further probe.

"September 15th, same year."

"Now look on page 28 and read that out loud." Jay's sullen demeanor influenced the sobering atmosphere.

As the appointed prosecutor of the impromptu kangaroo court thumbed through the pages, Jay picked the first paper up and stared at his photograph. He then tossed the "rag" on top of the table. The exaggerated motion caused an air disturbance, and the single lamp flame would flicker and all but go out. Although her concentration was temporarily interrupted, she refocused her attention back to the task at hand. Sheila scanned the second paper in hopes to find what the angry man wanted her to see. Short briefs and continuations of previous headliners littered the page but nothing caught her attention that would correspond to the serious subject of mass murder. Without saying a word, Jay leaned over and with a precise gesture pointed at the applicable section. Without bold print of any kind, the small message simply read:

The Times apologizes for the misprint of Officer Jay Devereux's photograph in place of the suspected killer, Officer Devin Pierce, on the front page of our September 12 addition. We sincerely regret any inconvenience or confusion the mixed photographs may have caused.

Sheila slowly dropped her head and stared at the floor. "I am so sorry. So, so sorry," she repeated. "How did they get the wrong picture ... or the pictures mixed up ... or how did all that happen; I don't understand?"

Jay drew a deep breath and reflected, "I was nominated and had won the *beat cop* award for the year and there was a write up about it all—but with the confusion of 9/11 everything got messed up, mixed up, and really f'ed up!"

Jay got up and dropped both papers back into the wood chest and slammed the lid down. "Come on, let's get out of here."

For the next several days, not much was said between the two; however, this time the reasons were more clear. Jay had decided not to reestablish a new residence at the old line-rider's shack across the canyon and preoccupied most of his hours carving on the cedar stump.

With her emotional state at an extreme low, Sheila felt remorseful about the breach of trust that she was responsible for. To make matters more depressing was the fact that Devereux had been unjustly accused and she too had been caught up so easily in the perception. She wanted to be home now and her thoughts were constantly of her mother, dad and sisters. She knew that by now they were most likely giving up hope and she pained for the misguided loss they must be feeling. Jay felt compelled to leave her alone more often and she did not like it. She understood his reclusive nature, but her sense of self-reliance was not the same. He never felt compelled to tell her when he planned on returning or where he had planned to go. He, however, did come back each time but she was still worried that at some point, he wouldn't.

*****

Sheila studied through the large kitchen window at the brilliant deep blue midday sky. The cabin was warm and she felt good today. As her hands worked the laundry, her thoughts of the plane crash and the morning after brought back a somewhat warm feeling. She was alive and within a short period she would be home and telling a lifetime of stories about the stranger who had rescued her. She drew an ever widening smile as she recalled the first time she had ever laid eyes on Jay and how frightened she was. Sheila even giggled as she could still see him falling onto the stove and burning his backside when she screamed. They had only known each other for less than a month, yet she had more experiences in those few days than most people would in a lifetime.

Although the wounds were deep and the scars indelible, Jay was virtually healed. Now and then scar tissue would bind and cause discomfort but by his superhuman tolerance to pain, it was not worthy of mention.

With sudden awareness, she felt Jay's eyes on her back as she wiped soap suds from the tip of her nose with the back of her hand. Sheila turned her head and before either realized it, both were trapped in full eye contact. Not wanting to be obvious, both just stared and with the passing of each moment, the environment grew more awkward. Finally, Sheila smiled and turned toward her laundry without saying a word. Jay felt once again consumed by her magnificent beauty and was spellbound by her smile. He had forgotten how stunning her smile was, and had all but forgotten how radiant her appearance in general was.

Later on that same evening, both Jay and his guest sat down at the dinner table for the first time in a long time. Although the conversation was light and somewhat guarded, both seemed to at last enjoy each other's company. After the meal, Jay even pitched in on helping with the dishes.

As Sheila whiled away the evening hours in the recesses of a novel, Jay engaged in his mystery wood carving. He had placed a visual barrier so the young lady could not readily see what his project was for fear of disappointment of the end result. Not all senses were diverted however, as the attractive odor of cedar filled the confines and added to the peaceful surroundings.

*****

Soon February was officially announced by the self-appointed timekeeper, Miss Gray. She had the only wrist watch for thousands of square miles and fortunately, the sports model had a full complement of functions; one of which was the basic date and time. Several weeks had passed since the confrontation. It was as though an unspoken rule had been established. The rule was that all major mistakes and misunderstandings of the past were just that, from the past. And by such, would remain non-worthy of readdress or reflection. This seemed to work out well as the two had gotten along most favorably and a friendship seemed to grow. The relationship was now constant, comfortable and even dependable with seemingly definite but unspoken limitations. There was no touching of any kind. It wasn't so much that the attraction was not mutual, rather that both seemed to understand the disorder that could result. Conversation was limited to pertinent daily issues and anecdotes. Never would it encompass past romances, money, politics, or religion.

Such reciprocal comfort was likely to change, however. On the evening of the second day of February, Jay insisted on preparing the evening meal. Mashed potatoes and gravy, canned corn, and large elk steaks with sautéed mushrooms were presented to a surprised young lady who was seated with great anticipation at an actual cloth draped table.

Sheila was not sure how her roommate knew, but it was her birthday. Not only was the celebration unexpected, but catered to with incredible preparation. She was not even sure where he got such a precious commodity as the potatoes. There was no cake or wrapping paper, but there were gifts, Jay assured her. She insisted that Jay sing her "Happy Birthday" but he declined with a declaration that of all his talents, singing was not among them.

"Come on," Sheila pleaded as she bit her lower lip in a luring way, "I will even sing with you."

Jay was suddenly lost in the sight of her incredible exquisiteness and had not heard a word that she had spoken.

"Hello, hello," she repeated, "Anyone present?"

Jay finally shook free from the spell and refocused his attention, "Now for the gifts."

"What about the song?"

"There is no song!"

"There is no song?" Sheila acted boo-boo lipped.

"There never has been-never will be." Jay's physical gestures were matter of fact.

"I know that there was a song 'cause I heard it several times in the low lands," Sheila was quick to inform.

"They don't have impending natural disasters in the low lands such as avalanches or stampedes. There is no song!" The mountain man would prefer to go up against a pack of wolves or even a cranky grizzly than sing such an idiotic song.

Sheila would giggle at the discovery that the mountain man possessed such an uncourageous trait on such a minor request. Jay was intrigued by such. He was not expecting Sheila to enjoy his discomfort so much, and she began to laugh uncontrollably. Jay found the moment amazing and wanted it to last forever. No matter how hard he tried, he could not help but be taken in by her charm. He suddenly felt obvious and embarrassed. In an attempt to free himself from her spell, he refocused his attention and placed another piece of wood in the stove that really didn't need it.

"I've got a couple gifts for you," he once again announced.

Jason realized that it had been fun up to this point, but he began to feel threatened as she pushed for the traditional serenade. Sheila dropped the subject.

"Really?" she mused. "And where did you go shopping? They better be good because I have been known to be high maintenance, and take things back for exchange." Jay found himself participating in her humor and jested with her in return. "Those were my suspicions from the very start," he said with a smile. "Stand up and keep your eyes closed," he was eager in his instructions.

Sheila thought she heard him rummaging under the bed but still did not open her eyes. He emerged with a large fur cape and gently cloaked the fair maiden in its protection. As she opened her eyes, she was amazed at how heavy the tanned hide really was. The long cinnamon/brown hair tickled her nose as she looked down and stroked the texture, and she began to giggle again. Taking a deep breath, she was barely able to contain her joy and she smiled at the rugged mountain man and simply said, "Oh, thank you."

It's not really a coat you know," Jay felt a little uncomfortable. "I don't really do coats all that well, so it's more like nature's quilt with sleeves."

She snuggled herself in it and then looked Jay straight in the eye and smiled. "I still want you to sing."

Jay realized her lighthearted request but stood fast to his convictions to spare her sense of hearing. "Ain't gonna happen, Miss Gray. The Pentagon won't allow it."

"Come on Jay, it can't be that bad."

"You know when I took Joe to Sky City entrance?" Jay asked. Sheila nodded.

"Well the dynamite didn't work so I sang Happy Birthday." Both Jay and Sheila began to laugh as they visualized the scenario. "Furthermore, if we are ever stalked by predators, just remind me to serenade 'em – that will surely cause 'em to dash!"

As Sheila attempted to compose herself, Jay pushed a large unwrapped box in front of her. Slowly she opened the top and peered in. A sobering expression was revealed by her face as she ripped the sides of the box and sat down and studied the magnificent craftsmanship. The unleashed aroma of cedar was almost overpowering. Jay had captured the ferocious expression of the bear, as well as the endearing facial features of the Nut. It was as though Wing Nut understood that the bear was vicious by nature and she forgave the beast.

"I can't accept this," she insisted as tears welled up in her large beautiful ebony eyes. Shaking her head, she would reiterate, "I can't accept this."

"Sheila." Jay was stern as he pulled the carving of Wing Nut and the bear from the box. "Nature gave you the bear skin rug, or coat, or whatever it is, but this gift is from me."

Tears streamed down her face as she took her delicate hand and passionately ran her fingers over the finished master piece. It was as though she wanted to experience every curve, every bit of the elegant surface.

"So that was what you were chipping away on for so long – I never suspected," Sheila was amazed. "I thought that you were just making a mess for me to clean up."

After Jay finished washing the dinner dishes he dried his hands and announced one more surprise; a moonlit skiing expedition that Sheila would never forget. This would be a late night adventure that no other person on the face of the earth would have the privilege to experience. Sheila was curious about the enchanted destination that would prompt such an expedition but no matter how hard she persisted for a clue, Jay stood solid to the secrecy.

For the most part the moon was full and magnificent. Its silver brilliance was magnified by the hard white crust of the deep snow. Jay was impressed with the speed in which Sheila effortlessly graced the winter wonderland. The view was spectacular and the company, excellent. The cross-country excursion was fast and every moment offered an opportunity to embrace the process towards the mystery with ignorant anticipation. But the best part, the surprise, was still a couple miles off Jay assured Miss Gray.

Within minutes, Sheila focused on a sight in the distance and became puzzled with the astonishing phenomena that began to emerge. Bellows of seemingly florescent clouds expanded into the air and then would slowly dissipate as it floated towards the canyon. She was curious, but maintained her silence as she understood that this must be the surprise. Besides, she knew that Jay would not tell her anyway. The mountain man continued thrusting his lead towards the vapor cloud.

Soon Sheila's curiosity was satisfied as a splendid wonderland unfolded before her. She stood astonished as hot water was boiling up from deep within the earth's core and surfacing in a pool surrounded by snow. Her focus was interrupted as she saw Jay begin to disrobe. With his back towards her, he attempted a considerate gesture of modesty. Soon he was slipping into the welcome warmth of the natural wonder and let out a deep, long, sigh. Without an invitation, Sheila voluntarily unfastened her skis and disrobed as well. Commanded by his sense of chivalry, Jay once again turned away from temptation and faced towards the canyon and away from Sheila as she consciously placed one foot timidly into the water, as to make sure that this was not all a mirage. Soon she too was enjoying the sensations of the natural hot tub by blissfully embracing all the spontaneous hot water the spring had to offer.

Nature's master mason had constructed the walls of the artesian phenomenon with rock and the past millions of years softly polished the surface with diligence and patience. The depth was inconsistent with the deepest areas up to five feet and the average, probably two. The water temperature was certain to be over a hundred degrees and with the contrast of negative 38 degrees atmosphere, the experience was surreal.

As a slight breeze drifted the vapor haze away, the couple watched in silence as the panorama extended its incomparable splendor. Rolling mountains reflected an indescribable feeling of visual pleasure as peaks in the distance presented themselves as a backdrop to God's masterpiece. Deep dark canyons added dimension and a sense of mystery. Neither Sheila nor Jay felt compelled to speak. They were in the midst of a wonderland for which words could not improve. The moment was full and time was endless.

It was quite some time before the silence was broken. As nature had created the perfect silence, nature would take it away. A lone coyote beckoned to the moon. It seemed to break the trance and both Jay and Sheila became aware of each other once again. As the endless volcanic heated water continued to pour into the confines of the tranquil pool, the two began to talk with generality about the past. It was as though the time was finally right and the exchange was something that needed to take place.

Sheila was of Italian/French descent and had enjoyed the fruits of her father's success. He was a self-made man with the bulk of his success stemming from the computer industry. Understanding that versatility was paramount to constant, stable success, he invested in multiple non-related ventures and it seemed that everything that he became interested in would achieve great financial prosperity. She had two sisters, Jasmine Rose and Isabelle. Her parents and sisters were now living in a large home in Colorado Springs. Although she was just twenty-six years old, she had already managed a sizable portfolio, as well as established herself as primary consideration in international modeling circles. She preferred to display her mind over physical attributes, however, and looked forward to the challenges and experiences of the business world.

After completing a short excerpt of her life, Sheila turned and studied the man who she suddenly felt an irresistibly attraction to. In the pale moonlight she could clearly make out the slightly weathered features of his handsome and dignified face. She remembered the photograph in the newspaper and somehow thought he might look better without the beard.

"What?" Jay asked.

"I didn't think about it at the time," Sheila was slightly embarrassed. "How do we get dressed when we get out of this thing?"

"Rather quickly," Jay said half joking, half seriously. "Otherwise you won't have to worry about another birthday."

"Why did you move up to the mountains and disassociate yourself from everyone down below?"

Jay looked off in the direction of the twin peaks as though to disregarded the question. "You know, you can almost see completely around the world from the top of those." Jay slowly drew his attention back around to the stunning face that had posed the question, "did you ever watch ants on an ant hill?"

Sheila was confused and could not comprehend the point of such a question. "I guess so."

"Ya' know, Sheila. It is incredible how millions of them have the ability to create their own city while through the very process chaos guides their every move. They eat, build, kill, and die while being amidst such bedlam, and by their own existence the chaos exists. They even make love in an urgent frenzy, I would guess, and after it is over they speed off in another direction on a new crusade." Jay took a deep breath and let out a sigh. "Collectively, they make the difference. Hell, they can even down a cow more than a zillion times their own weight; collectively. Individually, their death will go unnoticed. You could take your foot and stomp on a thousand and it doesn't even change their world. The survivors would just use their remains to build a higher city.

"I'm sorry, but I'm afraid that I really don't quite get your point." Sheila was still confused.

"The point is ... I guess that life is not something that we can arrive at. It's more like a process," Jay stated as a matter of fact.

"That's kind of cynical isn't it?" Sheila offered her observation.

"It would depend on how you looked at it." Jay smiled. "If you were to build a passion around the process and not such high expectations around the arrival, then you would be freed up to live life. Otherwise, you would work yourself to death for that one moment in life, all the while ignorant to the fact you would not be able to suspend that moment indefinitely, if indeed it had arrived at all.

"And what does all that mean?" Sheila was lost.

"It means that you can't live solely off of the past, so you should not prepare a future with thoughts of someday doing so." Jay thought that he had finalized the explanation.

"And, with that in mind, where do you fit in?" Sheila was still expecting Jay to qualify his theory.

"I'm no different than the ants," Jay said. "I just choose to build my mound on the side of the mountain rather than spend any more time competing for space on the ant hill."

There was a lull in the conversation as both the mountain man and the princess took in the scenery. The air was becoming crisper now and Sheila was beginning to consider submerging her shoulders and head underwater to keep them warm but then thought better of it. Initially, it would feel great but it would mean a death sentence on the way back to the cabin.

Sheila began to make snowballs out of the snow which was very near the edge of the natural spring. She then packed them hard and placed them in the pool and watched them dissolve. "Thank you for the carving of Wing Nut." She suddenly extended her heartfelt gratitude. "I'm sorry I trespassed into your past. I had no right, and I am sorry."

"I'm sorry that I got so angry, Sheila. Now, I am thinking that it was all for the best." Jay had also regretted contributing to the general anxiety of the moment.

"But you were right ..."

Jay put up his hand in a halting fashion and cut her short. "It seems that virtually every aspect of my past has been extreme." Jay began to reveal and, perhaps even concede, his history. "Extremely good or extremely bad without much average in between; I guess I'm pretty sensitive about some aspects."

Sheila wanted to reply but decided to listen and not interrupt. It had been a long time coming and now that it was here, she dared not mess it up.

"I was pretty good at handling a football in high school and so they gave me a shot at it in college," Jay's modesty revealed. "After that I went into the pros for a couple years and got paid a whole lot to do very little. It seemed that the more important I thought I was, the more they paid me." Jay began to create his own snowball and place it in the water. As he watched it, he went on, "I think they call it status paralysis. In any event, I was pretty high on myself and then when people that I once valued as friends tried to tell me about it, I would shut them down. Even Father Jim told me I was heading for an egotistical catastrophe." Jay paused for a moment as if to view his relationship with the priest with great favor. The good father was his chief adviser from Jay's college days at Notre Dame.

Breaking his trance, the ex-pro went on. "He said that I took the one commandment to a new extreme. The one about loving one's self. Anyway, I shut him down and let him know under no uncertain terms I guided my own destiny." Jay looked at the inquisitive face before him. "To prove a point, I went out on the field the very next day and maimed another human being. Oh, it was all legal and just and no foul was called because that's just part of the game." Jay once again paused and diverted his gaze off in the distant mountains again. "Anyway, I emptied my locker virtually before the game was even over and never looked back."

"Is that when you became a cop?" Sheila asked.

"Oh yes," Jay smiled; "Trading one extreme for another! I decided that now that I got so much money to do so little I would place myself in a position to do too much work for very little pay. One minute I was wearing a uniform and pledging only to feed my ego and signing sponsorship contracts with really obscene dollar amounts." Jay shook his head. "And tens of thousands of people would cheer just to see me walk out onto the artificial lawn. Then, I traded my number on the roster for a number on a badge and the new uniform got results too. My intentions were to make the difference and I was going to do my absolute best. One minute I was preoccupied with changing my world; the next minute, the whole world."

Sheila interrupted the now depressing Jay, "How did they get your picture mixed up with the other man's?" She figured that as long as he was talking about it, it might as well be put to rest as well.

Jay ran both of his hands through his hair and took in a deep breath. "I was to be honored as the Beat Cop of the Year. My picture was given to the paper the same morning that the kids died. Somehow, someway, due to 9/11 and all, it just simply got mixed."

"Why didn't you sue them?"

"Sue who? The paper said that the police department was at fault for giving them the wrong picture. The police department denies the mistake and points the finger right back at the Times. And the general public, who has the final say, points a finger in my direction and says an eye for an eye!"

Sheila was touched by the testimony and felt sadness for the trials of which had been unfairly inflicted upon her new found friend. She suddenly felt compelled to extend more than a token gesture of affection. She wanted to embrace him and let him know that she really cared. The beautiful woman was aware that the moment would be awkward enough clothed let alone nude, but the inclination was strong and the reason secure.

Somehow Jay could read her mind and felt extreme mixed emotions about the possibilities. He had not felt the tenderness of a woman's body next to his for several years now. The prospects were inviting, however, the emotional burden was too great and Jay found himself cowering as she eased closer.

"Well, it's getting late and we had better make our way back," he said in a raspy voice. Then, with a single bound, Jay catapulted his way out of the heated pleasure of the pool and into the brisk sobering effects of the winter night air.

Chapter Ten

The Building of an Empire

The days after Sheila's twenty-sixth birthday were far more pleasant with a great deal of laughter. With such laughter, friendship and mutual admiration grew. Although opportunities of physical contact were great, both adults avoided temptation and held fast to the unspoken pledge not to indulge; not even in the slightest. Even so, the alluring Miss Gray found herself becoming increasingly fond of the bravest but least boastful man she had ever known. Often she found herself staring at him and wondering why he never made a move to embrace her; to attempt to steal a kiss from her. She smiled at the thought of the many men who tried and were turned away. Now, on a mountainside many miles away from civilization, she had perhaps discovered the most civilized man in the world.

With the detailed confession in which Jay had revealed his past, communication had opened up between he and the beautiful lady, and in a great way, he felt the weight of the past taken from his mind. He no longer felt on constant guard. As a matter of fact, he was at ease, and subsequently, content with life. He was, to the best of his memory, the happiest he had been in years; perhaps ever.

*****

Soon there were subtle signs of spring. The sunshine was lingering just a little longer each day and the v-shaped formations of geese were beginning to pass overhead to the north again. Although snow in the high country was persistent in its lingering presence, one could see the speckled dark spots progressing into larger ones on the distant foothills of the lowlands. With the announcement that summer was on its way, came a deeper desire to worship the sun. This reverence stimulated thoughts and plans for such a time each day.

The mountain man had anchored deep feelings for the wonderful woman that had fallen out of the sky and into his life. He often wished that he had allowed her to embrace him — to feel her tangible charms press against his body — his mind. But the opportunity had passed so quickly and although his obvious diversion of such an advance, he understood that he would have to now take the risk and make the first critical move. He was not really prepared to do so, but with the passing of each day, came the inevitable awareness that soon she would be leaving.

It was early April. This particular day, the sun was high and the warmth of its radiant heat beat down on the south face of La Garita Wilderness. For all practical indications, this would be the first real sign that spring had come to the highlands. A large patch of grassland would appear, and by its existence, the knowledge of day travel would have to be suspended. The water saturated snow would no longer support skis or snowshoes during the solar periods. However, from nine o'clock at night to about nine the next morning, the landscape was frozen to a point that Jay and Sheila often enjoyed late night walks without the aid of skis or snowshoes. Their weight was supported by the rolling crystallized snow.

*****

By mid-April, definite signs of passion were in the air as the mountain man had built a gazebo which had been fashioned out of logs and wooden pegs. The construction was ingenious with only antique hand tools to aid in the production. Sheila loved it and was so excited when it was finally done. Weather permitting, the evening meals were enjoyed in the serenity of the structure and the visual vantage point of the canyon and the peaks were never disappointing. In the evenings, Jay often found himself fantasizing the construction of a large log home with a loft and a huge balcony, as well as ample living room, luxurious bedroom, and even indoor plumbing; on the chance that this may draw the lady's favor was worth consideration. Jay was constantly thinking of persuading Sheila to stay with indirect hints, but he could not manage the courage to address his feelings and ask her to ponder such plans. Somehow, maintaining the possibility was better than facing the risk of rejection, although the odds were, he felt certain, in his favor.

One warm afternoon, Sheila wandered out to see what Jay was doing. He was seated in the gazebo and appeared to be looking through several large rolls of paper which was laid across a table. At first, the dark haired woman approached unnoticed. When Jay realized her presence, he reacted with a start and became embarrassed.

"Let me see," she said. But with panic in his eyes, he attempted to hide the already discovered article of issue. As he backed away from her advance, he backed too far and before he knew it, he was flipping backwards over the gazebo railing. Unfortunately, he dropped the rolls in the process and by the time he had made his way back onto his feet, Sheila was holding them in her hands.

"That's personal!" Jay protested.

"I'll say it is," Sheila agreed. "The question is, is it personal for you or for me?" But Sheila was not mad. Her eyes slowly scanned every detail of the charcoal drawing which offered several dimensions. In all actuality, the entire history of the woman's stay was portrayed in true artistic fashion. The top of the drawing showed Jay and the Nut looking up at the belly of the plane flying overhead at tree top level and the wolves were scattering in all directions. Other sketches depicted the shooting of Mexican Joe, Sheila falling through the snow, and even her suturing Jay's injuries which were caused by the cousin of the grizzly. There were many others of which were done quite well; however, the one that caught her attention the most was the moonlit winter scene in nature's hot tub.

Jay felt obvious and anxious as he walked around the neatly built structure and once again stepped into its entry way. He felt as though he wanted to grab the drawings and erase them from her mind. He could grab them and flee, but he knew that his embarrassment would be too evident, so he chose to divert the damsel's attention.

"I have more drawings in the vault," he simply stated.

"That's nice, Jay" Sheila did not look away from a particular drawing in hand. "I'm still interested in this one." She slowly looked up and caught Jay before he could avoid her eye contact. He wanted to look away but it was too late. "You have kind of embellished certain parts of my anatomy, didn't you? So you did peek!"

Now, thoroughly red in the face, the wide eyed Jay was in shock and did not know what to say or do. However, what he did say, even he did not expect! "I just draw 'em the way I see 'em."

*****

One evening, a couple days later, Jay and the good natured woman were sitting across from each other at the table in the cabin. Both were aware that the time had come for Jay to lead the damsel out of the high country mountains and return her back to the congestion and confusion otherwise known as civilization. Her pattern had been changed and her life definitely took on a new dimension. As a matter of fact, she knew that her life would never be the same ever again. The experiences in Jay's world and the hospitality extended by him had made its mark. She knew that Jay liked her, perhaps even loved her, but she was fearful that she really was not welcome to be a permanent fixture in his life. She had given him several opportunities to extend to her a sign that his feelings were extreme; that she was desirable and that he wanted to take the next step, whatever that may mean. However, he had not responded. By Jay's inaction, Sheila would have to conclude that he had chosen solitude over companionship; loneliness over happiness. She was saddened by this, but would try once again to break through the hard exterior.

"Are we going to be leaving tomorrow?" Sheila was first to actually verbalize the probability.

Jay would respond only by nodding and did not lift his stare from the table top.

"How long will it take to get to the nearest phone?"

Jay was irritated. Not so much by the question but that such indicated that Sheila was more than ready to depart his company and embrace life as she had known it before. How could he compete with that?

"It takes as long as it takes," he simply responded. All of a sudden, he was compelled to despise her. He hated the way she had brought such a disturbance to his serene existence. And now she was leaving and he would feel a great void, for the pattern of his life had also been changed, and so completely. He leaned back in the dining room chair and placed his hands behind his head. His deep thoughts were interrupted by instinct and he became alarmed that an outside force was present. Something was lurking just on the other side of the door! He slowly repositioned the tilt of his chair to its intended upright position and placed his hand over Sheila's lips as to quiet her anticipated voice. In a whisper Jay announced, "Someone is at the door!"

Both Sheila and Jay watched with agonizing anticipation as the latch began to lift as if on its own. As soon as the latch cleared, the door burst open and in surged a frightening figure with a large hunting knife in one hand and the other poised as if, on the defensive ready. With a savage grin, the man advanced towards Jay as if in a wrestling stance. The difference was, this was no wrestler and the knife was obviously not a gesture of friendship. Jay slowly began to step back but the bookshelf blocked his retreat.

The intruder stepped closer and motioned to Jay with the blade as to entice him to engage. "Come on, boy! You can't get out of an ass kick'n so let's get into it!"

With such an invite, Jay chose to accept and slowly began to circle the room in attempt to somehow improve on his obvious disadvantage.

*****

The night was at its darkest as the young guard peered briefly at the vacant courtyard. Satisfied that there were no prisoners, he concentrated far beyond the compound and now scanned a hundred and eighty degrees around to the never ending maze of the consecutive chain link fences. There were seven such barriers. Each fence stood thirty foot high and was crowned with a circular accordion of razor wire. The obvious intentions of such obstacles were to discourage the notion of an escape. As the spotlight flashed past him and out into the early spring drizzle, he would take a deep breath and release it with a sigh. He then stretched out his arm and positioned his watch so that the reflection of the light would somewhat illuminate the crystal face. It was just past four in the morning and within a couple hours, he would be able to call it a shift. He felt fatigued as he directed his concentration the best that he could into the depths of the inner perimeter. He adjusted the collar of the department issue rain sticker. While doing so, he thought that he heard something and tilted his head slightly as to gain a better advantage. Yes, he had heard something but it would be too late!

Alarmed, the guard turned with swift reaction and was suddenly surprised to see a well-known convict standing at arm's reach.

"Mayhem!" The state employee had barely uttered the name when he felt a sharp piercing pain that ran from his chest all the way to his shoulder blades. When he looked down, terror gripped his very soul. As focus began to drift away, he recognized a shank that was masterfully embedded through his heart. The convict slowly withdrew the crude instrument and the guard gasped, then gasped again as he stared back into the deep hollow set eyes which belonged to the merciless inmate.

"Night night, piglet," Mayhem was pleased with the task he had just accomplished. The guard slowly staggered backwards and braced his back next to a retaining wall. As his life drained away, he slowly slipped to the concrete floor leaving a blood streak on the wall. The shank had been driven completely through his body. Slowly and deliberately, the inmate took his middle finger on his left hand and ran it along the flat of his blade. He looked at the fresh blood on his fingers, and then without hesitation lifted his hand to his lips and tasted it. A smile of satanic ecstasy slowly but distinctly broadened across the seemingly possessed man's face. He removed the officer's service revolver, took one last look at the still body and slipped into the shadows of the night.

Within minutes, eight dark, shadowy figures slid down the penitentiary wall and drifted one at a time in a stealthy crouch, across to the first stage fence. The drizzle by this time had turned into a driving rain, and although the escaping convicts were uncomfortable, they found luxury in knowing that visual detection of their activity would be greatly obscured. They paid little or no attention to the bloody water that was cascading out of the upper flight drain pipe which was emptying next to their feet. Their mission was clear, to escape at any and all costs.

Within a few minutes, the eight had breached the seven razor clustered obstacles and had run a distance of a mile or better to a pre-set rendezvous point. Awaiting their arrival was the two time loser on rape convictions, Joe Garcia. Even on the inside he went by the name "Mex" or Mexican Joe.

Joe had already opened the hatch gate to the half-shell camper which sat on the back of a "borrowed" 1975 dark blue ¾ ton Chevy pickup. A large man known as the "Knight," the "Black Knight" or "Esquire" took immediate charge by ordering everyone in the back of the transportation with the exception of Mex who was pre-designated as the navigator. Mexican Joe scooted across the seat to the passenger side of the truck as Esquire climbed in and slammed the driver's side door to the old beater. In the distance, the eerie pulsating shrill of an old military surplus air raid siren could be heard over the torrential downpour.

Esquire, the uncontested leader of the castaways, drove the old truck in a southerly direction on a back road which had been deemed a four wheel drive only road. A more accurate description would have been a goat trail. Time was of the essence and a comfortable experience was not to be had as the potholes and large rocks could not deny the aggressive manner in which the heavy truck was being driven. As the truck made its way back into the deep recesses of wilderness, authorities mistakenly placed the ATL (attempt to locate) bulletins throughout the nearby towns and blocked all expected routes. Air support was not possible because of the cloud cover, and the continuous downpour would hamper search efforts for the next forty-eight hours. This would prove to be just enough time for the desperate men to gain eventual access to a highway, and ultimately travel half the distance across the United States. Their intent was to become within striking distance of Mexico.

Inside the confines of the old blue pickup truck were a mismatched collection of misfit talent and unbound rationale. First, there was Mayhem. He was a thirty-one year old who had been a convicted murderer of a single episode however, he was suspected of numerous deaths that were non-prosecutable. He was on his third year of forty, knew the system well and was a dedicated worshiper of Satan. As a matter of fact, he had been convicted on a satanic ritual death. He was white, weighed 175 pounds, worked out often and was a whole lot stronger than he appeared.

Mr. Mayhem came by his jailhouse handle legitimately as he had no common sense and thus, no fundamental talent to monitor or restrict his impulses. He would rely on Esquire to handle all consequential thinking.

Then there was Sly, a mute from birth. He was expert in banking "transactions" and prided himself in "after hour withdrawals." He preferred to operate alone, and the one time that he had incorporated a partnership, he had been burned. After spending close to five years of an eight year stretch, Sly suddenly found himself block-mates with the same individual who had dropped the dime on him. The snitch had gotten off scot-free the first time around, but now finding himself in the Big House on a non-related burglary, he would soon realize, much to his regret, he was in all actuality condemned to death. Sly was found guilty of the execution and ordered to spend the rest of his life behind the steel curtains of the Illinois Penal system.

Sly was a thirty-four year old white male, weighing one hundred sixty pounds, had somewhat striking features and was intellectually acute. He had a talent of receiving intelligence and storing such for a rainy day. He was most instrumental in the success of the escape but was not pleased that the guard had been sacrificed in the process.

The third man, and most likely the one who processed the greatest amount of intelligence of the group was Drafter. He had been confined for only five years on a white collar conviction. He thought that he was smart enough to represent himself at trial, and subsequently had discovered that he had acquired a fool for a client. Drafter was anxious to rid himself of the unpleasant atmosphere for he which had unexpectedly found himself. He had thought at one time that he would endure the sentence and later emerge from the system to claim a nest egg of over a million dollars. The sum represented the fruits of an elaborate embezzlement. However, it was soon discovered that the life expectancy of a courtyard wimp would not outlast the sentence. Under Esquire's protection, Drafter would not only buy himself time but a ticket on the leader's coattails if he could mastermind the escape.

Drafter looked to be fifty with a diminished hair line and chubby cheeks. He, at one point, was pretty close to forty or so pounds overweight, but prison life had been cruel and if anything, he was underweight at the moment. He too, had been unaware of the added planned execution of the corrections officer and although depressed of such, dared not protest for he realized that on the outside, his life was now expendable.

James Eagle was of Native American descent, stood six foot, six inches tall and at over 230 pounds made a lasting visual impression. He was a quiet sort, who at one time had celebrated the amenity of being the most powerful man in prison. With battle scars from the past that would easily yield to the imagination, it never was quite known for sure why he was on the inside. He was nevertheless respected throughout the population and somewhat feared by the establishment. Eagle, which he most commonly went by, had a reputation of being hard to anger, but one who would never forget.

"Squeeze" had come by his name honestly as he was slight of build and maintained a girlish appearance. "She" had, without option, given into the unorthodox sexual indulgence from the first day in prison, and during the process, acquired several "owners." Also, without knowing it, Squeeze won the one-way trip ticket out only because the others feared his possible preconceived knowledge of the escape plan. He was notorious for snitching. Once on the outside, he was of no apparent use and thus on borrowed time. Really, it was a wonder that he was still alive thus far.

John Hamel, aka Blade Runner, was so named due to the remarkable ability to locate and procure virtually any and all objects of destruction. The shank in Mayhem's possession was subsequent to the Runner's talent for acquisitioning. Although well-muscled and extremely active with dead weight conditioning, his first concern was not so much the acquired physical attributes as his mental sharpness. If there was a most valuable player within the organized escape party, it would be the Runner. Not only had he acquired the necessary raw materials from the inside for the project, but he had lined up and arranged for Mexican Joe as the rescue source on the outside. And, this had been no easy task.

The seventh select member was Wells Gonzales. He was an undocumented visitor from Mexico who had been convicted of using an axe to decapitate another guest of the United States. Neither he nor his victim had legal credentials. Wells spoke broken English at best, but was valued for his savvy in his homeland and would serve as the liaison once the border had been crossed. He was of average build but strong for his weight and prided himself as an expert with a broad edge. He was upset that Mayhem been chosen for the guard carving, but his homeland was heavy on his mind and he was thus preoccupied with maintaining focus on the overall objective.

Then there was the Esquire; a man of enormous dimensions, weighing over 280 pounds and towering six feet, nine inches. From the very moment that his presence was felt at the "Mansion", few men, including the guards, had dared to cross his path. Those that did were not around for a second opportunity. He had been convicted of a homicide stemming out of a fit of rage, and although that was the only blemish on the official register, he had been suspected of twelve unusual circumstance deaths while in the system. Simply put, he ruled.

*****

"You sorry son-of-a-bitch!" Jay yelled as he lunged towards the ugly uninvited man. Sheila let out a shriek as the two men collided and much to her amazement, they began to hug which was definitely contrary to the expected combat. Sheila was poised with a butter knife and stood her ground a little longer, then placed the ridiculous weapon back on the table.

"Man," observed the shaggy stranger as he took a step back and studied Jay. "Looks to me ya' been winter'n perty fur."

Jay smiled and gestured in Sheila's direction. "Spook, I want you to meet Sheila Gray. Sheila, this is Spook McGuire."

Spook had not seen, let alone expected to see company in the Devereux house. To further confuse the spontaneous visitor was the fact that the young lady had to have fallen out of a fashion magazine as she was the loveliest sight that he had ever seen. "Well spank me on the ass and call Wilma!" Spook uttered. He paused for a moment and then studied her stunning features. Stroking his beard he asked, "She's your sister, no?"

"That would be a no." Jay wanted no misunderstanding.

"Some other type of relative, no?"

"Wrong again."

"She been here fur a spell?" Spook inquired further.

Jay began to laugh, "for the most part. Ever since Christmas."

"One hell of a present! Don't 'spose she is tired of your unrefined habits by now, huh?" Spook was hopeful.

Sheila realized that this frightful excuse of a man was friend rather than foe despite the dreadful appearance. To state that Spook was not a pretty sight was an understatement. He was a fright! Spook maintained deep set eyes that were so open as to reveal the whites more than the beady centers. His hair, facial as well as otherwise, was matted in every conceivable direction and must have been that way for the last decade or so. All things considered, he looked like the missing link or at best, a crazed escapee from a mental hospital.

In an abrupt fashion, the nervous Spook wiped his hand front and back on his rawhide britches and extended the still soiled limb in the direction of Sheila as a peace offering after the frightful entrance. With a tentative expression, Sheila surrendered her own. Spook unexpectedly clasped his hand around the young lady's wrist and lightly wrenched it as though a wild animal was ready to feast on it. What made the playful gesture all the more alarming, was the low guttural menacing sound emitting from the dirty visitor that was not that far removed from that of a savage beast during a feeding frenzy. Letting out a shriek, Sheila instinctively reclaimed her limb. She was angered by the abrupt prank but was able to appreciate the joke a little as the two men rolled about the floor hysterically indulging themselves in laugher.

Soon the immature pranksters were able to once again contain themselves and a pleasant conversation was attempted. "What are you doing in these parts?" Jay inquired.

"T'was up at the hot springs the other day and saw human signs all over the place! Thought som'n was a might wrong if'n ya' be tak'n a bath so early in the year." Spook turned his attention back to Sheila. "Don't reck'n ya'd care for a dip with me?" He was hopeful.

Sheila took a deliberate step towards Jay and shook her head, "Not a chance." She made it perfectly clear.

"Anyway, I was just pass'n through these parts and thought that I might stop in and give ya' some grief ..." Spook paused for a moment and with a slight nod in the woman's direction continued, "But, I can see ya' probably had your fill already."

Sheila was not a part of the conversation for the rest of the evening, nor had she any desire to be. She was content to spend her last night on the mountain absorbed in the serenity of a novel and pleased not to participate in the substandard communication with someone so illiterate. From time to time, however, she would look up from the book to stare at the handsome Jay Devereux. She was saddened by the thought of never seeing him again, but tearfully grateful for the experience for at least once. She entertained the fantasy, if invited, to maybe living a good portion of her life with such a magnificent man and on this mountain, but again, she had not been invited. Sadness began to consume her, and as she turned yet another page she felt tears trickle down her cheeks.

*****

It was inevitable that the darkness of night would give way to the ever approaching eastern glow. Dawn was breaking and with it came the natural anxiety of departing from deep rooted feelings that had been acquired over the past four months. To further stress the moment, was the discovery by Sheila that Jay intended not to escort her to the lowlands after all. It had been arranged, without Sheila's knowledge or approval, that Spook would be the acting guide for her deliverance from the La Garita Wilderness.

Sheila felt compelled to impose her thoughts on the subject of departing with such an untrustworthy and obnoxious individual. She soon would discover that her extreme concerns would fall on deaf ears. For some unknown reason, Jay had made up his mind that he would stay behind and his decision was final. Upon receiving the less than adequate farewell, Sheila found herself stomping from the cabin with a brisk gate. Exasperation overwhelmed her and at each step she became increasingly livid.

"Come on; if we are going to go then, let's go!" She said as she slammed the door.

"That's all fine and dandy," Spook took the initiative to let the young lady know that there would be no way that they could be traveling at this time of day. They would only have about three hours before the consistency of the spring snow was unsafe and every step would place them up to their midsection in slush. Not even snow shoes would be able to be of benefit. The only "solid" time to travel would be about 9:00 or 10:00 pm to about 9:00 am.

Sheila trudged past the waiting Spook and began to descend the mountain. At one point, her stomping caused a snow pack to settle, and she lost her balance and fell flat on her face. As she shook her head, the Spook assisted her to her feet where she abruptly pulled her arm away in a huff.

"Now don't ya' blame me for hav'n your little female tantrum," Spook said with a smile on his face.

"What is that supposed to mean?" Sheila demanded.

The Spook picked up his pack and began to descend at a reasonable speed, "It makes no never mind to me. Three hours are better than noth'n I guess. I mean what the hell; denial is fine and all, but only if ya' truly don't give a damn!"

"What is that supposed to mean!?" She displayed an expression of frustration with tears streaming down her face. At this point, Sheila broke off a frozen clump of snow and threw it at the uncouth man. As it hit him in the back of the head, he stopped and glared straight forward for a moment. Finally, he slowly turned around to face the now frightened young lady.

"Look Miss. I don't mind ya' hurting the one ya' love. As a matter of fact, I prefer it. For a nickel, I'd even go back up to the cabin and hold him down for ya." The scary figure walked back and knelt down as though to rest. "But I's got to tell ya, I ain't gonna put up with a beat'n I don't have com'n, no matter how purty ya' be!"

"I'm sorry," Sheila tried to extend her apologies.

The unsightly man slowly lifted his body as he struggled to stand, and as though not to address her directly said, "They always be sorry when they think ya' about to knock the crap outa 'em." Then in a more direct tone stated, "Now ya' get," and pointed up to the cabin.

"Cause I ain't gonna babysit a love sick kitten for the rest of the trip. Besides, ya' two got unfinished business."

Jay's mind was caught up with thousands of impulses that were all stemming from recall of the amazingly beautiful Sheila Gray. It seemed that equal and opposing forces were pulling the man in conflicting directions at the same time. He wanted desperately to run after her and bring her back and yet, he felt comfortable in some strange way with living alone and having things the same simple way as before. Jay placed both hands to his face and wiped tears from his eyes. "Hell," he murmured out loud to himself, "If things were meant to be, then they would have been."

Jay had been so caught up in his own thoughts and misery that he had not even heard the cabin door open again.

"That's bull Jay, and you know it!" Sheila scampered across the room, grabbed Jay by the shirt and pulled the surprised man to his feet. Jay attempted to gain his balance by stepping back; however, the aggressive intentions of the woman kept him off balance and he ended up struggling halfway across the cabin. With a thud, he felt his back slam against the wall, but Sheila had followed Jay's stumbling and was still pressing.

"You don't get it, do you?" She was half yelling. "You're not going to let God be the fall guy for all this! For somebody who thinks they're so damn tough, you're pretty Jell-Oie at times!"

Jay felt Sheila's grip soften and mistook the sign as her easing off the intensity. In all actuality, she was grasping for a better grip and in so doing, managed to secure a great amount of chest hair through his shirt as well.

"Jay," Sheila still commanded the floor. "I think I'm falling in love with you." There it was, finally official; nothing to hide; nothing to misunderstand.

The uncomfortable pain the mountain man felt as his chest hairs were being plucked could not compare with the total overriding joy he was suddenly experiencing from within.

"What?" He was stunned by the revelation.

"I love you, you damned fool!" She once again made it perfectly clear. Still holding tightly onto Jay's shirt, she pulled the tall man to her and for the first time passionately kissed him long and hard. Slowly, but deliberately, Jay pried her hands from his chest as the intense unpleasant sensations were beginning to take away from the moment.

Spook stood for a few seconds at the door seemingly amused at the scene. "Ya' all get through suck'n on each other's faces, we might wanna think about scoot'n on. Besides, all this heat from this cabin will start melt'n the snow at a faster rate, if ya' get my drift."

Sheila pulled back and looked at the man to whom she had just confessed to. They both studied each other's eyes as if to somehow make up for so much wasted time. Softly this time, she patted him on his chest and then held her hand firmly against his heartbeat.

"I've got to go." She was regretting the obvious. "They need to know that I am still among the living."

"Absolutely." Jay's mind was still reeling from the sudden unexpected embrace. Sheila reached up and with a touch as soft as silk, slowly stroked the hopeful face of the mountain man. "I've got things that I have to take care of," She paused with a warm smile, "but I promise that I will come back in a couple months." Once more she would kiss his longing lips and slowly withdraw. As she approached the open door, she turned and directed a heart filled wave by raising her hand and offering a slight nod, "I will be back and then we can build an empire together."

Within minutes, she was out of sight, but the fresh memory of her kiss lingered heavily on Jay's mind. Without conscious effort, he touched his lips as though to reacquaint the vivid physical feel. He had never felt so energetic or compelled with purpose in his entire life. He would spend the day and a great portion of the night seated at the lone table planning and sketching. Jay found that he was driven as never before and he placed his total focus on the dream that would dictate his every move and ultimately guide his destiny for the next nine weeks.

As he finally stood and stretched, he gave into the notion that it was time to retire for the night. He felt compelled to look one last time at the project he had set before himself. Even he would be amazed at the beauty in which the drawing revealed; a mammoth sized structure.

Chapter Eleven

El Paso

Squeeze felt uneasy as he peered out of the window of the small rundown quarters listed as room 112, Blue Parrot Motel. "Why can't we just get across the border?" He asked as he looked at the directional sign that indicated Mexico was only five miles away. No one in the room paid him any attention, so once again he posed the question. "Why don't we just go?"

Mayhem was slow to rise from the threadbare carpeted floor and cross the room. Taking great pleasure in antagonizing the undesirable effeminate Squeeze, Mayhem imposed unmerciful fear. Pulling the knife from his pocket, he placed the blood stained blade next to the nervous boy's throat and applied enough pressure as to just break the delicate skin.

"Maybe with a little more pressure I take all your worries away; what ya' say?"

Gonzales felt compelled to join in the fun as well. "Stick 'em, Mayhem," ordered the Mexican nationalist. "Stick 'em good or do you want me to show ya' how?"

Before long, everyone in the tiny room, with the exception of Drafter, Eagle and the Black Knight were chanting, "stick 'em, stick 'em, stick 'em!"

As Mayhem increased the pressure, blood began to trickle down the young man's pale neck, but even then, he dared not move for as ironic as it may be, he feared retaliation would certainly cost him his life.

"Alright," Esquire interrupted the entertainment in a low guttural voice. The chanting stopped. "Bring the whore over here," He directed from the only berth in the room. He waved a stainless steel revolver in a manner which indicated his intentions.

The restless Mayhem escorted the frightened Squeeze to the ruler's bedside and forced the wimp to his knees. "Let me off 'em, Squire," pleaded the cutter.

The Black Knight sat up and placed his feet on the floor. "Come on ...," the man holding the shank once again solicited approval but was cut short by a silent gesture. Esquire merely glanced at the knife bearer and then steadied his focus on the pitiful Squeeze. The squint was worth a thousand words as Mayhem withdrew the prison-made knife and walked back across the room to the window.

In all but a whisper, the Black Knight pulled the frightened lad close, "How am I going to be able to keep you alive? Look here, boy. You have no redeemable value. There ain't anybody here that gives a rat's ass about your scrawny existence. I'd suggest ya' relax 'cause you're making everyone anxious!" At this point, the boss pushed the lad away and placed the finishing touches on the climactic moment, "Now get your once tight ass away from me!"

Everyone knew that finances would be impossible to obtain once the nine fugitives breached the border. As a result, it would be necessary to pull a major job before leaving the country. The desperados also knew that once they pulled off the robbery and broke into Mexico, Squeeze and Drafter would be as good as dead. And, neither would be missed. If their bodies were discovered, their gringo status in Mexico would draw little interest, if even an investigation.

"What time is it?" Gonzales inquired.

Mexican Joe had the only wristwatch and thus was the only one qualified to answer. "Half past nine."

"What ya' say we kick it in the ass." Gonzales was getting fidgety.

"No time like the present," agreed James Eagle.

The Black Knight knew that there were too many men for the task. If they all walked into a bank at the same time suspicions would be certain. Besides, an armed robbery was no place for Drafter or the Squeeze. Gonzales and the Indian, along with Joe Garcia, would stand watch over the outside of the building, as well as babysit the two misfits. Sly was responsible for casing the establishment and bagging the spoils once the robbery took place. Mayhem was instructed to hold the elderly guard at bay at knife point and recover the unprepared man's sidearm. Blade Runner acted as the door monitor and would pose as if he were a patron of the bank. The only firearm at present was the stainless S&W that Esquire stood master over.

Esquire entered the Southland First National Bank when the signal was given by the mute. He could feel the adrenalin pump through his veins and he thrived on the excitement of such a moment. The Squire sensed that Mayhem was too pumped, but they were past the point of no return. As he scanned the luxurious surroundings, he was surprised that only a female customer was within the business. He glanced at Mayhem and a slight nod was given. The plan was to watch closely over the group of tellers while Mayhem took care of the guard. Esquire was not prepared for what was to take place next. The lone female customer suddenly let out a scream and dropped her purse on the marble floor. The lady was the first to see the man with the knife. She backed towards the main counter without taking her eyes off the daunting circumstance. The Black Knight quickly diverted his attention to Mayhem. The fingers of Mayhem's left hand clasped securely through the silver strands of the elderly employee's hair and he pulled the gentleman's head back from behind. In his right hand he had drawn the deadly blade deep into the guard's left jugular. As he drew the weapon under the guard's chin and across the throat, an ever widening spread of tissue expelled a geyser of warm, red, life sustaining blood. Mayhem would not stop the slice until he felt the blade connect with the victim's spine. The guard's eyes grew wide as though to grasp the reality of what had just transpired and then slowly and permanently closed.

"You goddamn fool!" The leader yelled as loud as he could. He looked at the Blade Runner who was watching the door. Runner shook his head and with hands out and palms up, then shrugged his shoulders in disbelief as the lifeless body of the security guard fell to the floor.

"What a fool!" the Black Knight reiterated, this time to himself but still out loud. Pointing his firearm at Mayhem, and then looking back at Blade Runner he instructed, "Get the gun from the guard!"

Mayhem reached down to recover the guard's revolver but it was not with Esquire's blessings. "No!" Esquire ordered. "Let Runner get it!"

"The plan was for me to get the gun, man," the indignant Mayhem protested. "I'm supposed to have the gun!"

"I'll plug you here and now if you don't back off and stay off!" The Knight made it perfectly clear.

"Man, I was supposed to get the gun!" Mayhem was still holding out. "That was the plan ... you said!"

Time was now more critical than ever and things needed to happen in an urgent manner. "Take the goddamn door!" The Knight ordered as he leveled a bead on the murderer, "Now!"

Mayhem stood stiff in defiance. He was obviously enraged at the Knight's response. His face grew red and his right hand worked the handle of the shank as it dripped blood down to a puddle on the white marble. Slowly he looked around the bank and all eyes seemed to be locked onto him. His concentration was soon broken.

"Come on man," Blade Runner patted him on the shoulder. Mayhem immediately swung around and poised the knife as if to stick his partner. "Relax man. Let's do this thing. Watch the door and I'll take care of what's left of the rent-o-pig." Slowly, the ruthless killer lowered his knife and glanced at the leader. With a look and a nod in the direction of the door, the gesture was extended and Mayhem finally complied with no further hesitation.

The Blade Runner peered down at the fallen security guard. Blood had already pooled from the victim's head and onto the earth-tone brown carpet that seamed close to the marble which caused an eerie contrast. Blade reached down and attempted to remove the pistol from the level-three holster but the holster was not designed to relinquish the weapon from anyone other than the guard.

"Take the whole damn holster and all!" The Black Knight was growing more impatient. "We have to get the hell out of here." Redirecting his attention back to the counter he, for the first time, addressed all employees, "Okay folks. By now you understand why we are all here. It should be obvious to what extent we are willing to go to get what we came in for! Who's in charge?"

With timid indecision a bald headed man with slight features emerged from what appeared to be an adjacent office. "Just don't hurt anyone else," pleaded the man with a quivering voice. Esquire viewed the small brass plaque which read "Vice President" next to the door from which the frightened, but courageous, man had come. Esquire motioned for the bank employee to step nearer. The administrator obeyed with regretful hesitation. As the Vice President stepped closer to the overwhelming size of the Black Knight, the contrast was all but comical. Esquire felt a growing impatience and grabbed the banker by the nape of his neck and yanked him hard.

"Now, I get the impression that maybe we got off on the wrong foot here." Esquire was eager to make his point. Looking at the terror stricken man face to face he went on, "Now we can make things a whole lot better or as you can see, a whole lot worse. I will even let you call all the shots. Now, which is it; better or worse?" At this point, the convict grabbed the bank officer's head and rotated it around so that he had no choice but to look at the dead security officer.

After a couple seconds the leader of the gang grabbed the banker by his tie and yanked him around once again. "Which is it; rough as 50-grit sandpaper or smooth as chiffon?"

"I don't want problems," said the Vice President. "Whatever you want, we will cooperate. Please don't hurt anyone else."

Esquire would now whisper, "If the bulls show up, everybody in the bank is going to look just like that." He then placed the stainless steel revolver next to the frightened man's face and forced him to look one more time, "any questions?" The man did not reply, he just nodded the reluctant confirmation.

"Now you didn't happen to call the police or set off the alarm, did ya'?" Esquire knew that any bank employee had ample time to set off the alarm and he was well aware of bank policies in regard to such. "Answer me, Mr. Nine to Five."

"I..., I..." It was apparent that the man did not wish to reply. Esquire felt for the small portion of the tie and grasped it firmly and began to pull. As the noose tightened, the man gasped for air, raised his hands and fell back against Esquire's lower chest. The women who had witnessed the murder of the guard began to scream with hysteria as she felt certain she was once again going to bear witness to another barbaric act.

"Get the bitch to be quiet or silence her permanently!" Esquire whispered in the bank officer's ear. The Vice President took one hand and loosened the tie which was binding his ability to take in a breath.

"Tonya, Sue, help Mrs. Weber," instructed the VP who had a grasp of the moment. "Take her into my office."

The Black Knight motioned for Sly to act as escort to the women as they entered into the office and then with sign language, instructed him to pull the phone out of the wall, bust up the computer and collect the lady's personal effects. Soon the accomplice would emerge from the Vice President's office with thumbs up and he proceeded to jump over the counter in a single bound. Once in the restricted area he began to cram currency into a yellow pillow case that had been "borrowed" from the motel. While this was taking place Esquire placed the muzzle of the pistol next to the banker's temple and ordered, "Get the rest of the skirts out here so that we can see them!"

As three more ladies filed out into the lobby area, the Knight pulled the frightened man around and looked once again into the man's terrified eyes. He would straighten the man's tie and collar and then place a solid double slap along the man's cheek, "Look's good my man. Now that we understand each other I want you to call off the dogs."

"They will still come." Now the bald, middle aged employee wished that he had never set off the alarm.

A sadistic smile came over Esquire's face. "Now listen, numb nuts," he impressed with a more direct tone. "It is very important that you listen and you do what is in your best interest at this point. It's all really simple. When the police call and ask for the code response, you better give them the proper code. If you don't, then I will turn everyone in this place over to the guy with the knife and allow the dude with the insatiable appetite for blood to do what he does best!"

"They will still come!"   Once again the bank officer overstated the obvious.

I know that, shit for brains!" The oversized convict shoved the man in the chest which forced him to the floor. "Now get your mind right before I dispose of you and we figure out a plan B."

Within seconds, the Vice President made the call and the police dispatchers were notified that the bank official had accidentally triggered the alarm. An apparent code word was given and the VP closed the conversation with, "That would be fine."

*****

Outside, Gonzales and the Indian waited patiently in the front seat of the stolen pickup truck. They felt confused with the occasional glimpse of the Mayhem at the front door. "That's not the plan," James Eagle stated, "Something's wrong, man. That's not the plan! Blade Runner is supposed to be at the door! "

Confidence had run out and Gonzales started the engine. As he grinded the transmission into gear and began to let the clutch out, the Indian reached over and turned off the ignition switch.

"You said it!" Gonzales was not pleased at the override on his decision. "Something is definitely wrong and I'm outa here!"

"We are here for the duration," the Indian made it perfectly clear. "Besides, I don't think you would want to be the one that skips on the Squire."

Anxiety grew as a patrol car with two police officers drove past the old blue truck and stopped at the front of the bank. Mexican Joe stuck his head through the boot between the cab and the camper shell. "What the hell is going on?"

"I'd say that the silent alarm got yanked," a disturbed Gonzales replied. "It's time to get the hell out of here!"

"Someone needs to let 'em know on the inside," said Joe as he watched with anxious anticipation as the two officers casually climbed out of their cruiser and approached the building on foot. It was strange but the policemen were responding in a casual manner.

Minutes earlier, Esquire had forced the bald headed man and a young lady to drape a plastic trash bag over the dead guard's head. After doing so, his body was dragged into the ladies restroom and left there. With the help of the Blade Runner, the bank officer was able to relocate a large planter which now covered the stained rug. If one looked closely there were telltale signs that something was not quite right. There was the peculiar off center location of the planter, the drag marks in the rug showing where it once was, as well as the signature in the carpet from which it previously sat.

By the time the police officers entered the bank, there were only two tellers and the Vice President that appeared in plain view.

"Good morning, Robert," said the first officer as he came in through the front door. "I take it that the damned system still hasn't got all the bugs worked out yet."

"No, not yet," Robert was deeply concerned that all hell would break loose if he did not get the officers out of harm's way. "Sorry for the trouble."

"That's why you pay taxes, "the first officer was jovial and wanted to visit. "Where's all your help today, Bob?"

"Corporate meeting downtown," the Vice President forced a smile.

Both officers turned and began to walk to the front door. "See ya' again tomorrow morning," joked the friendlier officer.

"Thank God," murmured the little vice president as they left.

With cautious apprehension the bad men walked out of the office. "You done a real good, Bob," taunted the ring leader. "Now that we have established good communications, let's see what you can offer us in the way of a safety deposit box."

Bob shook his head, "I can't do it. The vault door is set up on a time release." He was trying his best to stall as the issues became more sensitive, more personal. He knew most of the people who entrusted their private valuables and documents within the secure regions of "his" bank and he was not about to let them down. The money was insured. Private belongings, unless privately declared and insured, would be a total loss.

"This is garbage!" Mayhem pulled his only weapon and advanced toward the bald man who was appearing to have taken an unexpected step from courage and entered the realm of stupidity. "I'll get the bastard to ..."

Esquire put up his hand and interrupted the unstable Mayhem's aggression. "I've got it." The Knight then turned his attention towards the VP. "What a coincidence! You see this here?" He held up the guard's service weapon. "This too works on a time release. Within about fifteen seconds if you don't figure out how to accommodate me ..." Esquire paused while he lit a cigarette and tossed the still lit match on the short shag. "The first thing you are going to know is that you're not going to know nothing at all because I'm going to blow your goddamn bald head off." As he let out a long drag from the cigarette, he pressed the weapon against the man's forehead and cocked the hammer.

Esquire was taken aback by the stubbornness that had suddenly surfaced within the middle-aged gentleman. He once again refused to participate. "Ya' have a family, Bob?" asked the hostage taker.

"Only the bank," said Robert. Robert had never married in his fifty-two years of existence and dedicated his life in the hopes to advance through the ranks at the bank. In the last thirty years, he had pursued such a plan and perhaps that was why he felt compelled to stand fast.

The Esquire gently placed his arm around the shoulders of the determined bank executive and began to walk with him to the back of the bank. As he did so, he would whistle to gain the attention of Mayhem and the Blade Runner. Looking at the murderous Mayhem, he motioned to the door and said, "Stand watch, and while you are at it, see if our transportation is still out there." Now glancing at the Runner he nodded at the tellers who were standing in the lobby. Reading Esquire's thoughts, Runner gave a nod of his own and settled into one of many luxurious stuffed chairs that lined the lobby. Meanwhile, Sly continued to rifle through the drawers of each teller station.

As the two men walked around the corner and out of sight, Esquire got down to the brass tacks. "Bob," the Knight paused long enough to place the newly acquired handgun in his waist band. Suddenly there was a powerful right fist blow to Robert's midsection. Robert's body immediately sprawled on the floor. For the first time in his otherwise guarded life, he felt excruciating pain; he was sure that he was about to die from such intense agony. He began to cough up blood. The criminal then placed two of his fingers in the victim's nostrils and lifted him back to his feet. "Now that I'm sure I have your undivided attention, allow me to make a suggestion. You see; I'm not going to flirt around with you anymore. So, why don't you open the goddamned room before I let the blood thirsty bastard draw and quarter one of those females out there?"

Within minutes, the industrious leader of the escape squad was standing among the mounds of treasures before him. He had just reaped the greatest financial advantage of his casualty laden career. Hundreds of thousands of dollars, as well as jewels beyond comprehension were stashed in the safety deposit boxes. The delay was worth it and he felt certain that he would be set for the rest of his life. There was a glitch, however. What he did not know was that the two officers had returned and things were about to become greatly complex.

"The badges are back!" Mayhem yelled. "What the hell do we do now?" Without the constant governing from the gang leader, the misfit felt vulnerable and lost.

Undetected, Mayhem, Runner, and Sly hunkered in behind the refuge of the counter. The same policemen as before walked once again into the establishment and immediately asked to see Robert. With Robert still in the back of the bank, the young ladies were extremely nervous and were not sure what they should do.

"Where is Phil?" The older of the Officers was referring to the retired cop who decided to supplement his retirement benefits with a full-time security job. "Where is the old timer, anyway?"

The two officers did not expect the sudden thick atmosphere, and it became obvious that none of the ladies were willing to participate in friendly conversation. Sensing that something was not quite right, the younger officer stepped back from the counter and began to study the interior of the bank. A cloud of desperation seemed to infiltrate every cubic inch of space. Sensing the inversion, the veteran officer began to draw his weapon from its holster. Without warning there was the thunderous report of a .357 as the handgun responded to Esquire's intentions. There was a sickening slap as the bullet struck into the older officer's chest just above his protective vest. The officer took a step, then another and slowly sank to his knees. The first officer watched in horror as his partner balanced for a moment and then, with a trickle of blood streaming from one of his nostrils, he fell backwards onto his lower legs and then onto the floor.

The younger of the policemen stood motionless with his weapon still secured in its holster. He dared not move for fear that he would draw attention to himself. He felt his upper lip begin to quiver and sweat started to bead on his forehead.

"Seems you have a bit of a dilemma; don't ya, boy?" The Black Knight stepped near and began to walk around the frozen youth.

The young man said nothing but continued to stare at his partner. Soon the partner's body expelled the last gasp of air and a death rattle was detected.

Esquire looked into the young cop's eyes but this did not interrupt the trance he was in. The Knight snapped his fingers and still the man's focus was constant. It was as though the officer was aware only of his partner.

"Blade, get the guns!" The leader ordered.

"Police 32, Central," the dispatcher's voice broke through the air. Not even the officer's handheld radio would draw him from his trance.

"Police 32, Central." The radio once again broke.

"Ok, folks. It's time to split! Let's go!" Knight motioned for Sly to come.

"Central, this is Police 32," the radio transmission continued.

"We have a report of shots fired in the area of Stanton and 47th. An owner of Samuel's Dry Cleaners advises that it sounded as though a disturbance took place inside the bank. We have Units 10 and 44 scheduled at that location as of 0932 hours and then again at 0942 hours. It is unknown what their status is."

"I'm half a block away now. Go ahead and show me out at that address and see if you can raise those two units, as well as start a sergeant this way."

Mayhem, which was now stationed at the door, became irate. "The bulls are here, man. We waited too long! The bulls are here!"

Sly and the Blade Runner removed the duty belts, weapons and all the accessories from the officers with haste. It was obvious that one was dead and the other's mental capacity had diminished completely. The once brilliant conversationalist who had carried his badge and gun effectively still had not moved from his stance. Esquire walked over to the full front window, pulled the shades ever-so-slightly and peered out. The second patrol car had now entered a parking lot across the street.

"Now or never," the leader bellowed, "everyone ready?"

"I get a gun. You owe me a gun!" Mayhem, who had never felt content with just the knife, was now feeling the necessity to expand his arsenal for a more conventional weapon. "Ya' can't expect me to face them without a gun! Give me a goddamn gun!"

"Stop whining!" Esquire did not need this, especially at this time. His eyes narrowed and the tone of his voice became brisk. "If I'd wanted whining I'd have brought Squeeze!"

The brainless Mayhem did not care for the comparison but no longer wished to agitate the Black Knight further for fear of retribution. Instead, he and the leader watched in dismay as two officers from the distant patrol car exited their transportation and started their somewhat strategic advance. One was carrying a twelve gauge scatter gun and the other, an assault rifle.

"I want the cop's guns right now," the Black Knight ordered Blade Runner to bring the hardware. He quickly gave Mayhem the revolver out of his waist band, gave Sly one of recently acquired semi autos with two 15-round magazines and kept the two other handguns with full compliments of ammunition for himself. He then gazed out the window at the cops that were still advancing towards the bank. The one that had the shotgun had quickly positioned himself next to the closer patrol car.

"Central, this is Police 32. We are in position. All looks calm, too calm. You can go ahead and make your call." The hand held radio revealed the conversation between the cops outside and their dispatch.

"10-4, Police 32. Also, we have S-1 and S-6 in route and the lieutenant has been advised," Informed the dispatcher. "Please keep us aware of developments."

*****

Wells looked at the Indian. "It's getting a little crowded don't you think?"

"Change places," James Eagle instructed. "I'll drive."

"What?" Gonzalez was confused. "I can't ..." With the power of great physical persuasion, the Indian grabbed the Immigrant and pulled the man from the steering wheel. With relative ease he then pulled him up over his body and slammed him into the door on the passenger side. Gaining leverage from the steering wheel, Eagle pulled his own large frame into the driver's position and simultaneously started the engine.

"What are you going to do?" Mexican Joe still had his head midway through the camper and the cab and was now displaying complete panic.

"We're going in after our own!" However, a third patrol car was approaching and the Indian was forced to hesitate for a moment.

"What are we going to do?" Gonzales asked again.

The Indian shifted the transmission hard and the gears finally synchronized with a grinding protest. He felt the adrenalin rush through his veins as he stroked his clean shaven chin and attempted to counter the rush with a planned response to their current quandary. He would not waste the time or mental energy with giving Gonzales an answer.

"What are we going to do? We are not just going to sit here are we?" Wells was getting more persistent.

Without looking, the Indian grabbed the nagging inmate by the face and slammed his head against the inside of the pickup cab. He then shouted to the entire party, "get down in the back and stay down!"

"Central, this is Police 17 and 20. Place us out at 47th and Stanton." The third unit arrived near the front of the bank.

"10-4, Police 17 and 20, break; Police 10, Police 44, Central," The concerned voice of a female dispatcher was detected. "Police 10, 44, please answer your radio. What is your current status?" Dispatch would try once again.

"Man, I am not going back to the joint!" Mayhem could not contain himself. "I'm not going back to D-Block, man. It just ain't gonna happen!" He began to pace back and forth in the bank lobby.

Blade Runner looked with alarm in the direction of Esquire. "Man, the dude's losing it!"

"Squire," the infamous Mayhem broke the cardinal rule in divulging the Knight's identity in front of the bank staff. "We got to book, man!"

Instantly the leader became livid. Grabbing the mentally challenged Mayhem, he whirled him around and confronted him with only a couple of inches separating the two men's faces. "You're the one who started screwing it all up and now you're the one that's all panicked?!" The Knight could feel the barrel of Mayhem's newly acquired pistol placing against his chest. "Go ahead, you missing link! Do it! Because, I ain't goin' to die no matter what you try!" Esquire had a sadistic smile, "And you know it!"

Although Mayhem felt compelled to pull the trigger, he was consumed by the notion that the Black Knight was right. In accordance, he bought into the notion that the almighty Esquire somehow could live through anything. And through the process of attempting to kill him, he, Mayhem, would, without a doubt, have to endure the consequential wrath of the Black Knight.

"Central, this is S-1 and S-6. Please put us out at the scene. Have you made contact with officers 10 or 40?"

Esquire diverted his attention from the intense visual exchange with Mayhem and directed it towards the radio which was sitting on the cashier's counter. With slow deliberation, he relinquished his tight grip on the stupid man's collar, and softly patted the man's cheek.

The radio once again blared, "That's negative, sir. I copy that you are out at the bank."

"Affirmative," the sergeant responded once again. "Central, go ahead and make a land line confirmation."

Esquire looked back at Mayhem, "Everything is going to be all right as long as we don't crap all over ourselves. Now let's start moving before SWAT gets into the picture." At this point, the Knight walked over to a nearby phone and waited for the inevitable call from the police. He motioned for the Vice President to approach as Robert slowly entered the lobby from the back room. Robert was having difficulty breathing, for he had sustained cracked ribs from the Knight's vicious blow a few minutes prior. By the time that the administrator reached the counter, the phone rang; once, twice and then a third time.

"What do you want me to say?" Robert appeared to be a beaten man emotionally, as well as in spirit. It was apparent that he had given into the realization that nothing but destruction and certain death would ensue. Somehow, however, he felt compelled to at least give a token gesture toward survival; if not for himself, for the ladies that were under his charge.

The phone rang for a fourth time. Esquire frowned and in a stern, non-negotiable tone said, "Whatever you say it better be magical!" He then handed the small framed banker the receiver.

"Southland First National, may I help you?"

After a brief conversation of basic acceptance, the phone was hung up and Esquire patiently waited for the radio to grant confirmation of the dispatcher's interpretation of what was taking place.

S-1, Central," the dispatcher's voice again penetrated the air.

"Go ahead," came the simple reply.

"Sir, I just spoke to Mr. Spriggs by land line. He is one of the managers of the bank and he gave the correct response; everything seems to be alright."

Are you still on the phone with Mr. Spriggs," inquired the Sergeant. "And if you are, would you please instruct him to come outside and meet with me?"

"Sir, I had already requested him to do so, but he insists that he was in the middle of an important transaction on a different line and would not be able to. He then hung up. Do you wish me to try to re-contact?"

"That's negative," the Sergeant advised. "I am now instructing all personal involved to proceed with condition zebra. Repeat, code zebra and only the tactical channel is to be used. Please advise the Charlie Unit."

"10-4, sir. Charlie will be notified," Dispatch confirmed.

Esquire looked long and hard at the ever increasing total of squad cars that were collecting in front of the bank. He then looked across the street at the blue pickup that was still waiting in the adjacent alley. "I don't know what the hell a zebra condition is but I sure do know who Charlie is!"

"Who is Charlie?" Runner was curious.

"S.W.A.T.; it's got to be S.W.A.T. Now listen up!" The Knight insisted. "We have got to go right now before those bastards with the automatic shit shows up. Now everybody grab a bitch and let's scoot!"

"Sounds good to me," Blade Runner acknowledged as he approached the nearest lady from behind and placed his arm around her neck. He took comfort in the thought that now he would be able to screen himself from the cops.

Robert Spriggs attempted to come to the lady's rescue but would be turned away by Mayhem. "Let me go in her place," pleaded the bald man.

"The attraction just ain't there, but thanks for the offer," Blade Runner proclaimed. "Besides, you wouldn't be nearly as much fun to party with if we get outa this alive. Ain't that right?" And the Runner looked at the deaf Sly who seemed to understand.

*****

"We are going in after 'em," announced the Indian.

"We can't do that! They already have our only gun!" Neither Mexican Joe nor Gonzales was pleased at the prospects of such a suggested mission. "Like, nothing is in our favor! It is suicide! They are the ones that took so long and now that the dog crap has hit the fan we are going to get it all over us too? I don't think so!" Wells made his position clear.

"Maybe you're right," the Indian seemed to give into the obvious. He placed the old truck in gear once again and slowly began to edge the truck forward. Both Garcia's and Gonzales's eyes grew wide as the Indian drove cautiously towards the accumulation of patrol vehicles which partially blocked the street. "But we are either going to get those poor bastards out or they can deep six us too!"

"No way, man," Gonzales was ready to jump from the moving pickup truck and take his chances on foot if necessary.

"Just sit tight and don't cause me any grief!" Eagle ordered.

As the old blue truck approached the cluster of black and whites, an officer drew his concentration from the bank and faded back. Still in a crouch, the uniformed cop placed a commanding hand in the air in a halting fashion.

As the truck drew near, the Native American driver rolled down his window and stuck his head out. "What ya'got goin?" The Indian posed.

"We need you to clear the area, and now!" The officer instructed.

"What ya'got goin?" The Native American repeated the question.

"Nothing that would concern you, now continue on your way, please," The officer was becoming more urgent in his instructions. "We appreciate your interest but you will have to leave the area. Please do so right now."

The Indian pulled the truck alongside the cop and then turned the ¾ ton truck at a right angle as though to leave as ordered. By this time, the pickup was facing away from the bank in perfect alignment to the bank's double doors. The Indian stopped the antiquated transportation and grinded the shifter into reverse.

"Now what," the police officer was becoming less patient with the apparent ignorance of the citizen as he walked towards the back of the truck. Anger would soon transform into shock as the pickup began to back in abrupt fashion!

With spontaneity, the cop reacted by dropping his rifle and placing both hands on the tail gate which by now had overtaken him. With one swift jump, he vaulted his feet onto the rear bumper and grasped his fingers the best he could to the top of the half-shell camper. His precarious perch would serve its purpose only until the back wheels of the pickup jumped the curb and collided with an open door of a squad car that was parked on the sidewalk. This sent the confused officer reeling from the bumper and onto the ornate concrete entry way of the bank. Without regard for life or limb, the pickup continued to back over the officer's legs. With a grotesque snap, the remaining officers witnessed the undeniable fractures and then the shrill scream that seemed to originate from the base of victim's very soul.

As the truck continued to be driven towards the bank's double doors, one of the sergeants grabbed his radio. With obvious panic in the man's voice, he keyed the microphone and yelled, "We need help! We need help! Get Charlie here now! Send an ambulance!"

"Holy Christ," Blade Runner yelled as the truck crashed through the double doors and into the lobby of the bank. It slid halfway around and came to rest just inches away from the Knight.

"Bitch'n!" Esquire exclaimed with a renewed sense of restored confidence as the resolve to the current dilemma began to unfold. "Come on you silly bastards; the taxi is here!"

The employees scattered as the four desperados quickly tossed the spoils of their endeavor through the open rear window of the camper shell. Before ten seconds could pass, all the bad guys were aboard and James Eagle began trashing the interior of the lobby as he thrust the Chevy back and forth in an attempt to realign the truck for the exodus. Soon the beater was coming back through the same destruction it had caused. The policemen that had previously run towards the front entrance with the intention of recovering their fallen casualty had to take cover for fear of being hit by the now outbound pickup. With hub caps spinning off and the cops scrambling, the scraped up blue truck gained momentum as it caught air and then touched down with an ungraceful double thud from the sidewalk to the blacktop of the street.

"Don't shoot, don't shoot, don't shoot!" The first sergeant shouted into a bull horn as he ran into the street. "There could be hostages! Don't shoot goddamn it, don't shoot!" As the pickup sped to the next intersection and turned right, the sergeant slammed the bull horn to the pavement with exasperation.

"Central, this is Sergeant 6," the second ranking officer called for dispatch. In as calm a voice as he could muster, he continued. "We need several ambulances; contact the detectives and let the Chief know that we have at least one officer down, perhaps more." As he focused on the lifeless body now on the bank lawn, he let the microphone slip from his fingers and onto the floor of his patrol car.

*****

The truck was traveling close to eighty miles per hour as it turned off of Alameda onto south bound Texas Avenue. "There are only two follow'n us," yelled Squeeze.

Esquire crawled through the maze of live bodies and eventually to the front of the camper shell. Sticking his head through the passage way between the cab and the camper, he instructed the always dependable Indian to head for the residential areas.

"It will slow us down but I will place a sawbuck with ten to one odds it will hinder the pigs' progress more."

Suddenly, the truck veered from Texas Avenue and down an embankment, through a chain linked fence and into a residential area. A third patrol car which was pursuing on a paralleling service street was the only vehicle of advantage at this point. As the convicts guessed, the lone officer was instructed to proceed through the neighborhood of family homes with extreme caution.

"Central, Police 41," The traffic officer broke the air.

"Police 41, go ahead."

"I am currently following the suspect vehicle in the Mt. Bellow Subdivision. I need air support and ground backup now!"

"Police 41; be advised that we will have a bird in the air within approximately fifteen minutes. All ground units will be advised of your situation and the Captain orders you to stand your distance. Do not attempt to contact or apprehend alone. Do not endanger the general public further."

Esquire handed the two-way radio that he had requisitioned from the officers at the bank to Gonzales. "Let's see what this hot shit cop is made of," Esquire yelled over the roar of the loud exhaust pipes. "We have fifteen minutes to disappear and this is going to be our best chance. Let's not blow it!" The other convicts did not understand what the Knight was planning, but nodded their approval as if they had. He peered out the back of the open camper door and then returned his attention to the front. "Tell Eagle to turn down the alley and slow up a little."

"What?" Joe asked. He did not understand.

"Tell the Indian to turn down an alley and then let the cop catch up with us!"

James Eagle overheard the instructions and placed the rusted excuse of a truck in a side skid and then navigated down the next alley. With light blue smoke boiling from the tires, he steered through some trash cans and then slowed as instructed. The full distance of the alley was made up of expensive brick and mortar walls that flickered by and yielded no relief or options other than a tight, single lane. The Knight pulled a recently acquired semiautomatic duty weapon from his jacket pocket and grabbed Squeeze by the throat. "Everyone makes a sacrifice and guess what ... it's your turn." Placing the weapon next to the young man's chest, Esquire pulled the trigger twice and the jailhouse prostitute was no more. Esquire quickly pulled the body to the back of the truck and tossed it out as if it had no more value than used toilet paper.

Police 41 slammed on his brakes and locked up all fours, but it was too late. He could feel the front tires and then the rear tires skid over the victim. As his car came to a stop, his heart sank. Unexpected emotions began to pull the officer into an instant depression but he had no time to dwell on what had transpired. He felt sick from the tips of his toes to his throat. He was overcome by the undeniable urge to yield to nature's voluntary response to the event. He opened the car door and began to retch.

"Central, this is Police 41!" The convicts could hear the officer over the radio.

"41."

"Please notify the Captain and the coroner's office that we have a code frank (fatality) in the east alley of the 1600 block of Villa Grove. I think that this is a hostage."

As the pickup continued to speed away, the convicts rejoiced in the brilliance of Esquire's impromptu plan. The diversion had worked perfectly!

*****

For the next two weeks, a search was concentrated around the area of the border and Mexican authorities in Ciudad Juarez blanketed their side as well. No apparent clues of the disappearance could accurately be theorized. Fingerprints at the first crime scene combined with the positive identification of Squeeze's body gave the police confirmation of who they were dealing with and prison officials from the state of Illinois immediately flew to El Paso to, as it was mainly perceived, cover their butts the best that they could. What the law enforcement agencies did not realize was that the desperados were calmly biding their time at the Blue Parrot Motel within the same city limits of the town that they had terrorized.

Chapter Twelve

North to Colorado

A slight early evening breeze from the north gently rustled the budding aspen as Jay took a moment to gaze at the fruits of his extensive labor. A large multi-leveled area had been carved out of the mountain side with giant marble stone strategically fashioned and placed for a foundation. Flat marble was also cut, polished and laid with precision to serve as a magnificent floor for the lower levels of what was developing into a mammoth sized structure. The first two rows of the eight inch logs had already been peeled and locked into place to serve as the base logs of the new home. Jay concentrated on the plans he had drawn and seemed pleased at the progress that had been made thus far. Monstrous log pillars would be secured in place tomorrow. These standards were peeled ponderosa pine, one of nature's most beautiful yields, and the construction would support a thirty foot cathedral ceiling with large windows for southwest exposure. The view of the canyon and the distant pinnacles was breathtaking any time of the year and would serve as the main focal point for the rest of Jay's life. The remainder of the planned structure would be made up of various rooms and secluded refuges, as well as open dwellings and spaces of general occupancy. Not wishing to appear presumptuous, Jay had planned for Sheila's expectation of privacy in a specific room for her own personal refuge. It would face southeast so that the warm winter sunshine could greet her in the morning and she would be able to watch the moon at her pleasure during the night. The four thousand square foot structure would hopefully serve as a symbol for his love and dedication concerning the beautiful Ms. Gray. Jay was hopeful that such a gesture could inspire her as she obviously had him.

Love was the constant adrenalin that served Jay's strength and vigor for such an endeavor; a deep rooted desire propelled by a single kiss. The mountain man would accomplish tremendous exploits and achievements within a short period of time because of that kiss. Every day had a specific mission and with such a profound purpose, the man would have preferred to work on through the night as well.

To help expedite the giant masterpiece, Mr. Devereux summoned the expert work ethic of 41 undocumented helpers who seemed to thrive on the concept of 12 to 14 hour days. They were appreciative of the opportunity to showcase their talents and while they worked their magic on the project, their wives and children prepared the meals and took care of menial tasks. It was amazing that such a structure could gain such momentum without major construction machinery; just the hearts and spirits of hard laborers.

The land baron had purchased two "exceptional" mules which were promoted as the cream of the crop; the Cadillac in terms of beast of burden; the ultimate in animal flesh. On the "showroom floor" the animals appeared strong and healthy and the deal was struck with the veteran horse trader. Five hundred dollars apiece seemed a steal and Jay was certain that the ugly droopy eared pair would soon be worth their weight in gold. He clearly visualized, with some coaching from the rancher who sold him the pair, bundles of lodge pole pine being skillfully snaked from the East Ridge below Machin Lake to the location of the home site better than a quarter mile away. He could envision the back sides of the two mules trudging up the pathway with ears cocked, ready to respond to his every command. Cash exchanged hands and then it was time to load the crossbreeds aboard a borrowed trailer. Jay thought it a bit strange as he peered around. He was surprised that Mr. Funk, who professed to be the friendly lover of animals, entrepreneur of exquisite beast and apparent authority of animal husbandry, could disappear so quickly. Jay suddenly recognized that the task was his and his alone and proceeded to set forth to simply load the livestock. After all, how hard could it be? The once nameless duet would soon be abundantly blessed with a wide range of unflattering adjectives for which the definitions were not acceptable within a hundred miles of any church. For the next hour or better, Jay matched efforts, wit, as well as brute strength, against the two mules, but to no avail. They, at the most, would place their heads in the gateway of the trailer, plant their feet and lean with such force, the rope would vibrate like a G string on a violin. When the rope reached maximum elasticity and Jay tried to push the beasts from the rear, each mule responded by vigorously swinging its neck from side to side which resulted in the animals' heads slamming into the side bars of the trailer.

Jay began to realize that he had not chosen wisely. The mountain man scanned the corral for some indication of where the dog food liquidator may have retreated. He was willing to sell back the worthless animals and endure a loss in the process if necessary. Soon Jay became enraged when the sound of laughter assaulted his keen sense of hearing. The laughter was coming from within the confines of a nearby barn. His pride challenged and integrity tarnished, Jay focused on loading the simple, if not completely stupid, beasts.

Looking directly at the anticipated location of the hidden rancher, Jay stated out loud, "This is for you!" He then proceeded to roll up his sleeves and approach a mule he would later, at a more gentle time, refer to as Jug Head. Jug Head was standing hard and fast to the rear of the trailer with her head just inside the tail gate and the rope secured to the front of the trailer. Slowly the new owner bent slightly, placed his back under the rump of the mule and lifted. The mule displayed a premeditation of lifting her powerful rear legs and disposing of the discomfort she had felt for the first time in her life. As her rear legs were lifted into the air and her weight transferred to her front legs, her sensation changed from kicking to just not losing her balance. As a result, she quickly stumbled into the trailer before she was even aware of what had taken place. Jay slammed the half door to the trailer with due haste and then addressed issues with the second beast, of which he would name Idiot.

"OK, you mistake of nature. Either we can do this the easy way or the hard way; what's your pleasure?" Seemingly without hesitation, and to the astonishment of her new owner, Idiot gently stepped into the left compartment of the divided trailer and waited for the gate to be shut. Jay had accumulated virtually no knowledge concerning domesticated animals of burden, but at least this day he would reign as victor in the battle of wits.

In the days to come, Jay learned a great deal about the emotions and patience involved with becoming a dumb animal trainer. The prime time for conditioning and training animals of labor is ideal when they are young. Jug Head and Idiot had wills that seemed to be deeply rooted in concrete and tempered by several years of non-indulgence in the realm of hard work. At first, it was as though Jay would be predestined to allow the mules to watch as he proceeded with the scheduled work that should be theirs. The mountain man's patience was great however, and his resolve solid. The vision of bundles of logs, one after another, being gracefully lugged across the Alpine meadows would soon be exchanged for the reality of both creatures giving their all to deliver one or two logs at a time. At such a slow and deliberate pace, both human and mule learned to extend themselves for the sake of harmony and progress, and the creation of an empire began to take shape.

*****

"It has been fifteen days since the catastrophic Southland Bank robbery which left four dead and sent one other to the state mental institution …," The television anchorwoman announced.

"Turn up the news," Esquire ordered from his vantage point while he was lying on the bed.

"…two El Paso police officers, one Southland security guard and one prison escapee died in the bizarre holdup gone wrong. We will now go to Sam Downs for an on-scene report at the Southland First National Bank at 47th Street and Stanton. What are the latest developments, Sam?"

"Unfortunately, not all that much has transpired investigative wise," Sam would reply. "I'm currently standing in the precise location where fourteen year police veteran Harry O'Neil was brutally shot to death; one other security guard was stabbed to death and a third officer died after being run over, twice, by a truck just a few feet from here."

Sam Downs narrated while scenes which were filmed two weeks prior flashed across the television screen. "It has been two weeks ago yesterday that eight escapees from the Department of Corrections, Illinois, made their way across several states and entered this bank with an unknown number of suspected accomplices. As a result, over a hundred and seventy two thousand dollars in cash and an undisclosed amount of money and jewels which were entrusted within the security of personal safety deposit boxes, were stolen. Four people, including one of the convicts, died that day and all reportedly, at the hands of the armed robbers. Yes, you heard correctly. Police believe that the armed convicts actually shot one of their own as a diversionary measure which greatly contributed to their successful escape from authorities."

The frame flashed back to Sam. "It has been established by the El Paso Pathologist's Office that Stuart Mays, who had been struck by a pursuing patrol car the day of the holdup, had not died from injuries resulting from that collision. Instead, it has been discovered that the 28-year-old escapee had been shot to death prior …"

"OK, ladies," Esquire addressed the men. "It is time to rock and roll. Tomorrow morning before daybreak, we head for the mountains of Colorado."

Mayhem had his heart set on Mexico. "What ya' mean the mountains?" He demanded an explanation. "We're supposed to be going to Mexico where there are no El Paso cops and women are free and easy, huh Gonzales?"

"And that is the way the cops on both sides of the fence have figured it." The Black Knight qualified his decision.

Just then, an overriding statement by the news team on the television would confirm Esquire's anticipation. "… police believe that the desperate suspects previously described have crossed the river into Mexico undetected, and by this time may have traveled as far south as Mexico City."

Mexican Joe had given Esquire an alternate place of refuge and the Knight was delighted with the option. The La Garita Wilderness in the high Colorado Rockies would serve as the ideal hideout for the entire summer if need be. And, in the following autumn, when the heat had simmered a bit, they would descend into the motherland of homesick Wells Gonzales. In the meantime, the migration north would be a simple plan of adaptation with the ever faithful James Eagle purchasing a van out of the want ads section of the paper. John Hamel procured a license plate and registration from a vehicle of similar vintage which was scheduled to be crushed at a salvage yard and before long, the eight remaining fugitives were north bound.

*****

"Mom, Dad, I'm home!" Sheila shrieked as she ran from the yellow taxi and through the wrought iron gate which opened out into a cobblestone walk. The large house was of rust colored brick that harmonized well with the red tint in the stone walk; the four ivory colored pillars matched perfectly with the shutters and trim. It was an exquisite home. By the mere appearance, one would expect classical music emitting from its main living room. The lawn was perfectly manicured, so much as to give the impression of deep pile carpet, and the aroma of lilac bushes mingled with the clear spring air.

"Mom, Dad, where are you?" The long-lost daughter burst through the oak doors and into the greeting room. She paused for a moment to take in the visual appeal of the room she had not seen in so very long. Sheila breathed in deeply through her nostrils and held the sudden familiar mixture of hardwood floor blended with the ever appealing aroma of her father's pipe tobacco.

"Mom, I'm finally home ... where is everybody?" The young lady's face took on a disappointing expression.

Upon discovering that no one was home, Sheila soon immersed her cares, as well as her body in the luxury of a long desired bubble bath. As the bubbles rose up about her, she closed her magnificent eyes and smiled. Her thoughts were extreme, but happy. She wondered what the mountain man was doing. She missed him. She was thinking about the journey back to the wilderness that had extended its hospitality and so many reflections. But for now, she would bask in the suds as well as in the anticipation of being reunited with the people who were so dear to her.

Sheila pulled a giant Egyptian cotton towel from an organized pile. As she dried herself off, she placed an inadvertent glance at an announcement that was sitting on the night stand next to her mother's side of the bed. What caught her attention was her name in print on the front fold.   Her eyes grew wide as she realized that the announcement was for a wake … a wake in her honor!

"My Lord; they don't know that I am still alive! What day is today?   What month is it today?" She asked herself as she hurried around the house looking for a clue. Finally, she thought of the phone and picked it up and dialed for information. "Yes please, I need to know the present time and date …, as well as the month, please."

"The correct date and time is Saturday, June 2nd, and the time is 2:45 PM." The operator granted the information without question.

Sheila unintentionally slammed the receiver down and started to stare at the announcement. Quickly she picked the phone back up and said, "Thank you," but only a dial tone was humming. "Sorry," she still made an attempt to apologize although she really knew that the gesture was futile. Again, she said, "Sorry," and gently laid the receiver down.

Focusing on the message, she read the following:

As a special friend of our late daughter
Sheila May Gray,
We cordially invite you to attend a wake
In her memory

Location: *St. John's Rectory and Multi-Purpose Center*
Date: *June 2nd, 2014*
Time: *3:00 P.M.*

Sheila slowly opened the front flap and read aloud the inscription within:

It is our heart filled desire
to unite those who knew Sheila
to share and celebrate
the memory of her life
with family and friends.

Sincerely,
Mr. & Mrs. Charles Gray

Although Sheila did not necessarily consider herself as shy, she did not want to be a spectacle either. But, she knew that she was now destined to shock all who were about to attend the celebration of what was thought to be the closing chapter of her life. She understood that this would be a shock felt around the world. But she also understood that it must take place.

*****

There were cars parked everywhere. As the cab made its way through the maze of unattended automobiles, it was most apparent that this was going to be a much bigger deal than Sheila expected or wanted. She was hoping that her unannounced reunion could be more personal, more private. That was obviously not going to happen.

There was a dull roar of crowd conversation as Sheila slowly walked through the back door entryway and into the spacious room. She became acutely aware that there were so many more people than even the number of parked cars would have suggested. Slowly and with a methodical approach she continued to advance through the multitude that had gathered on her behalf. As she progressed down the makeshift isle, so did a wave of silence. Soon she found herself approaching a section where her mother, father, and sisters were seated. She overheard her father's reassurance directed to her mother.

"Sweetheart, we can do this thing. It will be important to our..." He paused as he became sharply aware that there was a wave of silence. With apprehension he began to turn around in his chair, slowly looking at each person in the seated crowd in an effort to understand the unscheduled suppression of conversation. There was not as much as even a whisper and all eyes seemed to focus in one constant direction.

Sheila stopped a few feet away and simply stood still, somewhat embarrassed at becoming such an unintentional spectacle. With a sudden realization of her presence, her father slowly rose from the folding chair and dropped the handkerchief from his hand. Although Mr. Gray was certain that he was in the middle of a visual aberration, he still had the presence of mind to turn back towards his significant other and offer her his hand. Whether this was a fantasy, a vision, or the actual presence of their daughter, he wished not only to participate but to share the experience with his wife. He gently grasped his wife's hands and helped her to her feet; turning slowly, as if not to frighten away the figment, he once again adjusted his focus on his beautiful daughter.

The unlikely silence still echoed throughout the event center as the parents began to walk towards the vision of their daughter. Although Sheila's sisters stood, they dared not advance. Tears began to stream down their faces as their mother and father approached Sheila, and holding onto each other, extended their free arms in agonizing anticipation that this might not be real.

As the three wrapped arms around each other, tears flowed and desperate hope would become ecstasy through such a tangible realization. The crowd began to rise and the eruption of emotion that was shared throughout came in a variety of responses from ovation, to simple weeping, as well as convulsive sobbing. No one understood how this could possibly come about, but all seemed more than just content with their ignorance. There would be plenty of time for reflection and discovery.

The next several days were hectic but each member of the family seemed to become progressively energized. There were people to notify about the airplane crash, as well as people to see and places to visit. It was as though everyone had a vicarious second chance at life and through such a realization came an incredible urgency to live life more fully. Values had seemed to realign and so had the meaning of life.

One evening, Sheila and her father sat by the marble fireplace and as the fire extended a peaceful flicker, Sheila began to expound upon her experiences of the previous months. This was a man that she trusted beyond all others – who embraced her when she inevitably scraped her five-year-old knees and placed a medicated kiss on a bump located on her forehead after she fell from a make shift tree house at age seven. He smiled as they both reminisced about the construction of an "elaborate" fort made from cardboard and discarded materials she had collected from around the neighborhood. The non-permitted endearing structure was the only blemish in an otherwise perfectly groomed back yard, but for the better part of a summer, a master piece which was allowed to stand. He found himself enduring extreme mixed feelings between thanking God that the apple of his eye had been spared, however, unexpectedly envious that a stranger, not he, had rescued her from the vicious jaws of the wild. Further, he felt uneasy with the unspoken discovery that his precious daughter was in love. He knew not the man with whom his daughter was referring, but the mountain man sounded barbaric and shallow. Charles Gray understood that his less than enthusiastic response would dampen the otherwise excellent evening, so he was content to restrain his apprehension and reserve his right to pass judgment at a later date. Thus, he requested an opportunity to visit with the mystery man and with the plane wreckage still to be investigated, an opportunity would be near at hand.

Sheila could sense her father's constraint but remained confident that Jay would be able to accomplish far more than just satisfy any preconceived reservations that her father had.

*****

Jay's muscles flexed as he heaved one end of a monstrous beam to his shoulder and then to a staging platform. After accomplishing the monumental task, he positioned himself to the staging area and once again, seemingly with little effort, lifted the peeled log to the next staging platform. Gradually the man with uncommon strength, both physically as well as of heart, worked both ends of the 400 pound log until it ultimately slid into its designated spot. Without hesitation, the mountain of a man placed a rounded wooden stake into the pilot hole located at each end of the beam. Then, with a one-armed thrust with a sledge, pounded the stake through, anchoring the beam to a cross member. The builder of an empire paused for only a couple minutes while perched on a horizontal support that was thirty feet from the rock floor. He marveled at the progress but would not tarry for long. He knew that the sweet princess, if she was true to her word, would return soon and with her, a possible desire to live on the beautiful mountain. By the creation of this extraordinary home, he was hoping to leave no margin of doubt in her mind.

Thirty of Jay's staff scurried about the complex contributing their efforts towards his vision while the other eleven carried building materials from a helicopter landing zone approximately a quarter of a mile from the construction site. The task was extremely tedious, but did not seem to detour the energy of the Spanish work force.

It has been said many times that you cannot teach an old dog new tricks. Once again, the fable would be severely challenged as Jug Head and Idiot developed a mutual understanding of the work ethic concept, and as a result assisted in the productivity as intended. They were able to double their tally with each trip. They too, had lost their winter fat and the frequent activity toned their muscles. Jay was also in training for he had never driven a team before. Instead of working mules day after day, he would harness them every other day and allow them to rest each day in between. This would allow him an opportunity to peel and place the logs on the mules' days of rest.

*****

The trip to Colorado was a long one with a constant avoidance of main highways and interstates. The desperados' main focus was a non-confrontational exodus into the mountains, not so much as to avoid complications with law enforcement as it was to avoid detection or suspicion by anyone. The Black Knight knew that if their existence in the country was in question, or their direction of travel was suspected by anyone, their destiny would be sealed; they most definitely would be located. With federal interest in the original "Los Ochos," the clan would be subjected to extraordinary preparations by law enforcement. This combined with the "never be taken alive" mentality shared for the most part by the now seven felons, their life expectancy would be nil if they were located. The Dark Knight was not opposed to a "Bonnie and Clyde" ending to his existence, but for the moment he had something to live for. Close to a quarter of a million dollars had been extracted from the branch bank and a lot of living could be had in Mexico for that much dinero.

Esquire insisted that no violations of the law occur during the relocation process. Drafter could take comfort in the notion that, at least for the time being, his life was not all that expendable. Still, he had great concern about his future and now that the Squeeze had been excommunicated from the clan before his very eyes, he had greater long-term worries. Self-preservation was foremost on his mind and until he could figure a secure way of escaping the wrath of the Knight, he would spend every waking moment figuring ways to appease each member of the career criminals. In order to accomplish this, he would, in some way, have to be of value to the collective tribe of misfits.

Mayhem was also an extreme liability to the mission. Upon several occasions he had demonstrated his inability to maintain any real grasp of self-control. This was brought on mainly by his natural talent to act on impulse and most often, at inconvenient times. He had caused grave mistakes which had not only changed a smooth bank job into a mass environment of panic and hysteria, but the subsequent needless murders placed a major adjustment in the direction of retreat. Unbeknownst to the stupid man was fact that he too, was on the endangered species list.

Gonzales and Mexican Joe Garcia were in marginal standing with the boss by their wavering loyalty but Joe still had an advantage over the transient party. He was the only one who knew of a hiding place.

Sly, Blade Runner and James Eagle were all solid in the notion of their leader. They had proven their loyalty and firm commitment under fire inside the joint, as well as on the outside. If there was any action on the outside, Esquire, without hesitation, could depend on them.

The trip went without a hitch until they entered the small town of Saguache, Colorado; a mere 80 miles from their destination. Esquire had relaxed too soon. What he had not planned on was a neighborhood watch program that had been in place before the concept was fashionable. On any given day, the small town boasted at best a population of around five hundred constant residents and every individual seemed to have an apparent heritage concerning the inalienable right to observe and then formulate an opinion about any other resident or visitor. What would make matters even more complicated was the fact that citizens would go to any extreme to involve themselves in the ritual. In short, everybody was a busybody; not only mutually watching each other through a separation of most often, a single pane of glass, but embellishing what they witnessed. By such an over abundant general behavior, everybody knew everything about everybody else, real or perceived. It was the most entertainment that anyone could hope for in such a small community.

At about 10:08 a.m., the van with Texas plates entered the city limits. The Knight had planned on the purchase of basic survival gear and weaponry at this stage of the trip for it was the last stop before heading into the wilderness. With the prospect of supplies being few and eyes many, he decided to backtrack to the larger towns of Monte Vista or Alamosa for such preparations. What he did not know was that the small town telephones were already ringing off the walls; transmitting information, no matter how accurate, to virtually every resident within the community. Mrs. Ward, who had the reputation of being the municipality's supreme "town crier," had spotted the suspicious vehicle first. Her residence of seventy five years had visual advantage over the grocery store as well as, the town's two gas stations. No one could pass without falling under such observation. Her perception was not always accurate but it was always voiced so strongly and with such colorful overtures that her broadcasts were sometimes more interesting than the *National Inquirer*.

"I just know that these are the bad men from Texas!" Mrs. Ward was feeding her own imagination as she informed her best friend of her latest sightings. She would switch the telephone to the other hand and drew the curtain back once again.

"They are so many in that little van and they are buying all sorts of food and putting it all in a little trailer," observed the busy body.

Before long, the Saguache County Sheriff's Office was called with the information that had the entire town buzzing. Veteran Sheriff, Benjamin Hall, felt compelled, eventually, to respond. At the age of twenty-three, he had been first voted in as the sheriff, but that had been forty years ago. With his reputation already legendary, he maintained a gruff exterior which culminated in a healthy fear within the community. Ben's presentation was often referred to as a "John Wayne swagger" and such a persona benefited him as a ten time unopposed elected official. Deep down, he was a caring man who had established a diversionary program for juveniles before the concept had been developed elsewhere. Every afternoon when school let out, he invited as many kids that wanted to participate to crowd into his office and after they completed their homework, he would indulge each child's imagination with a "war story" from the past. Every story had one common denominator; no matter how factual or made up, the sheriff always won in any confrontation and the bad guy always paid the "ultimate price," whatever that meant. He had also developed the art of motivating the juvenile congregation to greater heights and aspirations. As a result, there were hundreds of documented successful experiences. The walls of the Sheriff's office were covered with letters of thanks from prior generations that participated in the richness that came from Ben's Den Club. It was generally understood that his jail was almost always empty because his office was always full.

Mrs. Ward watched from her constant vantage point as the familiar primer-gray Willys Jeep of a vintage long past, drove into the parking lot of the filling station. It came to a halt behind the suspect van. Ben Hall slowly and deliberately stepped from the vehicle which bore a seven point star decal that was faded and beginning to peel at the tips of each point. The emblem of many years had been placed with great care on the hood of the government vehicle, and although now barely legible, still represented the distinct symbol of authority. This had been the first patrol transportation of the respected sheriff and if he had his way, the only one. The many dents and dings, along with the oxidized paint lent a greater personality and was a portrait of history, if not professionalism, by its appearance. Although there was a new Dodge Ram in the Sheriff's garage, the open-aired chariot was still Hall's first choice. That other "thing," Ben was often heard saying, was for parades and funerals, and for trips out of county.

With traditional caution, Ben approached the back of the van and keyed the lapel mic to his portable radio. "Lynn, this is Ben." What Ben had no way of knowing was that Lynn was acting as jailor and not dispatcher at the moment; she was tending to the needs of two inmates who required their daily distribution of medications.

"Lynn, this is Sheriff Hall", Ben would try again.

Without the acknowledgment, Ben proceeded to make contact with the strangers.

"Howdy, fellas." The sheriff of better than four decades greeted the first man who stepped out of the utility vehicle. "Where y'all headed?"

At first, Blade Runner was taken aback by the surprise appearance of the elderly law enforcer but as he further observed the features of the sheriff, he became amused with the apparent lack of threat the man posed. Blade thus engaged the "broken-down" cop with trivial conversation.

"Just head'n up into the mountains to do a little fish'n and camp'n," the escaped convict responded with complete confidence. The Indian and Gonzales exited the van next and stood by while John Hamel furthered the conversation. "Don't know where we could catch some big ones do ya'?"

Sheriff Hall surveyed the interesting attire each man wore. His eyes slowly ran the full length of the Native American. He was curious as to why the unshaven trio gave more of an appearance of destitute street folk than those about to embark on a camping excursion.

"Don't mind if I take a look at some IDs, do ya' boys?" The lone sheriff would inquire.

The Indian began to position himself closer, "the only one that is driv'n is Garcia," he offered.

"Don't matter, son," the sheriff was beginning to detect uneasiness with the subject's demeanor. "I want to see some identification now, fellas." He was taking a step back and repositioning himself with his gun side away from the strangers. What he did not see was the vulgar figure of Mayhem sneaking up behind him. With a knife at the ready and his beady eyes focused with intense despise on the law man's back, Mayhem had a smirk on his face as he advanced toward the unsuspecting sheriff. Without warning, Mayhem lunged. Before the beloved pillar of the community could react, the murderer had wrapped his right arm around Ben's neck and placed the blood stained point of the shank next to the sheriff's jugular vein.

"Ya' know how to say the Lord's Prayer, sheriff?" Mayhem's teeth were clinched as he spoke. "Make your peace, for there is no time like the present!"

Ben slowly raised his hands out in front of himself and spread his fingers as to surrender. Without so much as a fight, Ben saw that he was forced to concede the confrontation. In so doing, he realized that his life was not worth a plug nickel. "What is it that you guys want?"

"Whatever it might be, you can bet we will take it without your blessing." At this point, Esquire was making his grand entry into the sunshine of the day from the dark recesses of the van. "Now you would have done yourself real proud if ya' just stayed home and conducted gardening or tried to get a little action from the wife." The Black Knight spit tobacco juice at the ground near the sheriff's feet. "Ya' see, ya' created problems for us and now I have to figure out how to resolve 'em. Ya' got any suggestions?"

Ben, who was a brave man with several near death experiences, had never been taken so completely off guard. He stood no chance and the prospects of such angered him more at himself than at those who were for certain about to take his life. He had been careless and because of this he was about to pay the ultimate price! He thought of his wife of many decades and regretted the news that she would soon receive.

"Apparently you don't understand the gravity of the situation, old man." Esquire was irritated at the major glitch in the otherwise clean trip from Texas.

"Does it really matter?" Sheriff Hall would pose the obvious.

"Perhaps not to you, but that little lady that is sitting behind the counter of this gas station should be concerned. Ya' see, she can identify half of us." The Black Knight had struck a nerve within the sworn peace officer.

"Whatever business you have is with me!" demanded Ben. "You leave her alone!" Mr. Hall felt enraged and he took acute exception to anyone else being harmed. He had made his mistake and he was willing to live with it or even die for it, but the unaware employee of Jose's Gas Station must be left alone at any costs.

Ben could feel someone tugging at his Colt .45 Peacemaker. The Indian was working the weapon in an attempt to release it from the holster but was failing to do so. "Just take the whole damn thing - how many times do I have to tell you guys?!" Esquire bellowed. With a tremendous yank, the Indian spun the lawman from the death grip of Mayhem and sent the sheriff sprawling on the ground. Eagle had procured the gun, holster and gun belt with the single yank. The sheriff felt a five inch cut along his neck but could sense that it was only superficial. Without warning, the notorious Mayhem planted a solid kick into the lawman's stomach which sent the man reeling. As Ben Hall lay on the black top surface of the parking lot, he attempted to catch his breath. Soon the aggressor tore the seven point symbol which represented the sheriff's ultimate authority from the sheriff's vest.

"Get up and swear me in, Sheriff," Mayhem ordered as he helped the injured elderly gentleman to his feet and leaned him against the side of the van. He once again placed the prison made weapon to the sheriff's throat. "I want to be sheriff! Swear me in you ancient bastard!"

The others began to laugh with the amusement. Esquire in particular found himself intrigued. "What a concept, Mayhem."

Through the recognition of apparent approval by the Boss, Mayhem became even more focused on his demand. "Do it, Baby! Swear me in and while ya' do it pin the badge on my shirt like ya' supposed to." At this point, he handed the badge back to Ben for the unrehearsed ceremony. Ben opened his hand and stared at the emblem of designation. He then shook his head and let out a grunt.

"Do it man, or me and the chick will go around back and get acquainted!"

Sheriff Hall was tentative but nevertheless rotated the pin latch on the badge with his thumb and pulled the pin from its safety clasp. With deliberate hesitation, he gripped the repulsive man's shirt and placed the pin as though he was indeed attaching the badge. Then, with predictable response to opportunity presented, the sheriff plunged the entire shank of the pin into the criminal man's chest. Smugness was replaced by sudden and relentless terror as the murderer staggered back and looked at his own chest.

"You son-of-a-bitch!" Mayhem wailed. His counterparts began to laugh even harder as he stood with the star still secured to his left pectoral muscle.

"That's one of them there universal type badges, Knight." Blade Runner ignored the pain in which his previous cellmate would endure. "Ya' can wear it with or without a shirt!"

The sheriff stepped back as though to make space in which to maneuver. The Indian, who was directly behind him, stuck his foot out and tripped Ben. The lawman fell flat onto the ground staring upwards with the wind knocked out of him. Leaving the seven point star in place as though it was a badge of honor, Mayhem stepped over the helpless figure and quickly bent down, placing a knee on the ground and the blade of the knife tightly between the sheriff's legs. Ben displayed no more than a slight cringe as the dedicated criminal applied more pressure.

"I'm gonna split you from your stem to your chin," the blood thirsty man forewarned. The sheriff could feel sweat begin to trickle down his temple and into the receding salt and pepper hair.

Without warning, a sudden loud blast startled the group of felons! No sooner had they flinched than the unmistaken sound of buck shot whizzed over Mayhem's useless head and ripped a hole in the side of the van.

All eyes turned in the direction of the abrupt interruption as the unmistaken sound of the action associated with a twelve gauge pump slammed another 3 inch shell into the chamber.

"Get off of him!" demanded Mrs. Ward as she attempted to steady the bird gun. "Get off of him now or I will rip you a new orifice!" As she screamed her demands, she was advancing closer and closer as to not chance another miss. The old lady waved the weapon from side to side in a gesture to not exclude consideration of any of the group. Now, with a steady voice if not of the heavy weapon, the neighborhood voyeur placed further emphasis on the moment with a familiar line, "go ahead punk, make my day!"

Mayhem was hesitant in his obedience but he rose and stood straight with slow deliberation and faced the threat as though he were invincible. Gripping and re-gripping the shank, he would challenge the old lady. Her eyes would fall on the stream of blood that drew from the badge which was still sticking in the man's chest. Nevertheless, she held the shotgun true without any apparent fear.

Mayhem began to smile. "Lady I'm gonna make you crap your bloomers!"

"Mister!" Mrs. Ward held her posture, "I don't think so, but I will guarantee I will fill yours with triple aught buck!" With this, she confirmed her intents by aiming the shotgun at the convict's crotch.

"Christ!" Mayhem was caught off guard as he accepted the change of prideful priorities. "I would prefer to be shot in the face."

Esquire looked first at the determined old woman and then back at the expendable Mayhem. He realized that she was just as crazy as Mayhem and he began to chuckle. Time was wasting though and with the unforeseen complications it would be imperative to facilitate an evacuation immediately.

"Load up," The leader demanded. "It is time to get the hell out of this one horse settlement. James, you and Mex take the Jeep. We'll follow."

Sly had sensed that there was something not quite right when he felt the vibration of the shot gun blister inside of the van. The deaf man slowly positioned himself next to the sliding door and with a pistol in hand, carefully peered around the corner until he could see the old lady saying something to Mayhem. Slowly, and with precision, he aimed his weapon at the woman but Mayhem inadvertently obscured his target.

"Hold it where you're at," demanded the woman.

"Load up!" Esquire once again directed his clan. He, diverting his attention back to the courageous elderly citizen, "let it go, madam. You won our respect and you best leave it at that."

With Ben's life extended and the intensity of the moment apparently relieved, Mrs. Ward no longer knew what to do. She stood guard while two of the suspects loaded into the Sheriff's Jeep and the others into the van. Both engines started simultaneously and the van's tires began to spin. Soon both vehicles were leaving the gas station and Ben could not believe that he was still alive. Slowly he got up and brushed the dust from his pants.

"Sheriff, they've got your Jeep," Mrs. Ward exclaimed.

The sheriff smiled as they both watched the van and the Jeep disappear around a bend and travel west on Colorado Highway 114. He took the angry widow in his arms and planted an uninvited kiss on her lips. So unexpected was the advance, that Mrs. Ward tensed up with a shocked expression on her face. It was with an involuntary response that she accidentally squeezed the trigger of the twelve gauge shot gun and there was a loud explosion. The shot was dispersed harmlessly into the blue sky. Ben grabbed the gun with one hand while still holding tight onto the shocked Mrs. Ward.

"I didn't see any stars but I sure did hear thunder, how about you?" Sheriff Hall asked with a grin.

As Ben attempted to work the safety mechanism, he discovered that the button was rusted in place. He worked the action and by doing so he found that there were no other shells in the gun. He slowly bent down and retrieved what was left of the fragile old lady. Holding the spent shell casing up to Mrs. Ward's face and rolling it between his thumb and index finger, he proclaimed his discovery, "This is made of waxed cardboard construction!" The Sheriff quickly realized that the shell was of a vintage at least fifty years old. As he steadied Mrs. Ward, he inquired as to how long the gun had been over her mantelpiece with the firing sequence ready for discharge. Furthermore, how on earth had the old lady remembered that there was triple aught buck in the chamber?

"My late husband, Sam ... did you ever know Sam, Sheriff?" Mrs. Ward eagerly responded.

Ben found himself nodding although he was not all that interested in what the old lady had to say. He had other things to be concerned about, and he needed to notify authorities in surrounding areas to be on the lookout for the bad men.

As Ben started the five block walk back to his office, Mrs. Ward continued to reflect. "Anyway, he always said that the only manly way to kill something was to shoot it with double aught buck!" She paused for a second to catch her breath, "so I just figured if double was so manly, triple was even better. Furthermore, Sam said that nothing was more worthless than an unloaded gun. If you are going to treat all guns as if they are loaded all the time, why not cut out the mystery all together by just keeping the guns loaded all the time? Furthermore ..."

Ben began to chuckle to himself as he quickened his pace. "You won't find me arguing with your logic and how you came by it!" He thought to himself.

Chapter Thirteen

Crash Site

Jay watched with curious apprehension as the two helicopters flew in ever tightening circles overhead. The first chopper appeared to be a private conveyance and the second had a government seal of sorts displayed on the side. Jug Head and Idiot were not impressed with the aerial intrusion. With the ever increasing noise, both mules panicked and began to test the strength of their ties. The mountain man waved vigorously for the aircrafts to continue on, but to no avail. Finally, the helicopters settled softly into a clearing and Jay studied the airships as the engines began to wind down. Finally the doors were opened and the beautiful Ms. Gray appeared in the closest helicopter. Jay could feel his heart begin to beat rapidly and his breathing became difficult. It had been several weeks since he had last seen her and she appeared even lovelier than what Jay's vivid memory and imagination could recall.

Not wishing to appear overly excited, Jay slowly climbed down from the loft floor which was all but complete. By the time he reached the rough framed main doorway, Sheila was already in his arms. He would feel her soft lips reach his and then kiss him long and hard. Finally, she would withdraw and take in a deep breath. It would occur to him that this was only the second time that they shared such a passionate embrace.

"What in the world is all this?" Sheila was taken aback by such an incredible and unexpected delight. "This looks fabulous," her smile radiated her approval.

Soon, Mr. Charles Gray would reach the construction site. He took a moment to catch his breath, as well as study the mammoth structure, then focused on the large frame of the man who stood before him. The concerned father stared at the sawdust in Jay's hair and slowly drew his gaze down to his exquisite physique. With his shirt off and the sweat glistening, every curve, every cut of Jay's lean two hundred and thirty pounds exhibited a near perfect specimen.

"Daddy, this is the man who saved my life!" Sheila was excited.

Jay wiped off his hands with a nearby t-shirt and then extended his right hand not only as a gesture of politeness, but out of respect. The feeling was evidently not mutual, for he could detect the lack of enthusiasm in the token grip of the older man and he was surprised.

"I'm grateful," Mr. Gray expressed his lukewarm sentiment.

It was with sudden dismay that Jay felt challenged by the unexpected undertow of discourtesy. He experienced mixed thoughts between a preoccupation with remaining silent and weathering out the storm, or asking for the courtesy of explanation for such a provisional greeting. At the risk of alienating the father of the woman for whom he would build an exquisite domain and thus, perhaps, straining the relationship between father and daughter, Jay decided to accept things the way they appeared and not say anything contrary.

"I too, am grateful for the opportunity to make your acquaintance." Jay simply stated.

"I'm sure you are." Mr. Gray would turn away and glance down the grassed slope to the three men who were walking up the mountain. Looking back at Jay he said, "The Feds want to look at the crash site. You don't have a problem with that, do you?"

"Not after the suits round up my mules, I don't," the mountain man was serious. By this time, the two mules had bolted through the makeshift corral and had beat feet for the forest. Devereux knew that not only would it take a better part of a day to round the pair up, but repairs on the corral would also take time.

"Quite a little place you have here," the first of the government arrivals was breathing hard as he leaned next to the side of the building. "What is the altitude here anyway?"

*****

The fuselage was well hidden by the clustered green leaves of the high mountain aspen. It was surprising to investigators how little damage to the foliage had actually occurred. However, the accident had taken place in the winter so most of the impact had been cushioned by the snow. As the NSTB (National Safety Transportation Board) investigators continued to sift for clues and answers, Sheila and her father sat a few feet away and watched.

Mr. Gray let out a sigh, "it's truly incredible you were not hurt sweetheart."

"Plus, the fact that afterwards I didn't become a part of the food chain," Sheila was eager to point out. "What do you think of Jay?"

The young lady's father stood up and dusted off the area of his pants that had made contact with the ground. "I think it is about time I engage a little one on one quality time with the boy; kind of do a little male bonding, if you know what I mean."

Sheila also stood, "Now daddy, don't be over protective."

She was concerned as her father began to walk back up the steep slope of the mountain. "Be nice," she would take one last stab at directing a parent's initiative.

Jay was about done repairing the corral when Mr. Gray approached. "Good morning again," he offered, but the stern Mr. Gray would merely nod. "What ya' think?"

"About what?" Charles was being a little obstinate.

It was easy to surmise that the man's concentration was not on the wreck, but with Jay. Jay's conjecture would further direct that Mr. Gray was having difficulty in accepting the rugged posture in which Jay stood firm. Jay would make sure that his own patience would endure, "One hell of a landing, if you asked me."

"What is with the rather large structure?" Mr. Gray asked.

Jay smiled to himself as he recognized the inevitable, "A man's home is his castle; don't you think? I just thought that I would shape up the castle a bit."

"Mr. Devereux, my wife and I have worked extremely hard to assure that our children would receive the best of everything. They all have gone to the best schools and we have hired the best tutors.

We even prepared for their financial futures." Gray held a pole in place as Jay attached it to a post. "Do you have any concept to what I'm saying?"

Jay wound the bailing wire around the post and crisscrossed it over the pole. "I believe that you are eluding to the fact that you think I am exploiting the environment as well as atmospheric enticements of this mountain, coupled with the mythical advantage of being basically mighty enough to endure such elements. You have prepared your daughters for all possibilities except for this one. And now that you feel your main interest is vulnerable, you are willing to do anything to secure her future through your own definition and set of values." Jay tossed the fencing pliers on the ground and grabbed another pole. "Mr. Gray, I have not intentionally or unintentionally taken advantage of your daughter! Not by my way of thinking, nor by what I am sure your definition and standards are concerning acceptable conduct. I have not influenced her thinking, nor will I in the future. I have not violated her by mental indulgence or physical contact."

"I have misjudged your abilities." Sheila's father was impressed at Jay's intelligence; however, he tried to fortify his basic resolve. "Mr. Devereux, my daughter has a future and experiences she wishes to pursue down below in a world of opportunity. She's bright and beautiful and can excel in anything she wants to …"

"And what if she chooses to peak on top of a mountain?" Jay felt clever with the paraphrased challenge.

Jay understood that the gentleman was used to having his own way, without exception. Slowly, Mr. Gray pulled his sunglasses from his face and began to clean the lens with a shirt tail. Then he peered through the glass at arm's length, staring at Jay as though to sight him in. "Allow me to be blunt."

Jay appreciated the directness but braced himself for a threat. "By all means," Jay simply said.

"I don't think you understand who you are dealing with young man." The wealthy father's demeanor was offensive by the condescending tone. "I will not stand idly by and watch my little girl's life be swayed by a man who lives in a fantasy of conquer or be conquered; life or death!"

Maintaining his composure was difficult to say the least, but Jay understood if there was ever a chance to change this fellow's mind, it would have to be approached with a satin touch. Insulted, but not detoured from his resolve, Jay regrouped. "So what is the alternative? What are you suggesting, Mr. Gray?"

Misunderstanding the acquaintance's intentions, Mr. Gray jumped in with both feet. "In short, you leave my daughter alone. You spend just enough time to redirect her values back to my control and in exchange for your troubles, I will extend to you five thousand dollars in cash."

Jay felt his blood begin to boil and his face became red and sweaty. He would allow the pole to slip from his fingers and bounce on the ground at the intruder's feet. "I should knock you on the flat part of your ass, Mister!"

Still misunderstanding the mountain man's thoughts, Sheila's father would dig a much larger trench between him and the mountain man.

"Alright, Mr. Devereux. It will take some capital to finish off this monster project. Anyone can see that. A hundred thousand clams and you never see my daughter again!"

"I'm embarrassed for you, Gray. You have misunderstood my restraint as an invitation for bargaining," Jay was more direct. "At the risk of alienating you beyond repair, now may I make myself perfectly clear? Once again, my intentions have been, and will continue to be, honorable. My feelings are pure and I take great exception to your thoughts to be otherwise. You judge me by appearance and geographic placement only, and by such, you demonstrate great repulsion." Jay folded his arms as he stood solid. "Don't create an adversarial situation; not because what can be at risk between you and I. You have obviously drawn your conclusions about me. What is most at risk lies between you and your daughter!"

Placing his hand up in a halting fashion, Mr. Gray cocked his head and once again made clear his thoughts, "Don't attempt to decipher my intentions! I don't give a damn about who you are, where you came from, or how honorable you say your intentions are. I am completely indifferent to such matters! This is not the life for my little girl and if your lust was not in the way, you would know it. If I were you, I would take the money and run!"

What had at one time stood out as a basic concern for a daughter, now took on different direction as an obsession for her devotion. Jay Devereux was not afraid of the man who was angrily attacking his character but he had a growing concern for the damage that could be done if this impasse was not worked out.

"What do you know about me, Sir?" Jay would attempt to establish common ground in which the two could perhaps build. "What has Sheila told you about me?"

The preoccupied guardian still would not waver. "Unless you have an aversion to becoming wealthy, I would make one last appeal to your sense of decency and advise you to accept the money and make both of our lives much simpler."

"Money does not even fit in the equation, Mr. Gray. Our conversation has come to an obvious, unnecessary stalemate." Jay turned and began walking towards a point of the last sighting of his mules. "Good day, Sir!"

*****

Around midafternoon, the mule trainer had been successful in recovering his livestock and as he placed the beasts into the newly repaired enclosure, Sheila made her way back up the mountainside. "What are their names?" she inquired. "And where did you get them?"

Jay relaxed for a spell while expounding on his talents as a mule skinner (trainer/operator) and how he came by such a short experienced ability. As his story unfolded, Sheila warmed his heart once again as her delightful laugh brought back the memories of the mid-winter midnight skinny dip. He was amazed at how he could love her so much; however, he was puzzled on how he would be able to win over her patriarch.

"Do you want me to come back and stay a while?" Sheila finally asked.

Jay was hopeful that was why she was there to begin with.

"Nothing has changed," he looked at the large home he was laboring over. "You are why I am motivated to build a home that is hopefully fit for your approval."

Sheila's smile was broad across her face for she was happy that he still felt the same. "I will not be able to come back right away. I still have a lot to take care of. It will probably take another month or so." She drifted over to Jay and softly touched both of his hands with her hands. "And then I will spend the rest of the summer, all of the fall, and if you still want me, we can talk about the winter." She looked deeply into his eyes, "that will give us more time to finish your empire." She then paused and looked around, "how did you get all this built in such a short time; and all the materials? Where did they come from?"

"I had a lot of the stuff air lifted in; and I put the mules to work on snaking the logs up." Jay was cautious with his optimism. "If your dad will let you, I can tell you now that you are more than welcome to stay for the rest of your life." Feeling obvious, Jay's face became red with embarrassment. "...Or as long as you want; whichever comes first." He now attempted to recoil from his obvious display of eagerness. "I hired a bunch of folks to build the thing and they are all off right now celebrating something called Cinco de Mayo, whatever that is."

Sheila let go of his hands and stepped back. "What do you mean, if dad will allow it? He said something disparaging, didn't he?"

"He seems a little concerned about your future with the likes of me." Jay was trying his best to be diplomatic.

"And I guess I don't have any say so in this matter?" Sheila was becoming angry.

By no means did Jay want to come between father and daughter. "I think you should give him a little time to get used to me and the whole idea of all this. You have to admit, it is pretty unusual."

"So let me get all of this straight," Sheila said as she glanced in the direction of her father, who was once again climbing up the steep slope. "You don't want me to come back in a month?"

Jay was beginning to feel exasperated with being misunderstood by the father and now, by the daughter. "That is not it at all," he would try to make himself more clearly understood. "If I had my way, you'd stay from this point on." Jay took a deep breath for he knew he did not have much time. "It's just that in the coming weeks, please be understanding to your dad's reservations about me.

I'm a stranger to him; not only by acquaintance but in lifestyle. Plus, I saved your life and after all, if anyone feels that is their role, it's a father. How can he possibly compete with something like that?"

*****

Jay stood close watch over the now hobbled and penned mules when both aircraft slowly lifted off. Sheila was waving vigorously and throwing kisses through the bubbled glass. The helicopters would hover for a few seconds and then both would drift to the downhill side and quickly vanish behind the trees. For a few moments, an ever fading blade wash echoed off of the trees and then gradually from detection all together.

Chapter Fourteen

Return to Sky City

The star on the hood was obscured by the dust that now covered the stolen Willys. With a chain tied to the front axle of the van, the Jeep gave it's all to tug the two wheel drive vehicle up the steep switchbacks of the "4-wheel drive only" trail. The destination was the abandoned Sky City Mine. This was the very mine which had structures that sustained Joe's life for half of the winter. Esquire was not pleased that they had been detected in the little town of Saguache but he liked the notion that these great mountains could serve as an excellent refuge until an alternate plan could be made. Surely no one would think to search so deeply into the mountain range.

After traveling all day, the two vehicles stopped in a small meadow with a brook near the jeep trail. It was decided that due to the treacherous travel, night time progress would be even slower at best and most probably, foolhardy. As the group of men began to gather wood for a campfire, Esquire motioned in earnest for them to stop and listen. As the sound grew greater, each man could feel his own heart beating faster and faster.

"Find a tree and get under it, now!" The Black Knight yelled as loud as he could. "Choppers, choppers, choppers!" As his words were drowned out, the men were panicked, confused, and looking in all directions. James Eagle was breaking out in a cold sweat and great terror was reflected in his eyes.

"Get aboard sergeant! Get aboard! I'll keep 'em off ya'! Just get the men outa here!" The Indian had the 9 mm Glock clutched in both hands and was alertly turning side to side as though scanning for a target in the dense forest. Suddenly both helicopters zipped overhead and just as quickly, out of sight. "Sergeant shoot the flare, goddamn it! Shoot the flare before it's too late!"

The escaped felons watched with puzzlement as the Black Knight approached the wigged out Native American. "The gooks are gone, man. It's alright. Ya' did your job and they are all gone." Esquire extended his hand in the direction of the extremist individual who was obviously not entirely present. Not on this continent anyway.

"Give me the gun, man. They are all gone." Esquire ordered.

"No sergeant. They might come back." Eagle was convinced that the Viet Cong was at the forest edge and the evacuation team overshot the landing zone.

Gonzales ran to where Esquire was trying to reason with the displaced James Eagle. "Why were they on to us so fast? What are we going to do now, now that the bastards are on to us?"

As Gonzales drew near, the Black Knight grabbed Wells by the throat with one giant hand and squeezed. The frightened man's eyes began to bug out and the boss drew him near. "The choppers weren't looking for us, dumb ass. I'm deal'n with a man who has time warped back to Nam and your wiggin' out 'cause a couple of choppers pass by? Pull it together or you're no use to me." Esquire once again studied the man with the gun. Slowly he would release the death grip on Gonzales. "Come on Eagle. I need to field inspect your piece!"

For a quick moment, James Eagle glanced at the Knight as though the mentor was out of his mind and then refocused his intensity as if he saw an enemy shadow just beyond the trees.

"Let me have your pistol, warrior. While you inspect mine let me have yours."

The Black Knight removed the revolver of which he had tucked in his waistband, pressed open the cylinder with his thumb and tilted the weapon up so the black talon police issue cartridges would fall into his free hand. He then snapped his wrist and by doing so the cylinder slammed shut.

"Here ya' go, Chief." And he handed the firearm to the Indian. The exchange was made and the Indian seemed content, if not fully aware.

*****

The next day the two vehicles crossed the rutted high mountain pass otherwise known as Toothache Ridge and began to descend down the extreme steep decline into Canyon Diablo. Magnificent mountain ranges swelled up as the depths of the canyon began to swallow the small caravan. Down the dusty trail, the Jeep and van crept at times teetering over a precipice or grinding the under carriage over an unavoidable teeth-gritting boulder. The descent was tedious at best and life threatening at worst. Mexican Joe was well suited for driving such terrain and guided the Jeep's every move which served as an example to the second driver, James Eagle. With his senses fully restored, the Indian seemed to have suffered no lasting effects from his short trip back in time. With no helicopters present, his faculties seemed current once again.

The descent into the canyon would take a better part of a day. Once the achievement was complete, Esquire's spirits were substantially lifted. It had taken three days to travel the distance from the sleepy town to the Sky City Mine and he was sure that no one would suspect their location. He slowly scanned the abandoned buildings and marveled at the thought that anyone could have found such a place, let alone ferried in building materials. Upon their arrival Esquire motioned for Joe Garcia to approach him.

"You did real well," Esquire acknowledged the excellence associated with the choice for a hiding place. "You really came through for us at the prison, too. We owe ya'."

After settling in, Sly and the Indian took it upon themselves to spray paint the Jeep with primer black which oxidized upon contact with the dirty surface of the metal. Much was gained as the appearance of the transportation was far different than before and there was still a great amount of the paint which had been found in a storage shed for touchups later on. The Saguache County Government licensed plates were exchanged with the stolen Colorado validations which had been procured at a junk yard after the escape convicts first entered the state. It would take little genius to realize that the van would not ascend out of the depths of Canyon Diablo. It had accomplished its assignment so, when the time came, it would be burned beyond recognition.

Towards evening the Black Knight began thinking of long range plans of his migration to Mexico or perhaps other countries. He was quiet. The rest of the clan knew that when the boss was quiet, no one dared interrupt his thoughts. He would reflect a little on his life but mostly think about the complications of the journey just traveled. The Knight watched as Mayhem sharpened his knife. He was always sharpening the damned thing. Mayhem had been an extreme liability from the very first part of the trip. He created a dire circumstance at the penitentiary, had foiled the escape to the southern country and almost messed up the retreat into the mountains. The leader knew all too well that Mayhem must be dismissed from the group. He also understood that when Mayhem's perishable nature had reached expiration, others in the group would become paranoid and restless about their own possible expendability. Now was not the time.

Now that the bandits were no longer on the run, the group of men seemed comfortable with the new environment; for the first time in a long time, they were able to relax. Their demeanor took on a juvenile-like excitement as they began to explore the mine's many structures. The Sky City excavation had a history that would date as far back as the 1890's and was marginally active to the 1980's. However, due to the dozens of miles of near impossible terrain combined with the lack of substantial quality yield, interest had been lost and the rights had been relinquished back to the federal government. In the fall, big game hunters would invade the region, and perhaps an occasional expedition of weekend prospectors would visit during the summer, but for the most part, things would remain peaceful.

Finally, the Black Knight emerged from the sanctuary of his deep thoughts and walked from the largest cabin in which he had adopted as his constant domain.

"Garcia!" He bellowed.

Soon the member of the clan came running. "Yes Sir," he was eager to please.

"Where is the tunnel, or shaft, or whatever it is?" As enthusiastic as Esquire was about the prospects of feeling secure in such a great concealed hiding place, he did not relish the notion of not having an emergency avenue of retreat if necessary.

With flashlights the two men entered the damp dwelling of the main mining drift, and began to make their way to where Mexican Joe had last seen Jay Devereux several months prior. "Where does this open up?" asked the leader.

Joe stopped for a moment in order to respond. Suddenly he became aware of the tight quarters and began to struggle with his breathing. "What?" He had lost his concentration.

"Where the hell does this take us?" An indication of impatience laced into the Knight's tone as he repeated the question.

Refocused, Garcia breathed heavy and said, "it leads to another big canyon and a waterfall."

Ducking under various obstacles and sagging timbers, Esquire hurried on. "How close is it to other humans?"

"The only other person I know of is the bastard that forced me through this hole in the first place." Joe remembered well the journey in the dead of winter, as well as nearly being buried alive in an avalanche of snow and ice.

"What are you talking about?" The main man was somewhat curious, but mostly concerned that there was another possible human obstacle in the mix.

"Some bastard that has a cabin near Machin Lake and I had a little misunderstanding about a broad." Mexican Joe felt uneasy with the reflection. "And he left me here to die in this shaft."

"What do ya' mean, he left you here to die?" Esquire was finding it difficult to buy into the story; especially without details.

As the two continued to journey though the seemingly endless maze, Joe Garcia preoccupied himself with his embellished version of what had transpired. The new, but hardly improved story had Jay Devereux as the villain. Esquire had been inside the system long enough to know that ninety-nine per cent of a convict's stories will yield only a fraction of traceable truth.

Eventually, the two men arrived at an unexpected obstacle. First, the air became cool as though someone had opened a giant freezer door. The further the men proceeded, the colder the atmosphere. Suddenly, the two stopped and listened to what sounded like a water trickle down a rock surface. The hollow echo gave Garcia the first indication that something was much different than his last experience in the shaft. Perhaps he had made a mistake and they had gone the wrong way while navigating the many passageways. Soon however, the mystery became clear as they entered the area that would have normally granted them access to the boxed end of the Stone Cellar Canyon and Shadow Falls. Instead of the anticipated open end to the mine, there was a quartz colored wall of ice that reflected the light of the flashlights and gave a translucent hue. The avalanche had transformed into a watery ice wall that gave the characteristics of a glacier rather than snow. It was evident that the solid mass of frozen liquid was in the process of slowly melting; however, with the slide area facing the northeast, little sunlight would find its way around Table Mountain to assist in the seasonal process.

The Black Knight was not pleased with the lack of an exit from Canyon Diablo. However, he would quickly accept the inevitable and in doing so, began to retrace his steps back to the hideaway.

*****

For the next few weeks, Devereux endured the long hard days and short nights, but it was by his own schedule. The grueling pace of which he had set might have forced an average man with an average constitution to give in to the rationalization of lesser productivity or perhaps no gesture towards accomplishment at all. Noting the daunting size of the project, it was remarkable that the project was even started. But this was a true mountain man who had established uncommon ambition to support his visionary crusade. As impractical and whimsical as this dream may seem, Jay's energy was constantly propelled by the recollection of Sheila's soft touch; her magnificent lips on his. He was driven to thrust forth a full day frenzy for he constantly kept his purpose in front of him and with Sheila's constant image in his mind, the purpose was far from being fictional.

It was getting close to the time that Sheila said she would return to the mountain. The winter experience was still fresh in her mind. She had missed the place that bore no distractions. She found herself longing not only for the man who constantly tugged at her heart strings but the indescribable beauty of the highlands.

With daily anticipation, Jay found himself constantly glancing down the hillside in the direction in which he felt certain she would return. Every action began to take on a greater sense of urgency, and although it was evident that the great bulk of Jay's dream had been accomplished, he still was not content. He had hoped, unrealistically, to have the epic structure dried in by now. Most would have thought it impossible to be much beyond the foundation, but as he gazed at what was so far accomplished, his eyes would run from the base of the logs to the trusses which held the rafters. He had worked hard for many weeks now and his already magnificent physical attributes were even more enhanced by the rippling leanness of the muscles which were a byproduct of his ambition.

He would consider an excursion to the lowlands within the next few days. Although it was a two-day trip, just the distraction was considered to be a rest. On the day that he was to leave, Jay planned to get up before daybreak, complete his morning chores, and then harness the mules to the wagon. He would head down the mountainside in the early afternoon towards the Van Tassel Sawmill which was only operational in the summer months. The trip would do him good and he welcomed the break. The purpose was to purchase 1"x12" rough cut boards which would be used to form the roof. In a great sense, this would be a good step toward the dry in process and Jay was excited.

Chapter Fifteen

Lust in the Air

The exquisite features of the beautiful woman were enhanced by her sense of dress. The white shorts and midriff blouse appeared incandescent in contrast with the dark olive tone of her skin. All eyes took on an inquisitive study as she walked into the modest Dinner Bell Café in Saguache, Colorado. Her presence alone seemed out of place in the small town establishment. What made the spectacle more unbelievable was her escort, Spook McGuire. The two actually appeared to enjoy each other's company and after being seated, engaged in conversation which, at the very sight bewildered the rest of the patronage.

"So, when can we leave?" Sheila was excited about her return to Machin Lake. She had made arrangements at home to place her life on hold until such time she could discover her future with the handsome recluse who declared the Alpines his home. No, her father was not excited about one of his daughters running off to play house with Paul Bunyan, but with the help of her mother, he came to terms with the inevitable and finally granted his favorite "kitten" the begrudged blessing she had pled for.

"Tomorrow morning, early." Spook replied. He had spent the better part of the spring and summer working for the Saguache Sanitation Department. He had money for supplies and feeling the pull towards the mountains once again, he would welcome the opportunity to guide the ravishing Ms. Gray back to the La Garita Wilderness.

"We won't be able to go the same way we came out, ya' know," he would further advise.

A bit puzzled, Sheila briefly glanced across the room and became aware, for the first time, of all the eyes which seemed to be drawn in her direction.

"Why not? What do you mean?"

"They're replacing the bridge that leads to the Van Tassel Sawmill."

"And that means what to us?" Sheila inquired.

"The mill is about ten miles or so from the cabin." Spook attempted to make it clear.

"Why are these people looking at me, Spook?" Sheila was becoming more uncomfortable.

Spook smiled and stroked his freshly laundered but uncombed beard. Although it was evident that the roughly manicured individual had recently washed his clothes and bathed himself, perhaps at the same time, he was still referred to around town as a "Pig Pen." And, with the reputation of such grand distinction, he seemed content to maintain the identity.

"Well," he paused as he began to chuckle. "They think that you are my girlfriend."

"And why do they think that?" Although Sheila inquired she already knew the answer.

"Beats the hell outa' me." The bearded fright took on a serious demeanor and with a shake of his head he said again, "Beats the hell outa' me."

About this time, an elderly woman dressed in a full length pink and white flowered print dress strolled towards Sheila and her companion. Sheila could not help but notice the deputy's badge which appeared so out of place on the woman's oversized bosom. Thinking that the lady was perhaps mental, Sheila was apprehensive with the approach.

"You've got to be Sheila," guessed the silver haired Mrs. Ward. "I've heard so very much about you from Spook. You know how he exaggerates and all, but you're as absolutely delightful as he described; and so pretty, too." The woman then surprised Spook by grabbing him by his beard and shook his head gently side to side. "See, I told you if you took a bath it would make all the difference in the world." Then the lady looked once again at Sheila and while doing so, placed her hands on her waist. "My, you are a pretty one," she once again voiced her observation. "My name is Deputy Ward," she said rather proudly. Sheila was somewhat confused but willing to go along as the lady seemed harmless enough; after all she wasn't packing a gun.

"And do you own the place?" Sheila referred to the little café.

"Heavens no, child", Mrs. Ward laughed. "I can barely manage my own affairs. Besides, I work part time for the Sheriff's office in a volunteer sort of way." As she declared her importance, she would place a thumb under the badge and pull the star outward so that Spook's "girlfriend" could catch a better view. As she did, Sheila could see a metal name tag which revealed an engraved designation of Deputy BB Ward situated off center and above the seven point shield.

"And what is that for?" Sheila was inquisitive.

"For sav'n Sheriff Hall's ass, weren't it Mz. Ward?" Spook eagerly contributed to the conversation. He was proud of the lady who he considered his friend and frequent personal advisor while he visited the lowlands. At times she was about the only one in town that would pay any attention to him and somehow her recent importance extended to him, if only by association.

"I suppose so," Mrs. Ward said as she lightly smacked Spook alongside his head with the back of her hand. "Watch your language!" Redirecting her attention back toward Sheila, Mrs. Ward continued to speak to Spook. "Why don't you go play some pool or look at some beaded head bands in the display case while I visit a little with your friend?"

Within a couple seconds it was only the two ladies who were sitting across from one another in the vinyl booth. "And what do you do for the Sheriff's office?" Sheila could no longer suppress her curiosity.

"Child, I'm nothing but a busybody, hence the nickname BB." Mrs. Ward was truthful about her reputation and although at times her perceptions were speculative at best, she always strived for the basic facts. "You see, I lost my husband several years back and the way I figure it, if you don't have a reason to get up in the morning, then you probably won't. My reason; to see what all is going on. Every day is so exciting and there is so much to live for, even at my age."

"So you're not really a deputy?"

"Not really," was the reply. "A few weeks ago, I kind of saved the sheriff's bacon and they had a big to-do about it where the mayor said I was a hero and everything. They even gave me a medal and made me an honorary deputy." Mrs. Ward leaned forward and whispered, "The way that I kind of figure it is every community needs a hero. If it happens to be a woman over seventy, then it helps not only the folks that are kind of getting up in years but our gender as well - don't ya' think?"

"I would have guessed that you were just over forty," Sheila politely observed.

"Forty and some months!" Ward said and then with a giggle, "some months!"

The intrusive soul continued to take up Spook's place at the breakfast table for close to an hour. As the two ladies began to consume the generous portions of eggs, bacon and French toast, Mrs. Ward continued to do what she does best. She began to inquire as to what a nice, quiet girl like Sheila was doing with a slob like Spook. Sensing that the old lady was indeed Saguache's version of the National Enquirer, Sheila nevertheless felt compelled to lead the busybody a little astray. "I met Spook after crashing my plane in the mountains and fell instantly in love with the man," she would fib. "You know, this day and age it is impossible to find such a man."

"And what kind of man is that, child?"

"One that can survive anything, anywhere; you know, a mountain man." Sheila was confident that her story would be considered.

Finally the wisdom of the elderly woman would become clear. "And who is going to tell Devereux?" Ward interjected at the most timely juncture.

Both females broke out in healthy laughter as each realized the other's capabilities for warping the truth a little. By this time, the Spook's curiosity grew too great and he was compelled to return his untraditional appearance to the table and join the ladies for breakfast. As he did so, Mrs. Ward made it clear to him that she knew the truth. However, she promised not to divulge his fantasy secret to the rest of the village.

There would be unexpected benefit related to the intrusion of the breakfast guest. With the bridge to the mill dismantled, an alternate route would have to be established that would bring the beautiful female as close as possible to her destination. Through the advice of the old lady in the pink and white dress, it was established that the Sky City Mine was about as close as one could get.

Early the next day, Sheila and Spook had acquired the necessary supplies and a borrowed a Jeep from the town's vigil, Mrs. Ward. With anticipation deeply seeded within her heart, Sheila Gray and her unsightly escort began the last leg of her journey to the location of her true love.

*****

"The natives are restless, Sir." Esquire would look over the four men gathered before him and then brought his discerning eyes to rest on Mexican Joe who was addressing him.

"And you, Joe?" The Black Knight did not like being confronted with what he perceived as a possible ultimatum. "And are you part of the silent majority?"

"Sir?" Joe was confused at what the leader meant.

"What's on your mind?" Esquire was growing tired of the foresight Joe failed to muster, as well as the selfishness the four had displayed over the past few weeks. They had become whiners. The leader listened to the news daily on a portable radio and the heat was cooling only slightly. There was still no room for error. Their situation continued to be delicate and the impatience of the group could easily lead to their discovery.

"We would like to go to town and get some more supplies," Joe stated in a hopeful tone. We are running low on stuff and I thought that it might be a good idea before too long."

"And I suppose it would take all four of ya?" The man in charge was already beginning to dismiss the suggestion.

Seeing the idea beginning to fall apart, Gonzales stepped in with tentative demeanor to assist Garcia, "No, of course not. But we all could use a break from all this and maybe whoever wanted to go, could."

Esquire stroked his unshaven chin and acted as if he was really considering the idiotic inquiry. "I suppose that the old broad with the shot gun wouldn't mind takin' another crack at ya'."

"What about the blade man? You want to go?" The leader extended the possibilities.

Blade Runner did not reply verbally but just shook his head no as to indicate his recognition of the dangers of doing so and to confirm his solidarity to the Black Knight as well.

Esquire then looked at his longtime friend, James Eagle.

"I'm always with you, boss." James Eagle did not care one way or the other.

Esquire smiled an uncommon smile and said, "That is, when you're not trip'n back to the past."

The Indian also produced a smile and continued with what was on his mind. "Besides folks, if we get caught they'll overnight express our asses back to the great State of Texas. You know the place ... where they take great pleasure in the lethal injection concept. No, I'll stay here, thank you."

By this time, Sly extended his position by stepping close to the Indian and placing a hand on the man's back. Esquire picked up a wooden stick of which he had been carving and began to carve again. "I ain't gonna get my fanny sent back for a murder rap in Texas just because you bastards think you need to get your rocks off. We have enough supplies here for the entire winter if necessary, so here we will stay until I deem otherwise."

The four were not pleased with the lack of apparent appreciation or regard for their needs but they knew better than to go against the man who was responsible for their escape in the first place. Instead, they would remain content not to ruffle the leader's feathers again. Esquire understood there was a danger with their idleness, though. He also understood that at some point he must exterminate them. Their continuing existence was now a growing risk. Until such a plan could be devised and implemented, he would be forced to structure an occupation for the discontented masses.

"Tomorrow gentlemen, you are going to become gold miners." The Knight made his surprising announcement. As all eyes turned to look at the informer who would make such an astonishing statement, he would qualify, "That's right, men. You guys need a retirement plan and this will occupy your time. So let's make it pay. Garcia, it's your mine so you're the mine boss - put 'em to work."

Garcia, Gonzales, and the Drafter seemed completely converted to the notion and were willing to proceed with their new diversionary assignment. On the other hand, Mayhem was not inclined to hard labor; or smart enough to fake such. "I rip people off!" He exclaimed with impulsive selfishness. "I rob banks and do gas stations and liquor stores. I don't mine!"

"Look around yourself, crap for brains." Esquire was disgusted at Mayhem's lack of comprehension regarding the obvious. "There are not that many banks or gas stations around here for you to practice your skills. Now get your ass in motion and see what the hell else you can accomplish to please me today! Stop trying to piss me off!" Esquire flung the knife down onto the ground where it stuck between the ignorant man's feet. "Look at it this way. You would kind of like be building a portfolio."

"What the hell is a portfa,…fa,…fa, whatever you said?"

"Just get a shovel, bright boy. Preoccupy yourself with the task and you will never have to pull another job for the rest of your miserable lives; I promise you that," Esquire said while he thought about his sinister agenda. He realized that for some, soon, a mining accident would occur.

"It's not the same…" Mayhem was cut short by a wave of the leader's hand. "What?" He was puzzled.

"Shut up!" The boss would order. "Listen!"

In the distance, the faint but nevertheless distinctive sound of a four wheel drive was slowly creeping its way across the terrain.

"Take your places!" Esquire was moving off the porch and in the direction of the makeshift armory.

The others followed as Esquire hastened his stride towards the armory. An old powder shack that was built out of concrete had been used for decades by the miners to store explosives, but now it would serve as an arsenal. Esquire was secure in the notion that he alone had access through the door of the arms depot and by such an installation he could also take comfort knowing that the weapons within would not be used against him. He only trusted a select few of his group. There were several cases of explosives with a familiar stamped emblem: "Hercules Dynamite, 1957." This was unbeknownst to anyone except the leader. As he opened the heavy steel door, the distinctive odor of nitroglycerine burned his nostrils and gave him a reminder to be careful around the unstable substance. The rest of the men chose to stand outside the powder magazine and receive the weapons which were being allocated by their boss.

"Who do you think it is?" Mayhem asked.

"Mary Kay hasn't been by for a while - how the hell do I know!" Esquire badgered.

It sure ain't a lot of 'em, if is 'em," James Eagle made a calculated deduction.

Mayhem was suddenly afraid after the talk about being sent back to Texas and the certainty in which lethal injection had been forecasted. "How do you know it ain't the cops?"

"Cause we can hear 'em, numb nuts."

After the weapons were issued, each member of the gang was deployed in several different directions. Mayhem and Sly concealed themselves in the woods nearby and within plain view of the mining buildings. Drafter and Gonzales took a vantage point within one of the old mining shacks as John Hamel and Mexican Joe took up concealment behind the powder shack. The Indian had a long gun and was secured by boulders which acted as a gateway to the compound. The boulders boxed in any possible escape route. Esquire positioned himself in an old rocking chair on the front porch of the main building which by all appearances served as the assessor's office when the mine was operational. He posed himself as relaxed and whittled with non-purpose on a pine knob while the sound of the lone Jeep grew ever closer. Finally, after forty minutes or better, the vehicle appeared with its two occupants. At first, it was brought to a halt as though to survey the unexpected inhabitant sitting on the porch. Slowly, the old Jeep started again and as it approached, the Black Knight could see that the occupants posed no imminent danger.

Spook turned off the engine and sat for a moment attempting to analyze and decipher the unexpected which had unfolded before him.

"What's the matter?" Sheila inquired. "Is something wrong?"

"There ain't supposed to be nobody here." Spook seemed impatient and a little annoyed as he scanned the perimeter. "Ain't nobody supposed to be here," he repeated.

"You're on private property, boy," Esquire's husky voice penetrated the air. "No one's allowed past the summit of Tooth Ache."

"Who the hell are you?" Spook insisted.

The stranger flung the knife to the wooded floor of the porch where it stuck and quivered with vibration. He then rubbed his hand the full length of the carved wood and without apparent reason discarded it. He drew his attention to the odd couple and studied their transportation for a second. "I'm the man who tells people to get their asses off my land!"

"Ain't nobody owns this land, mister. Not since it got all tied up in litigation and the government took it back over." Spook offered that he knew a thing or two.

Sheila leaned over and grabbed her escort's sleeve and whispered, "Let's just go and let him have the place."

Still scanning the area Spook resisted, "That would be fine and dandy miss, but there ain't no other way unless you want to drive all the way to hell and back out'a here and wait a couple more weeks until the bridge is fixed. Personally, we have just as much right to be here as anyone else!" Spook turned his attention back to the oversized obstacle, "Who are you?"

"I'm the groundskeeper and you're out'a here!" The extremely large man now stood as if to accentuate his statement.

By this time, Garcia had positioned himself to a better vantage point and in doing so recognized the stunning features of an acquaintance of not so long ago. "That's the whore that shot me!" He exclaimed at the top of his lungs. Soon he was running down the small hillside yelling, "that's the bitch! That's the bitch!"

"Oh my God!" Sheila yelled. "It's Mexican Joe! Let's get out of here. Please, now!"

Spook responded by attempting to start Mrs. Ward's Jeep but the carburetor was flooded and the engine was too hot. The starter turned over, but the engine would not fire.

"Hurry, hurry!" Sheila was yelling.

Joe was within twenty feet when the antique motor coughed and then sputtered to a struggled start. Spook revved the engine twice and then let out the clutch. Dirt and dust spewed into the air as all four tires spun and the Jeep began to rotate counter clockwise. As the four wheel drive made one and a half revolutions, the angry Garcia placed both hands on the small tail gate and hung on for all he was worth. Spook steered the Jeep in the same direction from which they had come, but soon discovered another unexpected adversary standing in the roadway with a rifle at the ready. He was forced to react by over steering hard to the left and spun the Jeep in another half circle. At this point, the irate Mexican found his hands sliding across the rounded metal of the tailgate and slipping from the relic. The momentum tumbled him across the ground like a rag doll and dashed him against the legs of the unprepared Indian. Both found themselves helplessly sprawled on the ground watching the Jeep speed back towards the mining buildings.

An ever growing panic gripped both occupants of the fleeing vehicle as it seemed strange men bearing weapons began to storm in from every direction. Spook once again found himself compelled to steer hard left. As he did so, this caused Sheila to lose her death grip on the single brace bar which was attached to the dash. Suddenly she found herself tumbling from the topless transportation. Engaging herself in a full somersault, Sheila located her feet and began running for she knew her future sense of wellbeing depended on it. The endangered young lady scurried up a small hill and rushed into the darkening depths of the mine drift. Everything was suddenly black, displaying nothing but an empty sensation of an abyss. She would stop and feel for the walls, and in doing so, discovered a steel rod. Fearing that she made a grave mistake, Sheila turned with the iron weapon in hand and directed her attention towards the mine entrance from which she just ran. She was ready to face any pursuing adversaries. Soon the sun that lit the entrance was partially eclipsed by two shadowy figures. She could see that one of the subjects was holding a knife. Outside, the distinctive sound of the Jeep's engine could be heard laboring under the demands of its driver even after shots were heard. It was evident that the two unwelcome intruders within the mine were also experiencing difficulty in navigating through the consuming darkness. Now was the time. Trying hard to not make a sound, Sheila held the bar horizontally and readied herself.

"Here kitty, kitty, kitty," Sheila recognized Mexican Joe's voice. "Remember that little get together I promised you? Well, ya' ain't gonna believe the party favor I have in mind for ya'. Now come out, you cute little kitten. Come on. Ya' make it easy for us and we'll make it fun for you."

The woman with culture, with proper upbringing and purpose, realized the peril she faced. Her future was unavoidably disturbed with the promise of the most dreaded of intrusions to any woman. Somehow, someway, she could not allow this to happen. Sheila silently vowed that if she could *not* get away, she would have the inner strength to kill herself. Flashes of Jay passed before her eyes as she searched for purpose; a sense of courage to face the enemy and to prevail. She and Jay had a dominion to build. Yes, she would die if need be, but for now she would be content to redirect her energies outward. To extend all effort to oppose those who threatened her pursuit of happiness. With a loud scream she thrust her weight forward, simultaneously connecting the iron drill bar into the midsection of the two aggressors. Both let out yells and fell to the ground while sucking for air. With a quick exit, the terrified girl emerged from the mine with the bar still in her hands and stood for a moment to one side as if in anticipation of their pursuit. With such a delay, Sheila glanced down the hill at the Spook and the Jeep. With the motor laboring under full throttle, Spook was still steering it around in circles which flung rocks and dirt high into the air. There was a shot, and then another. Spook turned the Jeep straight in the direction of the road which lead out of the mine camp and guided the transportation best that he could between the boulders and then, out of sight.

Sheila's heart sank as she realized that she was left alone. She listened in hopes that the Jeep would stop but it did not. She realized that she must be fleet of foot and began to run along the mountainside in hopes that the men below her would not look in her direction. As she did, she could see the thick timber straight ahead. If only she could make it to the trees without being detected. At first, it was a hundred yards away but as she sprinted, the possibilities grew greater that indeed, she may reach the woods. Fifty yards and she still had not been noticed. At this point, Sheila turned and looked behind herself to see if anyone was following. By now, the woods were within ten yards and she could feel her lungs burning, but she began to feel a small sense of security.

"There she is!" Dread filled her heart as she heard yelling behind her. "Over there! The bitch is over there!"

Sheila was compelled to dash harder and through the trees she ran as fast as her delicate feet could carrier her! Again, she turned to look and by doing so, failed to see a low branch. At the last minute, she threw her hand up which saved her face; however, the branch would still knock her backwards and hard onto the ground. Panic mixed with a sobering realization that the branch had actually saved her life. As she scrambled to her feet, her eyes grew large as she peered with unexpected shock over a four hundred foot sheer cliff. The sound of the river reverberated up the steep walls and amplified the depth of the Devil's Pin Cushion. Sheila knew she had to think fast, and her mind was racing. Still, no one was in sight. With quick determination, she stripped off her bright red jacket and hastily tied it around a log. With a heave, she threw what she hoped to be a decoy over the side. Sheila said a short prayer and then let out a long chilling scream.

Garcia was the first one to appear. Breathing heavily he quickly looked over the edge. "Damn!" He exclaimed in a guttural voice. "Damn!"

"Where is she?" Gonzales appeared and was soon to bend over and place his hands on his knees as if to catch his breath.

"She took a header over the side!"

"No way!" Gonzales could not believe what Mexican Joe was saying.

"Yes, way!" By this time, Eagle was observing the depth of the canyon and could make out the red cloth half in the water and half out. "She was a looker but I bet she ain't no more."

What the desperados failed to realize was that Sheila had managed to burrow herself under pine needles, dead aspen leaves and other forest rubbish near a large pine tree. She held her breath the best that she could as she watched from beneath the debris. She was sure that if they did not hear her breathing they surely could feel the vibration of her heart beating. The three men were only a few feet from her now, so close as a matter of fact, that she could smell them and the odor turned her stomach.

"Why did the wench jump?" Gonzales turned and looked up the hill and past where Sheila was hiding.

"Where is she?" Sheila heard a fourth voice inquire as a progressive sound of footsteps came closer. So close as a matter of fact, she could feel the ground tremor. "Esquire wants you to bring her back untouched." The man was close enough that she could have reached out and touched his boot.

"Well, she ain't touched," Joe said. "As a matter of fact, she tossed herself off the goddamn edge." Joe shook his head. "She just friggen' lost it and ran over the edge!"

Blade Runner cautiously stepped to the edge and looked over. "You really have a way with women, Mex. Are you really sure it's her?"

"What ya' mean, man? I saw her jump." Joe took offense to being questioned so he felt compelled to lie. "She was screaming her ass off all the way down, too."

The Indian squinted but had difficulty deciphering what he was staring at. "She looks kind of funny down there. You best drag your sorry, worthless existence down there and make sure it's really her." The Indian then began to study possibilities other than what Mexican Joe declared occurred. He looked up the hill and around where Sheila was hiding as if to entertain the thought that she may have staged her own apparent demise. Sheila could see his face now and he looked as though he was responding to sensations and instincts unique to Native inhabitance developed through centuries by ancestry.

"Why do we have to go down there, man? I saw the bitch jump." Joe was eager to contest the Indian's order. Turning his attention back toward the canyon, he thought to himself out loud, "I wonder if she's still any good?"

"You're about one sick son-of-a bitch!" As crude as Gonzales was, he still was repulsed by the suggested possibilities.

Without taking his eyes off of the deep terrain, the Indian once again ordered the reluctant Joe Garcia one last time, "get yourself down there or I will see if you're any good after I toss your disgusting carcass off the cliff! Now did she jump or fall?"

"Fell; jumped-what the hell is the difference?" Joe didn't care much either way.

"A thing called credibility." James now looked right at Garcia. "And as far as the Knight is concerned, you're running kind of short on the stuff. Do what ya' think best. Just remember who ya'll be answer'n to." At this, the Indian turned and placed a foot on Sheila's right hand, pivoted, and walked up the hillside. Pain shot through her wrist and traveled up her arm, but she dared not murmur a sound. With tears welling up, she remained motionless.

"Where is everybody else?" Gonzales inquired.

With the sound of the footsteps growing ever fainter, the fourth man's voice was barely detectable now. "They're chase'n down Chicken Little in the Jeep," was the response. "Just make sure when you recover her body, you bring it back for Esquire to see."

Garcia took off his hat and dashed it to the ground only a few inches from Sheila's face. "The son-of-a-bitch wants proof? I'll give him proof. I'll stick it up his ass!"

*****

Spook brought the four wheel drive to a halt a little ways off the beaten trail and parked it under the shadow of a giant yellow pine. He shut off the engine, took in a deep breath, and held it while he listened. It was faint at first but he could detect the sound of the other Jeep. He could tell that it was being driven without regard for safety or consideration for machinery. He recalled seeing the burned out van and now realized that the other Jeep that was pursuing him had to be the sheriff's.

"My God," he thought to himself as it occurred to him that he had stumbled onto the hiding place of what was left of the "Texas Eight." It had to be them. He shuddered at the thought of how he left Sheila behind and now all he wanted to do was to take back the moment in which he had abandoned her. But, for now, all he could do was bide his time until the other Jeep passed and then return to the mine as quickly as possible. And what if she was dead? Or raped? Now he had time to really grasp the true extent of his actions he found himself overwhelmed with grief. Although he knew he had nothing to do about the aggressions of other men, he nevertheless wished he could take back that point in time when Sheila tumbled from the Jeep. Yes, he had worked with a sense of desperation to save his own hide, but somehow it did not seem worth it. In the recesses of his mind, his instincts pushed him to make this dastardly event right. What a coward he had been. And if he could not take back that brief time where everything went wrong, then he would have to be man enough to face Jay and tell him what had gone wrong.

His thoughts were interrupted by the sudden change in the rhythm within the other vehicle's engine as it drew near. Without any apparent reason, the motor was turned off and the silence that followed was cause for a level of greater anxiety. Spook drew a deep breath and held it as not to be detected, although the other Jeep was more than fifty yards away. What if they had spotted the tracks of his Jeep leading off the main trail? He had not planned on them slowing down enough to see, let alone stop. His mind was racing and confusion replaced good sense, but one thing was for sure, he would return to the mine. In the distance he could hear the roar of the river in the deep part of the canyon and the occasional chirping sound of an unconcerned bird.

"I can't hear 'em," a voice pierced the silence. The voice was incredibly audible and seemed much closer than the visual distance should allow. Spook's eyes narrowed as he slipped the Old Timer hunting knife from its sheath. Without intention, he rubbed his thumb nervously at a right angle across the razor sharp blade as he waited. Instincts pushed him to leave the Jeep and position himself to attack rather than wait any longer for his enemy to make the move. Quietly, he slipped through the trees as to gain a visual advantage. Then, he would stop dead in his tracks when he heard the motor start up again. Sheila's guide hid behind a group of aspens and that was when he was able to study his adversaries. The largest one, the one who had greeted him and Sheila when they drove into the retired mining settlement, was sitting in the passenger's seat with four in all to be reckoned with.

"Kick it in the ass," the large man ordered. "If he is ahead of us we have to catch up with him. If he is behind us, we can deal with him later!"

Spook watched with some feeling of relief as the black Jeep roared off. He rushed to his own transportation and started the engine. With little regard for the possibilities of detection, he drove as hard as he could back to the main trail and started, once again, down the tedious descent that led back to Sky City. The ride was rough and dangerous, but the thought of grasping his most regretful moment back from time, was now paramount. Whatever it took,

Spook needed to make this impossible circumstance better! Somehow he needed to rescue the magnificent Sheila Gray.

*****

The jeep traveled at an incredible speed through the boulder gateway and into the main courtyard which was surrounded by rustic mining buildings and tailings. In the center of the drive stood the Indian bearing the rifle which the Jeep all but collided with. Eagle did not anticipate the return of Spook; expecting instead, the return of his comrades, James Eagle found himself diving to the ground and rolling out of the way of the intruder. As the Jeep brushed past the surprised man, the front bumper struck his weapon and sent it spinning across the compound. Spook turned the steering wheel and the Jeep skidded around in a half circle. As the vehicle came to rest facing the Native American, the bearded Spook swiftly climbed out of his transportation. He did not take his eyes off the victim of confusion as he hurriedly retrieved the rifle which had been dropped.

"Where is the woman?" Spook demanded to know.

The Indian declined to respond. Spook worked the action of the weapon and once again made his demand clear. "The woman; where is she?"

"Stuff it!" James Eagle tested the stranger's convictions.

Spook raised the rifle slowly to his shoulder and took aim at the man's head. "No, whoever the hell you are, you can stuff it!"

"She's down over the edge by the river." Eagle nodded towards the Devil's Pin Cushion.

Don't lie to me! Ya' can't get to the river from this side." Spook knew this area well and he would not be easily fooled.

"Somebody might should have told her that," the Indian suggested with a shrug.

Still holding the rifle to his shoulder, Spook shifted his eyes in the direction of the canyon. "What the hell are ya' talking about?" Then he tilted his head in the same direction. "Show me!"

Slowly the two walked towards the woods and then proceeded through the trees. The distant roar of Satan's River was deafening as they approached the edge of the cliff. The Indian hesitated at first then prodded forth with a nudge by the barrel of the rifle. With a nod of his head, the Indian gestured down the canyon and to a clearing where the red jacket of Sheila's could be seen. Spook studied the colored object with intensity and found himself grief stricken with the thought that the wonderful young lady indeed was dead. His face became red and his breathing more rapid as he felt himself becoming enraged.

"She dies - so do you!" he demanded. As the rage rose, so did the gun to Spook's shoulder for the last time. A shot rang out and he suddenly felt a sharp pain across his forehead. He felt confused and dazed. It was as though everything was growing dim and in slow motion. He squeezed the trigger and felt the rifle recoil. He watched as the Indian flinched but Spook still had enough awareness to realize that the bullet missed its mark. Spook went down to one knee and blinked his eyes until he could see a little better. In the distance he watched as two figures crouched and then ducked behind a tree. He refocused on the man who stood before him and marveled at how brave the stranger seemed to be. The Indian did not attempt to run. He was not begging for his life, nor did he appear crazed. He just stood there and looked at Spook with cold steel eyes. Spook had never killed anyone before, nor was he about to begin with the unarmed man. Spook looked in the distance where the Indian's allies were still hiding. Such a distance was too great for a handgun and they had been lucky with grazing his head with their first shot. It was apparent they knew Spook had the advantage at this point. He could pick them off one at a time if they were so rash as to show themselves.

Without warning, Spook became sick to his stomach. As he recalled his abandoned charge a mere forty minutes before, he once again felt worthless. First, he had left Sheila which created a condition where she must fend for herself and now he could not even punish the men who had driven her to the point where she perished. His mind raced and his awareness once again surfaced as the dreaded sound of the other Jeep came ever nearer.

"Don't follow me! It won't take much of an excuse for me to off ya'!" Spook yelled as he began to run up the incline.

Spook reached the courtyard just as the bellow of dust could be seen. He stood for a moment and mentally took in the inevitable. Placing the gun between the seats he climbed in the Jeep and started the motor. He was not sure what to do, so he just revved the engine and stared at the gap between the boulders. It was as if he was in a trance. Soon there was a gunshot and a then a second. The third creased across the hood and brought Spook back to his senses. He looked down the hill. All three men of whom he had ordered to stay had disobeyed and were now advancing with confidence in their numbers. As Spook looked back to the boulders, he realized that it was too late. The black Jeep was already bearing down on him. With instinct driven by necessity, Spook shifted his Jeep into first, popped the clutch and the race was on. Garcia, Gonzales and Eagle ran to cut off Spook's retreat near the large rocks. With no clear place to go, Spook changed direction and steered up the hill and before even he could realize the full consequence of his actions, he funneled Mrs. Ward's Jeep into the open mouth of the mine drift. He gripped the steering wheel and slammed on the brakes as total darkness engulfed him. Spook could hear the other Jeep coming up the hill behind him and he fumbled for the light switch. Finally he found it and pulled it on. The two yellow beams lit the way well as he was surprised at how much room there really was. Spook grabbed the rifle and turned in the seat as to fend off the persistent foes. He aimed for the radiator which would permanently disable the other Jeep and grant him a clean get away. Soon the Jeep entered the manmade cave and Spook began to shoot. At first, it seemed that the bullets could not phase the determination of the bad men, but all of a sudden, the vehicle veered first to the left and then overcorrected and slammed into the heavy timbers of the underground structure.

Spook wasted no time directing the antique Jeep down the tight alleyway and out of sight. He could hear shots over the roar of his engine but he felt comfort in knowing that the shots that were directed towards him would be in vain. The tunnel had already curved and direct line of sight was no longer possible.

The further the frightened man traveled, the more he felt relaxed and he began to drive more carefully. Although the mine was extremely old, the dry Colorado atmosphere helped preserve the interior planks and timbers and no obstacles presented themselves. Spook continued to distance himself from the carnage he had left behind. After a lengthy distance, he could see the welcome sight of the light at the end of the tunnel. Jay's glacier had finally melted to a point of reasonable access and the Spook wasted no time in sliding the old lady's Jeep down the post-season glacier that had now formed a shoot. Nature's process had created a smooth decline to dry dirt and extended Spook's access past Shadow Falls which otherwise would have been an impasse for the vehicle. He had accomplished the impossible! He had escaped the wrath of those who would do him great harm, driving where no other would have dared go and now he was free again. As the Jeep carried him across the untamed meadows and to the foot of the north face of San Luis Peak, he was smiling at his accomplishment but that would be short lived. He soon remembered the most delightful woman he had ever seen. He remembered her smile and their friendship, and the way she allowed him to feel important in the little town where before he had been nobody. Tears began to intermingle with his bushy beard and the dried blood from the grazing wound on his forehead made him appear all the more a fright. Soon his uncontrollable sobbing was echoed off the trees of the La Garita Wilderness. He stopped the Jeep, removed himself from the marginal comfort of its front seat and fell to his knees. With both hands over his face, he continued to be hysterical until he fell asleep in the evening glow of the western sky.

Chapter Sixteen

Silent Rage

Jay paused as he took time to listen to the early morning vocal competitions between Red Winged Blackbirds. Their songs filled the air as if to announce the arrival of the woman he loved; the woman who had inspired him so. It seemed that all of Jay's senses were more acutely in tune to every sound, smell, and sight. He was standing in the third story window of the mansion and for the first time began to absorb the true dynamics of his accomplishment. He wasn't as far along on the project as he had hoped, but then again, with a project this size, you never are. At the beginning of the summer, when his imagination was fresh, he thought that he could have built the realm by himself; however, after realizing the true magnitude of the project, his undocumented crew had accelerated progress on what would have otherwise turned into a hopeless venture. He insisted on paying them better than they expected, always cash at the end of each day, and treated them with the respect due every human. In return, they insisted on a full day's yield which traditionally started at 6 in the morning and ended sometimes near 9 at night with a traditional two-hour lunch and siesta break midday.

Now that the structure was nearing the final stages, Jay bid farewell to his southern assistants and opted to dry-in the daunting structure by himself. As each member of the crew embraced their employer and bid goodbye, he insisted on handing them an envelope containing a note of appreciation and a non-solicited thousand dollar bonus. As the long string of manual laborers trailed off, mutual admiration and respect had been established.

He took in a deep breath and exhaled. What a marvelous morning it was. He could smell the scent of Blue Spruce intermingling with the freshly peeled Yellow Pine logs of his home. It was as if this day was somehow made just for him. He wished that the lovely Miss Gray was by his side. She too, could share in the wonders that this morning seemed to hold. It had been a long time and he marveled at the realization that he never once doubted her return. Jay understood that the conflicting feelings that had been exchanged between her father and him were an important obstacle, but for the time being Jay would not allow this to tarnish his faith in the future. He smiled as he thought about the many experiences they shared. In a great sense, it was as though time had not existed before she had stepped into his life. That the true worldly sensations had not come about until he and the Nut witnessed the plane glide overhead and crash into the trees. From that point on, every breath, every motion seemed to have been etched with its own indelible distinction in the archives of his mind.

Abruptly, Jay's thoughts were interrupted by a peculiar noise. All of his energies were now drawn to identify the sound and he was puzzled. He was certain the actual sound of an engine was emanating from behind him near the top of the Continental Divide and deep into the designated Wilderness. Jay listened as the surging of the motor gave way to the knowledge that it was a land bearing vehicle laboring greatly over terrain in which reasonable expectation would not, nor would Federal Government law, allow. With the exception of 660 acres which was deeded to Jay, all else was Wilderness by Federal decree which required him to bring all building materials in by animal or helicopter conveyance. Jay's sense of wellbeing instantly changed to anger. He was not sure how or why the vehicle was on his mountain, but the discovery was distressing and the notion that someone was actually violating God's untouched sanctuary, intolerable!

With a frown on his face, Jay watched the terrain above in anticipation. Finally, the vehicle which was causing so much noise appeared and began its descent towards Jay's new home. Jay slowly placed his hammer in the belt loop and began to walk down the stairs to confront the unknown.

Before the Jeep reached Jay's location, he could hear the panicked yell of the driver. Jay stepped from the building and studied the approaching carriage as if to try and understand its purpose.

"They killed her!" Spook yelled as he drove what was left of Ward's transportation nearly into the confused mountain man. "Jay, there was nothing I could do!"

Jay half drug the panicked Spook from the Jeep and then stood him up straight. "What the hell are you talking about?"

"They killed her, Jay. And there wasn't a damned thing that I could do about it!"

Jay was paralyzed by the thought that Spook could be referring to Sheila. His eyes narrowed and he gained a better grip on Spook's shirt collar and drew him near. "Spook, make it damn clear to me what the hell you are talking about!"

"Sheila," Spook braced himself for the fury he knew was to come.

The blood drained from Jay's appearance and his eyes took on hollowness. Slowly he let go of Spook's shirt and stepped back. "How do you know that she's dead?"

"Man, I did everything I could. I even went back for her and everything!"

Jay again gripped Spook's shirt so tightly that the old fellow was beginning to have difficulty breathing. "Spook; I'm only going to say this one more time. What in the hell are you talking about?!"

"They chased her off into Devil's Pin Cushion. I saw her body at the bottom." Spook leaned against the Jeep and began to tremble. "We had no idea that the bastards were there until they were all over us!"

Jay released the grip on Spook and sunk to his knees. He just stared at the ground. Slowly he turned his head and looked at the great mansion of which he had raised as a symbol of his love for the most magnificent woman he had ever known. How could she perish? After all, she had promised to return to him, to build an empire together.

"Who are they?" Jay would now extend a concentrated stare at the messenger. "Was it Garcia at Sky City?"

"Him and a whole bunch others I'd never seen before," Spook was still prepared for a thrashing at the hands of Jay. "I think they are a bunch of convicts from back east someplace. They even killed some cops in Texas."

"And how do you know that?" Jay insisted that Spook qualify his assumptions. "Cause I'm pretty sure they were driv'n Sheriff Hall's old Willys."

Jay had heard about the Sheriff's run-in with the suspected Texas killers when Jay was purchasing lumber at the lumber mill. He also knew that Garcia had spent hard time and would have most likely created relationships and connections while in the joint.

"Get the hell out of my way, wonder boy!" Jay stepped with determination toward the driver's seat of Mrs. Ward's Jeep.

"Man, I did everything I could. There was just so many of them!"

Without saying another word, Jay climbed aboard and started the Jeep. It was as though the devil had consumed his entire existence. His eyes were glazed and fixed, looking straight ahead as he grinded the gears into place.

"They've got guns!" Spook yelled.

Slowly Jay diverted his gaze to Spook. "You stay here and hide under my bed if you feel the need," he simply said as he released the clutch.

Spook went limp with shame and watched helplessly as the madman began to pound the Jeep into the unforgiving steep terrain in the direction of the Great Divide. "You weren't there! You don't know what it was like... there were so many," the dejected Spook said more or less to himself. Spook had been short on dignity to begin with and now he felt completely depleted of such. He had given his best, but his best meant very little as it could not bring Sheila back. He was willing to go back and sacrifice his life if Jay would have deemed it necessary. But, he had not been invited or even wanted. Confirmation finally reared its ugly head and he knew to his core that he was an utter and complete failure.

*****

Only Esquire and Garcia were not present. They were searching for a descending path into the Pin Cushion so that once and for all Miss Gray could be confirmed as deceased. James Eagle, who had been placed in charge, stood guard along with Sly and the Blade Runner. Esquire deemed Mr. Mayhem and Drafter untrustworthy and in need of constant babysitting. Esquire figured Gonzales to be of neutral worth at this point. Only the Indian would possess a firearm.

Drafter attempted to play a tune on an old upright piano which had been left behind by the miners. From all appearances and aroma, it had served more as a packrat's refuge for the last several decades than an instrument of music. Nevertheless, with most the notes out of tune and others missing all together, the man continued.

Jay Devereux emerged from the darkness of the Sky City West Portal on foot and walked in the direction of the less than pleasant sound. The fragmented music drew his direction and unconcerned with concealment, Jay advanced towards the obvious occupied structure. He had left the Jeep at the far end of the East Portal as it could not traverse the steep shoot back into the mine drift. It was unfathomable that the man had successfully travelled the distance of the shaft without a guiding light. In his haste he had not brought a gun and the odds were mounted against him. Still, Jay was not concerned. It was as if Jay had already decided that this mission had a predisposed conclusion. As far as he was concerned, there would only be a need for a one way ticket. Without fear or caring, the mountain man entered the boardwalk that skirted the front of the main building. It did not occur to the occupants within the rustic structure that this was an intruder. As a matter of fact, he went unnoticed as he stepped through the front door of the assessor's office. He stood for a moment and calculated what lay before him. Taken somewhat back by the sudden appearance, Mayhem stood up and drew his shank from a makeshift sheath which was tucked under his belt. Stepping closer to the unexpected guest, the murderer waved the blade as though to intimidate. Jay did nothing in response but just stood motionless. Mayhem began to step to one side, but Jay looked straight ahead as if not to notice. The others raised and looked at the stranger with confusion. How could he have driven into the compound unnoticed? What was this peculiar man's intention? Mayhem stepped closer and placed the knife towards the intruder's neck.

"Wrong place at the wrong time," the ruthless killer sneered.

With lightning speed Jay crossed his right hand over Mayhem's hand and grabbed the fist that held the knife. With tremendous leverage working for him, Jay swiftly shoved the man's arm towards the water stained ceiling. There was a loud pop as Mayhem's shoulder separated from its socket and Mayhem let out a loud scream. No longer needing the leverage, Jay let go of the injured man and quickly side-kicked one foot in the center of the man's chest. This sent the convict reeling across the floor and into the Indian who was in the process of drawing a 9 millimeter pistol from the convenience of his belt. As the two men plunged to the floor, the gun slipped from James' grasp and spun under a large antique potbellied stove.

"What the hell's your problem?" Blade Runner had retrieved the shank which Mayhem had involuntarily surrendered. "You some sort of bad ass, ain't ya?"

Jay did not reply. He just waited and stared straight ahead. Mayhem remained on the floor while the other four men began to cautiously surround the stranger. Sly and Wells Gonzales made the next move. Both were compelled to lunge at the lone figure, and as they came in from each side, Jay simply stepped back and quickly placed each of his hands back of their heads. By doing so, he was able to direct Sly's head into Gonzales's and both went down without a struggle. Drafter was unaccustomed to violence, but he found himself somehow duty-bound to participate. Without hesitation he tackled the uninvited visitor. As they tumbled to the floor, the Indian jumped forward and prepared for an aggressive assault. Both Drafter and the Native American held Jay down while Hamel placed the homemade knife to the mountain man's neck. Slowly he rubbed the sharp blade ever so lightly across the skin and the skin instantly peeled as it parted. Blood began to streak down the neck and inside Jay's shirt. With a sadistic smile, Hamel pulled the blade away, "prepare to meet the devil, whoever you are!"

Before Hamel could thrust the knife into his victim's chest, the overpowered stranger focused energy into a kick which connected the heel of his boot to the chin of his knife wielding threat. There was a crunch as the convict's jaw shattered! Unbearable agony further accentuated the already surprised expression on John's face. John

Hamel let out a pain filled scream which caused him to discover a new level of excruciation. All at once he lost interest in the offensive posture and slumped to the floor with the spark of aggression extinguished.

Jay Devereux struggled to stand. The Indian could feel the man's extraordinarily powerful body begin to lift. Not wishing to face the stranger on even ground, Eagle responded with a crashing blow to Jay's forehead with a huge right fist. This forced Jay backwards onto the flat of his back and would serve to daze the mountain man if only for a second. Jay raised his head a little only to have it met with another blow, this time to the side of his face which drew stars and made his right ear ring. Before he realized what was taking place, the Indian pulled Jay to a sitting position and then raised him to his feet by pulling his hair.

"Grab the son-of-a-bitch!" James Eagle instructed Drafter. As Drafter secured the half conscious Devereux, Eagle guided Jay's head around to face Mayhem. Mayhem was still holding the grossly deformed shoulder and grimacing in agony.

"Stick the mother!" Eagle ordered.

Mayhem began to stand, took one step and a half of another, rolled his eyes up into his head and fainted. As he fell to the wood floor, dust rolled up around his body.

"I'll cut the bastard!" The familiar voice of Gonzales yelled. With a single drop of blood streaking down the crease of his upper lip, Wells stood up and walked over to where Hamel had dropped the knife. "I'll cut his damned heart out!"

Jay's senses were now coming back to him. As he desperately tried to focus, he could make out the vague shape of Gonzales staggering closer. With a couple more blinks, he saw what he thought was the knife striking out at him and he reacted by twisting to his right as hard as he could. This resulted in the blade missing his chest but slicing a superficial cut across his ribs. At this precise moment, all pain, all hatred and all the rage within once again surged forth and with clinched fists Jay shouted, "You will pay the ultimate price! Not I!" Raising his right foot high, he brought all his weight to bear solidly onto the heel of his boot and subsequently transferred the kinetic energy down on the arch of the Indian's left foot. Jay could actually feel the bones in the enemy's foot crush. James Eagle let go of the steel grip around Jay's arm and then the powerful Indian fell to the floor without so much as a word.

Shocked at the sight of the interim leader falling, Drafter also let go, however, it was too late. Dedication to a fraudulent career had not built intestinal fortitude within the likes of such a man let alone outward strength. He was a small man both by heart, as well as appearance. Jay's solid right cross would knock the forger completely out before he crashed into the wall and slithered to the floor.

"It's time to get stuck, stranger!" Gonzales was holding the knife waist high and was working the duct taped handle nervously with his right hand.

Jay glanced for a brief moment at Sly who was just now beginning to pick himself up off the floor. "Suit yourself," Jay gritted his teeth. By now, Gonzales was nervously switching the knife from one hand to the other in an apparent attempt to distract the mountain man and keep him off guard. Sly slowly raised himself to his feet and looked around at the devastation before him. Finally, he realized the intruder had his back to him and Sly figured it was an excellent time to attack. The deaf male figured wrong. Hearing the advancing footsteps, Jay moved to one side and then grabbed the criminal as he passed by. Giving a great heave, Jay tossed the aggressor into the waiting blade held by Wells. With a mere gurgle emanating from Sly's lips, the mute looked into Gonzales's eyes for a lengthy moment and then, slipped to the floor.

By this time, the Indian managed to stand again and hobble his way in the direction of the potbelly stove. "Keep 'em busy and I'll blow his ass away in just a minute." The Indian had lost interest in continuing the physical contest.

Jay looked at the knife that Wells had just pulled from his ally. Not only was its blade red with the blood of the mute, but his hand as well. Jay watched as the Indian struggled to bend down next to the stove. For the first time during the entire episode, he considered the possibilities of continuing the fight or, the better judgment to flee but it was too late. Eagle was now pulling the semi-automatic from beneath the cast iron stove and pointing it in Jay's direction. As the lone mountain man searched for cover, the urgency of the moment created a slow motion sensation within his senses. What made things all the more pressing was it seemed that everything outside his control was moving much faster. As quickly as he could, he pulled the upright piano from the wall with a mighty yank and shielded himself behind it. He heard three shots but none would penetrate the double oak construction of the antique upright. At first, he slowly pushed the instrument in the estimated direction of the shots. The small rollers would not turn, so he placed his shoulder just above the key board and pushed for all that he was worth. The piano gained surprising speed as it skidded across the hardwood floor until the back rollers sunk into a soft spot in the old wooden floor. Momentum toppled the heavy musical instrument over and the thing came crashing down onto Mayhem and the gun wielding Indian. Simultaneously both men let out swear words and collapsed under the great weight. With instinct, Jay swung around to face the last of his present adversaries. The once aggressive Gonzales looked around the room. Drafter was still out for the count, leaning against a corner of the room. Sly was currently sitting upright on the floor and appeared to be holding his intestines in while gasping for air. Blade Runner was flat on his back, trying with all his might to breathe through his now swollen, deformed jaw. Gonzales' gaze would fall on the Indian and Mayhem who were motionless under the piano. Slowly he eased his grip on the knife and the blade fell towards the floor and stuck. He found himself now staring at the man who, with few words, had challenged unfathomable odds. The man who was covered in blood soaked clothing, but who had conquered all. Gonzales studied the mountain man as he took off his blood soaked shirt and discarded it on the floor. Gonzales chose to wisely concede without saying anything.

Jay looked down at the cut across his ribs and took in a deep breath, "Where is Garcia?" Jay asked.

Wells Gonzalez was surprised that this warrior knew the enemy by name. Wells nodded in the direction of the Devil's Pin Cushion. "They're trying to find a way down to the bottom."

"Who?" Jay demanded clarity.

"Esquire and Joe Garcia," Wells simply replied.

*****

Esquire turned his head as if to more closely listen. He stood and looked up the hill.

"What's going on," asked Garcia.

The Black Knight did not respond. He felt something was wrong and quickly pulled a revolver from his pocket.

"Man, what the hell is it?" Mexican Joe was feeling increasingly uncomfortable with Esquire's sudden sense of alarm.

With stern resolve the Black Knight frowned at Joe as he wished to convey a response of silence. Slowly the giant turned his attention back up the hill and crouched. Esquire and the Mexican were in a small clearing and so it was not difficult for Jay to observe their every move. "Drop the gun!" Jay yelled.

Esquire flinched and began to study the perimeter more closely attempting to locate a source of the demand. He began to smile. "And if I don't?" He dared pose the question. The Black Knight anticipated that Spook had returned in order to recover some self-respect and perhaps a reward from citizen's arrest.

"Who is it?" Garcia whispered as he was baffled at the keen senses of his leader.

"How the hell do I know? It ain't anybody with our best interest at heart - I'll tell you that much!" Redirecting his voice, the Black Knight once again studied the terrain above him. What's your name?" Esquire was still unable to locate the man that belonged to the mystery voice.

Jay watched as the two individuals desperately tried to find him. Jay had recovered the semi-automatic from where the Indian had dropped it, but what the Black Knight did not know was the gun was rendered non-functional. It had been irreparably damaged in the fight and would serve only as a prop at best. Jay stepped from behind the concealment of the large Ponderosa Pine.

"Toss me the weapon," he instructed once again.

Taken off a bit by the unsettling discovery that this was not Spook, the Knight placed the pistol down by his side. He then peered at Mexican Joe who was just standing with his mouth open. "Do you know him?" Esquire asked.

With his natural limited capacity, Garcia had forgotten about Devereux. Joe was now consumed with concern.

"Joe!" Esquire was growing impatient with the lack of response by the Mexican. "Who is he?"

As if having been shaken from a sound sleep, Garcia looked at the Knight. "Devereux! Jason Devereux! He lives on the other side of Table."

"What does he want?" Esquire studied the forest in anticipation that the mountain man was not alone. "Garcia!" Joe was still not paying attention to his boss. "Pull your head out of your ass and answer me! What's on this guy's mind?"

"It's because of the skirt. He's here because of the skirt!"

Esquire was confused by the reference and no longer tolerant of Garcia's lack of clarity. "Garcia, we don't have a whole lot of time to screw around here. Now drop the mystery talk and tell me what the hell you're talking about."

"The skirt, boss; you know, the bitch that fell off into the gorge. That's her old man." Garcia declared.

"Kick the damned gun towards me or I'll plug you from here." Jay raised the pistol at eye level and placed the bead on Esquire's forehead as he approached the two men with an obvious display of caution.

The Dark Knight considered making a run for it; however, when he realized the distance to cover, he changed his mind. Besides, if Devereux was going to shoot without provocation, the convict figured he would have already done it. Esquire began to kick the gun forward but then stopped. Sensing it best not to give the weapon to Jay, Esquire bent down and picked the piece up by the barrel and threw the 9 mm into the depths of the Devil's Pin Cushion.

Jay was not pleased at the reaction of the convict. He had banked on having the workable gun and now there wasn't one. He would adjust however, and subsequently maintain the illusion. Jay stepped from behind the last cover and marched confidently toward the last two men between him and his objective. "Joe, come here," he demanded.

"What do ya' want?" Joe Garcia was hesitant.

Esquire looked at the brave man and tried to determine his convictions. The blood had dried around Jay's neck but the Knight could tell the mid-chest wound was seeping. He was puzzled as to why the man had not just shot them both, but knew the longer he could delay such an occurrence, the greater the chance for survival.

Hatred once again swelled into every fiber of the mountain man as the repulsive, frightened Garcia stood close and began to tremble like a frightened dog. This was the man that had intruded into Jay's life and had now stolen from Jay the most precious discovery of his life.

Jay stepped close to Joe who was now paralyzed with fear and pressed the firearm next to the man's forehead. "Tell me all about it, weasel!"

"About what, Jay?"

"Why did you throw her off of the mountain?" Jay's teeth were clinched as he spoke. "Did Sheila beg for mercy?"

Joe's eyes grew big with fright and he began to become hysterical. "Please don't kill me. I had nothing to do with her death!" He blubbered. "She jumped. I didn't make her do it."

Jay was incensed by such cowardice display and he was driven beyond the boundaries of self-control.

"So what you're telling me is that she just was out on a walk and decided to leap off the goddamn cliff?" Without removing the gun from Garcia's head, Jay directed his attention to the Black Knight who was inching his way closer. "Not on your best day!" Devereux warned the huge man.

Jay looked back at Joe. Jay's face became distorted with immeasurable anger as he studied the pitiful excuse for a human before him. "You're dog crap," Jay announced and with a sudden impulse slammed the gun alongside Joe's head. The man fell to the ground with not so much as a grunt and lay motionless; perhaps dead. Soon, however Garcia showed signs of life and groaned. Jay bent over and grabbed the despicable man by the hair and began to drag him towards the edge of the cliff. The Black Knight watched with increasing anticipation as the mountain man placed Joe's head over the edge and then stepped back. As the cobwebs began to clear, Garcia became fully conscious and opened his eyes to the great vastness of space. He let out a panicked yell and began to scoot back from the rim. He then felt the cold steel of Jay's weapon on the back of his neck.

"Go ahead," Jay said. "Jump!"

The Mexican shook his head and grabbed clumps of native grass as if in an attempt to not be persuaded.

"Go ahead and get up and take a casual step. I'm not forcing you to do it. I'm merely suggesting it as an alternative."

"An alternative to what?" Garcia wanted to know.

"Of getting a bullet through your already hollow head!" Jay whispered close to the Mexican's ear.

"Ya'll have to just go ahead and shoot me because I ain't tak'n the dive!" Joe felt faint and blood was beginning to trickle out his nose from the blow to his head.

Jay had enough with the contemptible bastard, "Turn around!" Jay ordered. "I want you to see this coming!"

Joe slowly pushed himself back from the edge and stood up with little help from his equilibrium. He tried to focus on his attacker, but with great difficulty ended up squatting, closing his eyes, and balancing his hands on his knees. Recognizing that the Mexican was dazed, and not wanting to spend much more time with the individual, Jay slapped the man across the already sensitive face with his left hand and Joe went down in a disgraceful clump next to the sheer cliff. Joe began to sob.

"You're one courageous handful with that gun, ain't ya?" Esquire was grinning as if he challenged the stranger to make things even. "Put the piece down and what ya' say you and me get it on."

Jay turned and glared at the big man. "Your turn is coming!" Jay had made his intentions clear. "I've got a better idea. Since you appear to have such an aversion to me having the damn thing I will do you one better." At that point, Jay tossed the Smith and Wesson semi-auto to the giant.

Puzzled but not stupid, Esquire was cautious. Bewilderment did not persuade his intentions from a quick resolve. The career convict raised the gun and took precise aim. "What a fool," he said as he attempted to pull the trigger. The trigger resisted the pressure and he laughed. "The mechanism is broke. My, ain't you the clever boy?"

"Broke by the misfit that was trying to use it on me," said Jay.

Without further conversation, Jay stepped forward as if to now make his intentions complete. The Knight attempted to work the action but it was jammed as well. As if to conclude that the situation was a minor distraction which would only serve as a delay to the inevitable, Esquire tossed the worthless gun into the depths of the Devil's Pin Cushion, "Have it your way, huh?"

Again Jay declined comment. Instead, he crouched in a ready position and began to circle the gang's leader as if to look for an opening to attack. He recognized the size of the man but it did not matter. Nothing mattered anymore. With his precious Sheila Gray now gone, he had nothing to really live for other than the purpose at hand. And for that, Jay felt he had the advantage over the giant.

The two locked up arm in arm and there was a struggle for leverage. Esquire was surprised at the strength of the shorter Devereux. With such comparable height difference, Jay was able to lift the man up off the ground and thrust him on his back. The Knight would not let go, and as a result Jay found himself slamming to the dirt as well.

Jay rolled away from the other man and sprung to his feet in a ready posture. He was surprised that the larger man had accomplished the same initiative and once again they were face to face. The mountain man sensed that this foe was of superior intellect, as well as a dynamic physical specimen.

With the intensity and power of two great bulls fighting to the death, the battle raged for thirty minutes or better until both men were too exhausted to continue. Both would then lie on the ground several feet from one another and stare at their formable foe while gasping for air and resting for the next unregulated round. Jay's left eye was now swollen shut and his nose was obviously broken. The torso wound was not bleeding any longer as dirt had filled the gap and clogged the gash.

The Black Knight was not unscathed either. He had underestimated Jay's strength; his endurance driven by intense desire. He knew the pain that pulsated from his ribs was generated from broken bones next to the sternum and breathing was most difficult, and at this altitude, nearly impossible. His right hand throbbed, indicating that it too was broken. Upon many occasions Esquire had engaged in hand to hand combat before, but never had the battle raged so long, nor was it so clear that both combatants agreed about the unspoken conclusion. To the convict's dismay, the mountain man was first to stagger to his feet and once again approach. For the first time in the Esquire's violent life, he realized the concept of possible defeat.

Jay stood before him as if to pay the courtesy of waiting until the large man was ready. As he did so, he flexed his chest muscles and rolled his head slightly as if to summon awareness to his attributes for the final round of the final bout. Esquire stood and extended his hand as if to see if it still functioned. Great pain penetrated his senses as it was confirmed that the hand was indeed broken.

This time, the Black Knight felt compelled to make the first move as if to mask any liabilities related to his own physical condition. He lunged towards Jay but he missed and found himself sprawling on the ground. As the large frame began to lift off the ground, Devereux placed a swift kick to the man's stomach and Esquire flipped onto his back. Blood began to flow from his nose and mouth, and he gasped for air. Jay grabbed Esquire by the hair and helped the giant to his feet. Sensing victory, he let go of the hair and jump kicked both feet dead center into the convict's chest. The giant exhausted all air from his lungs and let out a painful grunt followed by a gasp for air. The larger man staggered, fell into a tree, and then slipped to the ground. Jay stood over the defeated Goliath as if in a quandary of what to do next. Suddenly, there was a sharp stabbing pain in Jay's side and he turned to look directly into Wells Gonzales' eyes. With a smile on his lips, Wells withdrew the knife and then slammed the butt of the handle into Jay's temple. Everything went black and Jay slumped to the ground.

*****

Jay Devereux opened his eyes and blinked. He could hear Satan's River off in the distance and became aware that he was looking into the depths of Devil's Pin Cushion.

"No", he heard a voice command. "He's all mine!"

Slowly the Black Knight staggered to his feet and pushed Gonzales out of the way. "Give me the goddamn knife!" he ordered. Wells obliged and Esquire grimaced with mounting agony as he grasped, as best he could, the bloody handle of the shank with his broken hand. Placing his fingers of his left hand through Jay's hair,

Esquire contracted his hand into a fist and pulled Jay's head back to expose the true worrier's throat. Placing the deadly blade next to the broken man's jugular, Esquire would extend one and only one courtesy. "Make your peace Mountain Man, for this is your last breath."

Raising his blue eyes toward the heavens, Jay simply said, "What lies behind us and what lies before us are tiny matters compared to what lies within us. I grant you permission to take away my whole existence if it should make yours better."

Chapter Seventeen

The Cavalry

Sheriff Hall held two fingers to the right side of the headphones as if to assist in the reception of the helicopter pilot's transmission. "We are going to lift off and hover at a distance," stated the pilot. As the turbine began to increase in power, the Sheriff gave thumbs up, but never looked back at the chopper as it started to lift from the ground. Instead, he kept his concentration on the old mining buildings which gave little indication of being occupied. His eyes were deliberate as he scanned for the anticipated resistance, but there was none. Perhaps they were too late. The Sheriff watched as the borrowed twenty-member Gunnison Police/Sheriff strategic entry team members quickly scurried about in four teams of five, searching what was first deemed as secondary structures. The pulsating chop-chop sound of the helicopter eventually receded into a distant minor distraction as it would pair up with three others of its likeness, approximately a mile or better to the south. The United States Army had extended their services in the way of aircraft transportation but was prohibited by law to directly engage criminals or enforce state laws. Furthermore, it had been made painfully clear that the crew would not be able to even touch the criminals once they were apprehended.

"Sheriff, TAC 1," the tactical leader's voice broke the radio squelch.

"Go ahead TAC 1," The Sheriff responded.

"We have cleared all outlying structures and are now approaching the main target." The voice was one of experience. "Still, there is no sign of activity; however, there is recent evidence of human intrusion - looks as though they may have split, so keep an eye out to the rear just in case they flank us."

The Sheriff was most grateful for the assistance by the highly trained organization and stood ready as the on-scene incident commander. "Proceed at your pleasure", he simply responded.

He patiently watched from a vantage point behind a large rock with a sniper and spotter who were overseeing the outer perimeter. Two teams entered the Sky City Assayer's building. The Sheriff felt anxious while anticipating the discovery of the convicts, but confused by the lack of resistance on the gang's part. Several minutes passed without visual advantage or radio traffic from the TAC teams. Ben Hall felt a great urge to key the microphone and ask for a disposition, but he maintained his position of quiet vigilance.

Finally silence was interrupted. "Sheriff, this is TAC 1."

"Go," the Sheriff eagerly responded.

"I really think that you are going to want to see this," the response was cause for curiosity. "We have five on ice but we weren't the ones that put them that way. These folks must have royally pissed somebody off!"

Soon the Sheriff entered the business room and he was taken aback by the destruction and such total devastation. The piano was still lying on two apparent unconscious men. Blood was evident all about and virtually every injury imaginable was witnessed.

"This is a damned war zone!" the SWAT team leader understated the obvious.

"What do you mean, someone was here before us?" The sheriff was confused and was hopeful for an explanation.

"We didn't do any of this." The Gunnison Undersheriff smiled as he looked around. The damage was here before we breached the door.

"Who the hell…" The Sheriff was unsure as to what to think about it all.

"One man, so says the dude over there." A team member pointed at the yet to be identified Drafter.

"Who?" inquired the Saguache Sheriff.

As the piano was being lifted up and set back on its small rollers, the Undersheriff leaned back on the frame and peered out into the La Garita Mountain Range through the broken panes of a window. "The convict doesn't know."

"What the hell are you talking about?" The Sheriff wanted answers.

Still looking at the outlay of the mining buildings, the team leader pulled a stick of gum from a pack and placed the wrapper in his vest pocket. "One stranger walks into a room filled with bad ass derelicts, kicks the mucus out of them and then leaves without even stating his beef; most likely saved us a lot of potential grief."

"How many are dead?" The Sheriff was certain with such havoc there would be cold bodies.

"Not a damned one," said one of the team members. "It's as though someone just wanted them to suffer a whole bunch. Nobody's dead!"

Sheriff Hall approached Drafter and studied the man. He hardly looked the desperado type. "Who did all this? Where is he now?"

Drafter just sat for a moment and stared at the floor. As his eyes lifted to look at the Sheriff, he shook his head. "How did you know where we were?"

"A young lady that you tried to rape was able to walk a distance and found people who had a satellite phone." The Sheriff was to the point.

"Not me," Drafter protested. "I don't rape, I don't kill, the only thing I did was push creative paper."

"Where are the others?" the Sheriff insisted.

Drafter drew a deep breath, "Esquire and Mexican Joe are trying to find a way into the Devil's Pin Cushion and I think that is where Wells Gonzales might be, too. They are trying to get down to… Oh, she made it out alive?"

"Incoming!" The sniper report came across the compound on every officer's hand held radio. "Incoming. I've got two closing, approaching on foot - and one, no make that two, more subjects approaching from the canyon west. No weapons visible. Four subjects, no weapons in view!"

The two alternate tactical teams that were outside the main building spread in a semi-circle as Garcia and Gonzales walked into the staging area. A sergeant began to spout orders, "Prone out convicts! Lay down with arms out and palms up!"

Both Wells Gonzales and Mexican Joe were quickly cuffed and legs shackled. Joe was compelled to protest the rough way that he was being body searched. "Man, not so goddamn rough, man. Be gentle. I don't hide noth'n there; you don't need to be searching there. What, you lonely or someth'n?"

"My grandmother is in a whole lot worse condition than you convict, and she don't bitch and moan as much as you," stated one of the observing officers.

"And how often do you push her face into the dirt and grab her by the balls?" Garcia was having trouble breathing with a knee on his neck and his hands being pulled up behind him. He would cough as every time that he took in a breath he was taking in dust.

"Only on her birthdays," the officer would reply.

"We still have two more on approach," The sergeant reminded his detail. Don't tarry with those guys. We still have unfinished business."

With Joe and Wells secured, the officers lined the compound as Esquire came into sight. Draped over his arms was Jay Devereux who did not appear to be alive. As he staggered into the open area between the officers, Sheriff Ben Hall came out of the office and into the street. Out of respect for the Sheriff and all that he had gone through, the officers did not wish to intrude in the final arrest. A team leader gestured with a pair of handcuffs dangling from his index finger. "Care to do the honors, Sheriff?" the cop simply asked.

All eyes were vigilant as the huge frame of Esquire finally struggled to approach the Sheriff as the Sheriff stood his ground. With deliberate hesitancy, the Black Knight came within arm's length. Both men stood for an extended moment and studied each other.

"Hello Sheriff," Esquire broke the silence. "You look well."

"John T. Sampson, aka Black Knight, aka Esquire, I presume?" Sheriff Ben Hall inquired with a formal tone.

"Among many others aliases, may I assure you," confirmed the Knight. "We really didn't have time at the gas station to be properly acquainted."

"The time just wasn't right. Things seemed too pressing," the Sheriff responded.

Esquire took a few steps towards the assayer's office and laid Jay down on the porch. "Think you may want to look after our boy," he said as he turned back towards the Sheriff.

By this time, the first and second teams began bringing the walking wounded from the office out into the open. As Esquire watched, he shook his head and snickered. "The boy was sure pressed about that young lady." He then turned and readdressed the County Official. "Where do we go from here, boss?"

Sheriff Hall nodded in the convict's direction and said, "I never really figured you as a quitter. I always thought you to be one of those who would insist on a blaze of glory, exit stage left." The Sheriff observed that Devereux was still breathing. He watched as officers began to take care of the mountain man. "Why didn't you finish him?"

As the sheriff used double cuffs to secure the giant's hands behind his back, the Esquire responded. "Sheriff, it just seemed pointless. I killed a lot of men who I had placed in a position to where they welcomed death. I never before had my ass kicked by anyone. And then after doing so, he gladly offers himself as a sacrifice rather than snuff out my life. I can't say that I really understand it, but I will say that today I discovered a better man and it wasn't me. Just maybe that's something to preserve rather than take away."

Esquire watched as officers began to evacuate the last of his clan and stretch them out on the boardwalk. "Sheriff, we can only take just so much from this world before we have to start paying it back, don't you think?"

"How in the world do you think you are going to pay back anything?" The Sheriff asked.

"There ain't no way, boss. All I can do now is give a down payment at Brownsville when they hook me up. That's about all I have left to do," the big man stated as a matter of fact.

"You found religion?"

"Hardly," Esquire truthfully replied. "I'm just tired of things my way. It just didn't turn out as gratifying as I thought it would." With that he looked up and studied the military choppers that began to circle as to announce their descent. "The spoils of the bank are in the powder shack," the Black Knight extended his final gesture of surrender, if not goodwill.

*****

The Sheriff walked into the reception area of the Gunnison Valley Hospital. "Devereux's room please," he inquired.

"Sir," the receptionist paused as to detain the man's presumptive entrance into the secure area of the medical facility. "I will have to call the nurse's station and get authorization. He is not taking visitors at the moment."

"Whatever it takes," the Sheriff was impatient but not rude.

Within a few minutes a doctor approached the Sheriff and escorted the law man into his own personal office. "My name is Doctor McMurren and I oversee ICU. We have a major dilemma, Sheriff Hall," the medical man of distinction seemed perplexed. He was looking out of the window of his corner office. "I have been in this business for a long, long time and I am at a quandary as what to do for Devereux."

"He is that bad off?" The Sheriff was quick to surmise.

"Physically he is banged up, bruised up, cut up and basically spindled and even mutilated, and even at that he's in far better shape than most people that I examine on a daily basis." The doctor lowered the blinds and redirected his full attentiveness to his visitor. "He, in my estimation, is a perfect specimen even in the battered condition he is in. But it seems that your boy has lost total will to continue. His condition is critical and he is getting worse. As a matter of fact, he is unconscious as we speak, and I really don't give him 48 hours. Although his body has taken a severe beating, a CAT scan has shown no intrusive penetration into the vital areas, but he still remains unconscious. It really makes no sense."

At this point, there was a knock from outside the office and Sheila entered uninvited. "Where is Jay?" She postured with resolve. "Where is Jay and is he going to be alright?"

The Sheriff got up and offered his hand, "You must be Sheila Gray."

"Who are you?" Sheila inquired of the plain clothed official.

"Saguache County Sheriff Benjamin C. Hall, at your service. We talked on the phone."

Sheila instinctively offered her hand in gesture but was still preoccupied with the fact that Jay had been hospitalized.

The Sheriff looked over to the experienced doctor. "Would you care to see a miracle in medicine, Doc? You happen to be looking at the remedy, I suspect."

*****

The single room was quiet with the exception of the heart monitor's continual beep... beep... beep. There seemed to be a constant lull in every breath Jay took in and then he would exhale. It was as if he subconsciously contemplated not even bothering with the next cycle.

Sheila entered the room alone. As she gently placed one foot in front of the other, she was hesitant for a moment. With noticeable difference, the heart monitor picked up in its audio repetition. If her attention was distracted, it would be for only a second for then she continued her approach.

"Jay," she whispered. "Jay, come to me." She reached out with her delicate hand and so gently touched his fingers. "You need to do your part now and come to me, Sweetheart." Tears began to streak down her cheeks as she looked at his face. "We have an empire to finish together; a life to share."

For the next several hours, Sheila sat and read to Jay. Occasionally she would glance up at the monitor in hopes that there would be another noticeable difference in its rhythm. There was no difference since the first brief moment when she had entered the room and it had been so long. As a matter of fact, progress was nil and she was becoming disheartened. With deliberate frequency the head nurse would check on Sheila and make sure that she was being well taken care of.

For several days, Jay's condition would not improve to any noticeable degree. Sheila was losing hope and the strain was taking an evident toll. Eight days had passed since his admittance. The head nurse opened the door and peered around the door frame with intentions of being brief. Sheila was sobbing quietly and clutching Jay's hand tightly. At the foot of the bed was a small puppy that resembled the probable likes of Wing Nut in his adolescence. The puppy had somehow managed to uncover the injured man's feet and was feverishly licking Jay's toes as if in a gesture to do its part.

The Nurse opened the door wide and pointed at the forbidden intruder. "What is that?!" The lady of posture demanded.

"I'm sorry." Sheila acquiesced. "I thought that the puppy would help. I should not have snuck him in. I'm sorry."

"That's not a puppy!" The lady frowned. "I know that 'cause we don't allow puppies in this place!" Then the lady smiled. "It must be a hemostat the way it is clamped on to Mr. Devereux's toe like that! Yep, it's a hemostat 'cause we allow those... as long as they are sterile."

As the nurse continued to enter the room, Sheila looked up into the concerned expression of the health provider. "I don't think that he really wants to come back," Sheila stated the obvious.

Instead of sympathy, the wisdom of the nurse began to show through. "The way that I understand it, he fought for you, is that right?"

"He thought I was dead!" Sheila exclaimed.

"Maybe, but nevertheless, he fought either for you or the memory of you. That's hardly the point." The nurse held her ground.

"Then what is the point?" By her nature, Sheila was trying to ask the question and still be polite.

"It appears to me that he literally gave his all for the love of you. Now it's time that you fight for your love for him!" The nurse was still stern.

"But I have been touching him and talking to him for days and he hasn't responded. I *am* here for him!" Sheila was taking exception to the implication.

"Yes, I know you most definitely have done all that, hon. But with the soft way that you caress his hand or touch his face, he does not know if it's a memory or a dream. He has no concept of where he is and that you are actually here." The nurse turned and began to walk out of the room. "It seems to me, if I were you, I would be fighting for the man I love rather than letting him slide into an everlasting never-never land." The door automatically closed and although it seemed that the nurse had left for the sake of more important duties, she had not. She was peering through the small window with hopeful anxiety.

Clearing the tears from her eyes and then her cheeks, Sheila looked at Jay with determination. She had no idea what to do at this point but she felt certain that the nurse proposed a valid train of thought and she was going to do something! She would be damned if she was going to allow this man the option of leaving her behind.

"Jason Thomas Devereux! It is time to get up and look alive!" She began to tug at his right arm as if in attempt to raise him in a sitting position. "Look alive!" She ordered again. You're not taking the easy way out! You made me promises that you *will* keep! You taught me to be strong and now it's time for you to step it up, Buster!"

Although Sheila did not possess the strength to lift Jay forward and keep him in an upright position, she did manage to pull him to one side of the bed where she was forced to brace herself against the wall and against him to keep him from actually slipping to the floor. As she summoned all her energy to stabilize the condition which she had caused, she was unaware that Jay's eyes were open and staring at her.

"Is this heaven?" Jay asked. "Am I in heaven?" he repeated.

With a gasp she looked at his face. Collecting herself she replied, "Don't flatter yourself!"

At this point, she let out a shrill yelp as she no longer possessed the leverage to keep Jason on the bed. With a thud they both landed on the floor.

With a smile, Jay stated the obvious, "Nope - this isn't heaven. I expected that there would be less nagging and a little more comfort."

"Where have you been," Sheila screamed. "Damn you, Jay Devereux, you scared the hell out of me!"

"Nope, it ain't heaven!" Jay reiterated. "But it's most likely the closest that I will ever be." With this, he reached up and then brought her down to him and kissed her with endless determination.

As the nurse began to walk back toward her station, there were tears now in *her* eyes. With great vigor she clapped her hands together and exclaimed, "Now that's what I'm talking about!" Then she instructed, "Ok, people. It's time to start doing this health care thing we do! Let's make that difference!"

With guarded reluctance, a second nurse began to walk toward the room where the alarming calamity was coming from. "What about the noise?" she asked.

"Honey, it ain't nothing that they can't handle! Besides - I'm thinking they will be making that kind of noise for countless years."

With that, the assisting nurse shrugged her shoulders and walked toward a different patient's room.